Goldeneyes

Goldeneyes

DELIA LATHAM

ISBN: 9798223954057

Cover Art by Heaven's Touch Designs, Delia Latham
Published by Heaven's Touch Books
First Edition, 2008 (Vinspire Publishing)
2nd Edition, 2023 (Heaven's Touch Books)

Heaven's Touch Books
dlathambooks@gmail.com

Dedication

In memory of my parents, Obie and Luella Dawson, who moved to California from Texas during the Great Depression. They raised eight kids with very little money, but lots and lots of love. We didn't miss and don't regret the luxuries we never had back then…but we sure do miss Mom and Dad now.

Part One

1936

Chapter One

A BODY LAY SPRAWLED across the doorway to the Lamont Limelight.

Clarence Camden, owner and publisher of the weekly newspaper, stood over the fellow in a bit of a mental quandary. He did not, for a moment, believe the man was dead—an occasional nasal snort emitted from the reeking heap of filthy rags and even filthier flesh crumpled at his feet. Even so, in his current state of sleep bordering on unconsciousness, the intruder barred Clarence's way not only to his desk, but to his first cup of morning coffee. Why, the gall of the pathetic excuse for a human being!

Finally, he reached across the inert body and turned his key in the lock. Not a small man, he found it no easy task to make his way through the door, briefcase in hand, while avoiding any contact with the smelly bundle of humanity on the ground. Having done so, he discarded the leather case and turned back to the problem outside his door.

Clarence dropped to one knee but did not shake the man. Such an action would have required touching him, and unfortunately, the odor emanating from the ground discouraged contact of any kind. He spoke loudly instead.

"Hey! Hey, mister! Are you all right?"

No response. Clarence groaned. He pulled a pair of driving gloves from his coat pocket and slipped them on with an unpleasant grimace. Even then, he allowed his hand only tentative contact with the other man's shoulder as he administered a half-hearted shake.

"Wake up, sir! You really must move along now."

The uninvited guest rolled over onto his back, producing three immediate results. Silence hit with almost shocking force as the rattle and roar of his snores ceased as if turned off like a waterspout. The new position revealed a face that could have used a shave several days earlier.

The final result produced the only reaction from Clarence—but it was strong and demanding of results. The movement stirred up an almost unbearable stench.

Clarence rocked back on his heels, disgusted and incensed. "That's it," he muttered. "No more mollycoddling!"

He rose and strode to a small room behind the front office. A moment later, he returned, a large metal pitcher clutched in both hands. At the open doorway, he scowled at the drunk man.

"I hate to do this, mister, but I've got a business to run here." With that, he dashed the frigid contents of the container full in the sleeping man's stubbly face.

That drastic action elicited precisely the reaction he had hoped for. The pathetic fellow's eyes snapped open. With a sputter and a low curse, he struggled to a sitting position.

"What the Sam Hill?" A baleful glance landed on Clarence, still wielding his icy weapon.

"I'm sorry to interrupt your slumber, sir." Clarence calmly watched his erstwhile incapacitated visitor struggle to rise from his now soggy place on the ground. "Allow me to introduce myself. I'm Clarence Camden, the owner of this establishment, which I fear you mistook for a free motel. I need you to kindly remove yourself from my doorway, so that others may enter without climbing over your body, which— forgive me for saying so—is far from a pleasant olfactory experience."

On his feet now, if a bit unsteady, the other man cast him a hateful glare.

"You kiddin' me, man? I don't understand your fancy, high-falutin words, so don't waste 'em on me. Why in blazes are you tryin' to freeze my rear off with that icy water? Talk about rude, mister—that was cold!"

Clarence was unperturbed by the onslaught of verbal wrath.

"I have already explained my actions. You were blocking the door to my place of business. I had to climb over you to get inside. And since I see you prefer a bit plainer language, may I suggest that a bath is definitely in order? Your stench is quite intolerable to any sensitive nostril!"

"Well, *excuse* me!"

Highly offended, the uninvited visitor cast Clarence a look that might have frightened a lesser man. His eyes flashed a burning anger, and Clarence found himself taken aback by their unexpected beauty. Golden, they were. No other word for it. Not brown, although that's probably how the man himself, with his preference for a simpler use of the English language, would define them.

They were large and framed by lashes so thick and dark that even Clarence—not as a rule given to studying the facial features of other men—couldn't help but notice. Not brown, not yellow, but somewhere in between. Even "amber" provided only a weak description of their striking hue.

Golden. That was the only precise way to describe the stranger's unusual eyes.

While the inebriated fellow continued to rail and curse at the mistreatment he had suffered, Clarence studied him. He stood just over six feet tall himself, and the man now giving him a peppery, expletive-laced dressing down towered at least an inch taller, in spite of his slouchy posture. Matted and tangled hair, like his beard, should have been cut days ago, but it grew in thick, black waves. Women might find that hair quite touchable, should the man ever think to wash it.

Though thin to the point of emaciation, his sharp features no doubt made single women's eyelashes flutter and pinked their cheeks. Yet nobility had little part in his description. Those disturbing eyes were deep golden pools of bitterness. Clarence found them empty and cold, though in all fairness he supposed their owner's current anger could be somewhat responsible for that. A weak chin also bore some clue to the stranger's character, though it sported one of those little dents women seemed to find so attractive.

So lost was Clarence in assessing the other man's appearance that the intruder's colorful tirade went mostly unnoticed until he felt his arm gripped with unexpected strength.

"Are you listenin' to me, man?" the guy demanded.

Clarence cast one, pointed glance at the dirty hand on the sleeve of his coat. "Take your hand off me, sir."

The stranger emitted a bitter, unpleasant bark of laughter, but his fingers unclenched their grip on Clarence's arm.

"Don't want me to touch you, do ya? What, I'm not good 'nuff? Who do you think you—?"

All at once, the irate man swayed, and his face went white beneath its surface grime. Fearing he would pass out on the floor yet again, Clarence overcame his personal revulsion

4

long enough to steer the unpleasant fellow to a small bench.

"You'd better sit down. Wait here, and I'll get you some water."

He hurried from the room, and when he returned a moment later, his visitor's demeanor had undergone a complete change. Sitting on the bench in the little lobby was a crushed and beaten man who elicited an unbidden sympathy in Clarence, despite his determination to feel no such thing.

The stranger sipped at the water, avoiding eye contact. A tear slid down one unshaven cheek. Uncomfortable now, Clarence said nothing, and the other man finally looked up and directly into his eyes.

"Look, man, I'm sorry. That cold water musta froze my pickled brain. I had no call to talk thataway to ya."

He nodded, a grudging acceptance of the man's sincere apology.

"Thing is, I need yer help. I guess I ain't runnin' a very good chance of gettin' it after all that, am I?"

Clarence held up a finger, then closed and locked the front door before answering. He preferred to have no customers until he was well rid of his caller. Still, something in the stranger's face tugged at his sympathetic nature, despite every attempt to quell the reaction.

He cleared his throat and lowered himself onto the edge of a hard, high-backed chair across from Mr. Goldeneyes. "Well, I guess we'll never know, sir, if you don't tell me what it is you need."

A brief flare of hope illuminated those incredible eyes, making them compellingly beautiful. He dug into the pocket of his threadbare jacket and pulled out a crumpled and torn sheet of paper. Shoving it toward Clarence, he spoke in a rush, his voice hoarse.

"I ain't got two cents to my name. But I need to put an ad

in yer paper. I gotta find her…for my wife."

Clarence picked up the grimy scrap, gingerly holding it between thumb and forefinger.

"Pleez bring her bak," it read. "Her mother greves."

Confused, he raised his gaze to meet that of the man across from him, who watched his every move—as if his golden gaze could swerve Clarence's decision. "I think you'd better tell me what this means."

The shaggy head fell forward, and heavy eyelids dropped over his eyes. When he spoke, shame and embarrassment warred for supremacy in his raspy voice.

"My name is Jack Kelly." Not a mispronounced syllable, not a suggestion of profanity. Then he spoke again, and the words themselves were profane. "I sold my baby girl."

Clarence wilted like a punctured balloon. He sank against the back of his uncomfortable seat, drew in a deep, bracing breath, and let it slowly out again.

"Wait right there! Excuse me, Mr. Kelly. Did you, uhm…" He paused. Closed his eyes, gave his head a little shake. "Did you say you *sold* your baby girl?"

"Yes, sir. That's what I said." Kelly seemed fascinated with something around the region of his feet.

Clarence's hands curled into fists. He drew a deep, burning breath and bit back an instinctive wave of fury. "We probably need something a little stronger than water for this discussion." He stood, and took a quick hold on the front counter, unprepared for the tremble in his long legs. Kelly's unpadded confession had him feeling sucker-punched.

He pointed down the hall to a small washroom. "Why don't you go in there and freshen up a bit? I believe you'll find a razor and some soap on the shelf above the sink, if you care to use them. Who knows, I might have even stashed an extra comb up there at some point. Do what you need to do, and I'll brew us up some coffee."

Kelly nodded and shuffled down the hall, his shoulders slumped, his head hanging. Clarence watched him for a moment. Then, without a plan or any intention to speak, he heard himself say. "Are you, uh…are you hungry?"

Jack Kelly turned and gave Clarence a long, distrustful look. But he nodded. "Yessir. I reckon I am."

"I'll see what I can do."

The door closed behind Kelly, and Clarence allowed himself to use the wall for support when he slumped against it, without a clue about how to handle the upcoming conversation.

Kelly disappeared into the washroom, and Clarence opened the front door to peer down the street. As he had expected, young Vergil Campbell was just arriving at his shoeshine post, where he would work until well into the afternoon, catching some of the local businessmen on their way to work and others as they ventured out for lunch.

Cupping both hands around his mouth, he called out to the lad. "Vergil!"

The boy looked up with a sunny smile. He waved a hand at Clarence then used it to nudge his once-dapper newsboy cap an inch higher. "Mornin', Mr. Camden!"

Despite the drama unfolding in his office, Clarence couldn't help a return smile. Virgil's open, honest countenance brought about that kind of response in all but the most cantankerous of townsfolk. But right now, he needed the boy's assistance.

"Can you come here for a moment, son?"

"Sure thing!"

Grabbing his shoeshine box, Vergil sprinted up the street,

arriving at Clarence's side only slightly winded. He dropped the box at his feet and used the back of one hand to brush a blond curl out of one eye.

"What can I do for ya, sir?" he asked. "Need'jer shoes polished up?"

"Actually, I could use a shoeshine, but I don't have time right now."

The boy's expression fell, and Clarence quickly continued. "What I do need is breakfast!" He pulled some bills from his pocket and handed them to the young entrepreneur. "Would you mind running over to the Breakfast Nook for me? Ask Bonnie for three or four fried eggs and several slices of bacon. Oh, and I'll take a bit of that gravy of hers, too—and a couple biscuits. Tell her I'll return her dishes later today."

Vergil grinned. "You got a big appetite this mornin', Mr. Camden."

"Yes, well, I'm a big man, kid. Think you can get Bonnie to hurry it up for me?"

"You betcha! Anything else?"

Clarence pulled out a few extra coins and dropped them in Virgil's shirt pocket. "For your trouble, son. I appreciate your help."

The boy's grin all but split his freckled face. "Aw, now, Mr. Camden, there ain't no call for you to do that!"

"Perhaps not. But you might miss a shoeshine or two while you're doing my bidding. So just take that money and go get me something to eat."

"Yes, sir!" The boy whirled and raced back down the street.

Clarence grinned, then closed and locked the door again. He didn't expect anyone in for another hour or so—not even Agnes, who manned the front counter like a drill sergeant. If someone did show up, he'd just have to think of something for them to do elsewhere.

The coffee pot in the small kitchen behind the newsroom had seen better days, but Clarence refused to trade it in for a newer model, despite Agnes's constant little verbal jabs, and those of the two reporters he'd finally had to hire last year. He insisted that new pots did not produce the same kind of flavor his well-seasoned one afforded and pretended not to notice his employees smiling behind their hands.

He poured two mugs of the steaming black liquid and placed them on a sturdy table—every bit as ancient as the coffee pot—which he also stubbornly refused to part with. Then he wandered back out to the lobby.

Only the tattered rags he wore made Jack Kelly recognizable as the same man who'd disappeared into the washroom mere moments ago. The matted beard was no more, and the face once hidden beneath it still bore the ruddy shine that comes from a good scrubbing. Water and a comb had tamed his tangled hair into something resembling normalcy.

He stood in the middle of the room, unease written into the set of his jaw and the constant back-and-forth shuffle of his feet against the wood floor. Ready to run at the slightest provocation.

"Mr. Kelly?" Clarence spoke softly, in deference to the other man's obvious nervousness.

Kelly looked up, his eyes even more striking now that the filth had been scrubbed from around them.

"Come on back. I have coffee made. Oh…give me a moment, please."

Clarence hurried to the door, in response to three firm taps. Vergil, of course, wearing that irresistible sunshine smile, both arms wrapped around a picnic basket. Having almost forgotten he'd sent the kid on a mission, Clarence relieved him of his burden, which bore no small heft. Why, that loaded basket must weigh at least half as much as the boy who'd carried it from Bonnie's Café, three blocks up the road.

"Bonnie says not to forget where that basket came from." The boy's eyes held a mischievous spark. "She sent a message for ya too."

"What message is that?" Clarence asked, as if didn't already know. He'd heard it a few times before.

"Well, she said, 'Vergil, you tell that newsfeller, iffen I don't see my basket and my dishes by closin' time, I'm gonna have his head!' That's what she said, Mr. Camden, and I ain't a'kiddin' a'tall."

Clarence laughed. "Thank you, Vergil! I'm sure she meant every word, too." Not that he was worried. Bonnie barked loud and bit not at all.

After locking the door again, he led Kelly to the kitchen and began unloading the contents of Bonnie's package. "Have a seat. I'll get you a plate. Eat first, then we'll talk."

The other man needed no second bidding. He dove into breakfast as if he hadn't eaten in days. He did not, however, resort to the coarse manners Clarence expected. He ate politely and with considerable restraint, considering his obvious hunger.

Clarence's natural newsman's inclination to notice details took in the fact that Kelly was left-handed when he lifted a forkful of fried eggs to his lips. He also wore a wedding band on that hand, plain gold but for three tiny blue inset stones—the middle one slightly larger than those on each side.

Kelly went suddenly still, his fork halfway to his lips. "Somethin' wrong?"

Clarence shook his head, appalled at his own poor manners. "No, of course not. Please excuse me. I was just noticing your unusual wedding band."

Lifting his hand, Kelly studied it for a moment, a sad smile teasing at his lips. He drew the ring from his finger and handed it to Clarence. "It belonged to my wife's grandfather. She wears a matching one."

"It's quite striking." Clarence murmured, even as he noticed a slight imperfection on one of the stones, a tiny chip along the setting. But then, the piece was quite old.

He returned it to Kelly, who slid the wedding band back onto his finger. Standing, he carried his plate to the sink and rinsed it before returning to the table.

"I gotta find that baby, Camden. If I don't, I can't never go back home. I can't face her! And without my Annie, I'm lost." His voice broke, and a muscle worked in his jaw as he clenched his teeth. "Lost, do you hear me?"

"I hear you. What I don't understand is how you could do such a thing in the first place. How could you sell your own baby?"

Kelly bowed his head and used his arm to brush at his eyes, which threatened to let spill the tears collected in their golden depths.

"I'm a slave, man. Can't you see that? I was desperate for a drink, and I didn't have two red pennies to rub together." He laughed harshly. "Musta been the devil sent that fella to work the field with me that day."

Clarence's head snapped up. "What fellow?"

Kelly shrugged and shook his head. "Don't know his name."

With a sigh, Clarence got up to pour himself another cup of coffee. "I think you'd better start from the beginning. Tell me what happened. I'm curious how two men get around to turning an innocent baby into a piece of merchandise!"

Kelly made no attempt to defend himself other than a quick shake of his head. "It wudd'n like that. Wudd'n like that at all." He looked up at Clarence, who made no effort to disguise his disgust with the other man's actions. "I'll tell ya what happened, but don't be breakin' in none. I only wanta say it once."

Chapter Two

SIX WEEKS EARLIER

WHOOSH…SMACK!

They were the only sounds to be heard in the scorching cotton field. The whoosh of descending blades, the hearty smack upon contact with the earth. A number of hoe-wielding occupants worked the endless rows, attacking pesky morning glories and any other unwelcome weeds that dared to take root there.

Jack Kelly and a newcomer chopped ahead of the others. Well matched in speed, they worked nearly side by side, yet few words passed between them. The persistent heat had sapped even the energy required to maintain a conversation.

Abruptly, Kelly hooked an elbow around the long handle of his hoe. Pulling a red bandanna from his pocket, he mopped at his sweaty face and gazed out across the budding fields, shaking his head at the visible waves of heat dancing across the tops of the plants.

Finally, he stuffed the large handkerchief back into a hip pocket. He stretched his tall, thin frame as far backward as he could, then back and forth in each direction, trying to work out the kinks from having chopped since early morning. "Hotter'n all git-out," he stated.

The other fellow nodded. Following his co-worker's example, he took a moment to clear the salty moisture from his own eyes. He fanned his hat back and forth, trying to create enough air movement to constitute a cooling breeze. Sighing, he set the worn piece of straw back on his head and stretched the aching muscles in his neck and shoulders.

"It surely is. I've never seen anything quite like it."

The men stood quietly for a moment, both of them wishing they were close enough to the ends of their rows to get a drink from the water tank. That not being so, they turned reluctantly back to the job at hand.

Kelly glanced furtively at the other man. His co-worker was obviously not afraid of hard, hot work, but no one knew much of anything else about him. He and his wife had shown up at the farm labor camp about a month before and moved into one of the rickety shacks just down the dirt road from his own.

The cracker box shanties in Corman's Camp were identical: tiny two and three-room dwellings, hastily thrown together to provide barely acceptable shelter for farm workers. Corman's was just one of many farm labor camps that had sprung up in California to accommodate the influx of immigrants from dust-blown eastern states.

Most folks in the camp were eager to make friends as well as new lives in this agricultural land of promise. A large number came and went, moving from crop to crop in the productive San Joaquin Valley, never staying in any location long at a time. One never knew who their neighbor might be from day to day, but the pitiful little shanties never sat empty.

This couple, however, kept to themselves—the man

being seen only in the cotton fields during the day or sometimes buying supplies in the general mercantile just up the road in Lamont. His wife was never seen anywhere, unless one were to count the infrequent occasions she had been spotted after dark hanging clothes on the line or taking them down.

Plumb fishy, iffen ya ask me. Clearing his throat loudly, Kelly cast his line, determined to find out more about this quiet stranger. "How ya likin' it in Corman's Camp?"

"It's all right, I suppose." The other man gave a shrug of his broad shoulders. He did not look up as he answered, and his speedy destruction of the pesky weeds never slowed. "Hot."

"Yeah, 'tis that." After a moment, he asked, "How's the missus?"

Glancing up briefly, his partner shook his head. "Okay." He paused then added, "She's okay."

Kelly cast another sideways glance at the poor fish struggling on the end of his line. He narrowed his eyes and set his jaw, for some reason utterly determined to reel the other man in.

"Well, that's good then," he said. "Don't see 'er out much. Thought she might be ailin'."

A lengthy silence ensued. Then, just as Kelly was debating whether to jerk hard on the line, his catch gave up the struggle. "She's ailing, all right," he said. "The woman's grieving herself to death for want of a child."

"No young'uns, huh?"

"No. We lost a little girl about a year back, just trying to get her into the world. It was a bad time for the missus. Real bad. I thought…well, I thought I would lose her, too."

Kelly grunted, suddenly wishing he had not tried so hard to draw his co-worker out. It was becoming obvious that this fellow thought himself something pretty special. He could tell by the fancy way the man spoke his words. *Yet here he is, choppin' cotton right alongside 'a me! So much for a fancy education and purty words.*

"Congratulations on yours, by the way." The stranger's voice broke into his sour musings.

Kelly's head came up. "Beg pardon?"

"Congratulations," his partner repeated. "I heard you have a new baby."

He wished his co-worker had not heard that little bit of news. It made this subject even more difficult. "Yeah, well. Thanks. A week ago."

"I wish I could do something to help her through this." The other man was obviously talking about his wife again. His otherwise pleasant voice roughened with a deep love and concern that were uncomfortable subjects at any time, in Kelly's opinion. Unfortunately, it seemed that, having broken his silence, the other fellow could not stop talking.

"Nothing short of a baby's going to make the woman happy, and the doctor says she can never have one. That poor little girl who died nearly killed her trying to be born."

Kelly cleared his throat, fervently wishing he had not caught this particular fish. He had never heard such obvious pain in a man's voice. It was almost visible, winding its sinuous way through the shimmering heat waves.

"Don't seem fair," he muttered.

"No, it surely doesn't. But then lots of things in this life aren't fair. Still, a woman who wants a little one as badly as mine does, seems like the good Lord ought to give her at least one."

"Uh-huh."

"Lord knows, I'd do just about anything to see her smile again."

Kelly did not reply, and the conversation died as abruptly as it had started, much to his relief. He was feeling the torment of his own demons by then and could not have cared much less about the private misery of the woman in the shack down the road.

The two men returned to their previous silent, steady chopping, each caught up in his own private war. Once again, silence reigned in their little corner of the blistering cotton field.

Whoosh-smack!

The old cuckoo clock on the shelf in the front room struck midnight. Its persistent chirping irritated Jack Kelly's already frayed nerves as he paced back and forth across the small room.

"Shut up! Shut up!" he growled beneath his breath, casting an anxious look at the crib in the next room. When no signs of disturbed sleep were forthcoming, he breathed a grateful sigh of relief. The last thing he needed right now was a squalling infant to further vex the burning demon within him. He had promised his wife he would not spend a cent on liquor. New babies meant new expenses, and those things must come first.

So far he had kept his promise; he'd had no choice. Every penny he earned with his hoe, day after blistering day in the cotton fields, was swallowed up in scratching out a meager existence.

There never seemed to be a penny extra, to say nothing of the few dollars a bottle of whiskey would cost. With the addition of this new offspring, who knew when he would be able to quench the gnawing demon of thirst that drove him insane?

He had to put food on the table and a roof over their heads. The arrival of more children would only make that job harder, and it was obvious Annie did not intend to stop at one pregnancy.

Another glance into the small bedroom revealed no unwelcome stirrings from the crib. A bright moonbeam, however, lay across the bed, and Kelly's tormented gaze fell on the lovely face of the woman he had married. He had considered himself a lucky man when she said yes to his proposal, despite her goody-two-shoes, Bible-thumping parents. If he loved anything on this poor excuse of an earth, he loved Annie. His perfect wife.

Their home might be barely more than a shack, but it sparkled, and she was a real wonder in the kitchen. He could not remember her voice ever raised in anger, even when he had fallen through the front door, dog drunk, a week after she married him.

Kelly's fevered mind wandered to his conversation with the poor fish in the cotton field. Had it only been eight or nine hours ago? It seemed an eon; every moment without the drink he craved was an eternity.

There's a fella who don't know how lucky he is. Only has to worry 'bout that pretty little gal and hisself. I bet he could buy a bottle of whiskey if he wanted one!

With the thought, an idea was born, full-blown and itching for action. He stopped pacing for a moment, shocked to the core by the undiluted vileness of the seed taking root in his mind. He stood staring at the crib against the far wall and shook his head as if to toss out the evil thought.

"You're crazy," he whispered. His heart pounded painfully against his chest; little beads of sweat dotted his forehead and chin. "You've done gone stark, starin' mad!"

And perhaps he had, for suddenly he found himself across

the room, gazing down into the hand-me-down crib. He was horrified at the darkness within his imagination, yet knew full well he hadn't the strength of mind or will to resist its powerful pull.

One more almost desperate glance at his wife's face…if she would only wake up, he would have to forsake this notion, and perhaps he could rid himself of the unforgivable intent. Indeed, Annie did stir a little and drew a deep sigh, almost as though she heard his desperate mental cry. But hers was the sleep of utter exhaustion, and she slumbered on.

A few moments later, Kelly slipped silently out the back door of the little shack, clutching a tiny pink bundle in his arms and blinking back the tears of shame and self-loathing that sprang unbidden to his eyes.

He closed the door behind him, careful to make not the slightest sound as he stole through the back yard and around the house to the dirt road that fronted it. Moving now with purpose and determination, he slipped from shadow to shadow, toward another little shack just down the lane.

Standing for a long moment in the darkness beneath a large, gnarled old cottonwood tree, he held the little bundle close to his heart. "It's best like this," he whispered. "It really is best for everybody."

One awkward stroke of a tiny cheek, then he strode to the front door and gave it a few firm raps. A light sprang up in the front window, and he breathed a sigh of relief. A moment later the door swung open, and he entered.

Exactly thirty-two minutes later, Kelly left the house, his arms empty. Hooked to his worn khaki trousers, a cheap pocket watch read 12:42 a.m. when he stepped back out into the moonlit night. He glanced furtively all around before slipping into the beckoning shadows. Head bowed, hands shoved deep into his pockets, he stole back the way he had come.

And at just after four o'clock in the morning, before the sun rose over the distant mountains, a piercing scream filled the dark camp, jolting the slumbering inhabitants of several nearby houses out of their much-needed rest.

They'd heard the bone-chilling cry of a mother bereft of her child.

Outside the newspaper office after his conversation with Clarence Camden, Kelly could not remember where he had left his old truck. He headed toward the bar, knowing that would be the most likely place to find it. He had no intention of going inside, though. He was through drinking. Never going to touch the stuff again.

Sure enough, the truck was there, half a block up the dusty road from the Whistlestop. He grinned when he saw the beat-up vehicle. It looked as if it had seen the wrong end of a crusher, but the old rust bucket could always be counted on to get a man where he wanted to go. He and Annie had come all the way from Texas in it, and it was still hauling his sorry bones around—when he could afford to put gasoline in the tank.

In spite of the noble promise he had made to himself and to Clarence Camden, Kelly stopped at the vehicle only long enough to give the faithful old flivver an affectionate pat. Then he hurried right on down the road and through the door of the Whistlestop.

The newsman's coffee and kindness had sobered him up just half a hair too much. With whiskey dulling his brain, he didn't have to see Annie's tormented eyes every time he closed his own. The cheap booze wrapped liquid gauze around his bleeding heart and eased the awful pain of knowing he would never hold his wife in his arms again. Not until he could put that baby back into hers.

Not that Annie knew it had been him who took the child. Had she known that, she might have killed him with her bare hands.

Kelly could not understand it. People had been losing children all down through the ages. Somehow they seemed to get past it and go on with life. He had thought Annie would, too.

But from the moment she looked down on the empty place in the crib and let out that bone-chilling, terrifying scream, he had known she would never get over it. For days, he watched helplessly as she sank further into a pit of despair, rising from her bed only when she had no choice.

Her once-beautiful silvery-blond hair hung lank and uncombed around her face, which, in just a few days' time, had taken on a sunken, skeletal appearance.

Nothing consoled her. She screamed out in the night, heart-wrenching shrieks that sent ice coursing through his veins. Even awake, Annie was not fully conscious of her surroundings. She sat for hours rocking back and forth in a non-existent rocker, her beautiful blue eyes distant and unfocused. She was lost and alone in a place he could not follow.

And he had put her there.

"Make it a double," he told the bartender.

When he locked up at two a.m., that gentleman had to all but physically remove Kelly from the Whistlestop.

"You gonna be okay, man?" he asked, supporting him with one hand as he turned the key in the door with the other.

"Get on outta here!" Kelly swore as he shook the man's hand off his arm. "Just leave me alone."

"Whatever you say." The barkeep rolled his eyes and

walked away.

Kelly staggered around behind the bar, hoping to find a partial bottle of something strong in the garbage bins. The one he now clutched in a death grip would be gone long before the night ended.

But someone had gotten there before him. Another obviously inebriated fellow hung half in, half out of the biggest container. A vagabond, Kelly figured, blurrily assessing the situation. One of the many wanderers who came through on the railroad, hanging out in town just long enough to steal a bit of food and as much strong drink as they could carry in their pockets.

He stood off a ways, swaying in the nippy night air, patiently watching the old hobo burrow in the stinking bins for his own kind of treasure. Soon the other man let out a triumphant yelp and slid to the ground beside the trash containers.

"I'll share mine if you sh-share yours." Kelly's voice was slurred, even to his own ears, and he sniggered. *Guess I must be drunk again. Oops!*

The old fellow blinked, instinctively hiding his hard-earned booty behind his back. Then he belched and broke into gales of inebriated laughter. "Sure, pal! Welcome to my p-palace. It's a p- arty!"

In no time at all they were indeed having their own little pity party, each of them ranting about the unfairness of life, each trying to one-up the other on the scale of hard knocks.

By the time his new buddy stopped talking and slumped across his lap, Jack Kelly had made up his mind. He'd strike out across California, searching every farm labor camp in the state.

He would find that fancy fellow and his pretty wife and make them give the baby back. Perhaps they would do it on their own if he told them the truth about Annie. If they insisted, he might even refund their money, though he'd have to work awhile to come up with it.

He needed to get on the road fast because he had a hunch that newspaper fellow just might take his story to the sheriff. Camden had as much as told him he couldn't keep it a secret. But he had agreed to run some kind of ad, making a plea for the return of the baby, so Kelly pretended to understand.

Do-gooders! Why can't they all just mind their own doggone business, anyway?

Angry now, he shoved at the smelly hobo lying across his legs.

"Get up, old codger. I gotta get outta here."

The old man did not move, and he sighed. Some folks simply could not hold their liquor.

"Get up, I said!"

He gave the fellow an impatient shove, but the stubborn old coot simply rolled over onto his back from the force of the push. Glowering, Kelly raised a balled fist, ready to do whatever it took to be free of his drinking partner. All the liquor was gone now, and he had to get the old truck in gear before Camden and the sheriff found him.

Something stopped him short of slamming his fist into the other man's face. He squinted his eyes, trying to get a better look in the murky darkness of the pre-dawn morning.

The old man's eyes were open. Terribly, unblinkingly, chillingly open.

"Awww, fiddle flakes!"

This was just great. The last thing he needed was for the police to follow him when he left town. And if they managed to somehow connect him with this old drunk, he might be in serious trouble. What if they thought he killed the miserable old codger?

He pushed the old guy off his lap and staggered to his feet. It was past time to go.

Back at the truck, he fell into the driver's seat where he sat gripping the wheel and staring off into space. Despite the large amount of alcohol making its way through his bloodstream, he found himself thinking with total, crystal clarity.

After a moment, he started the vehicle and shifted it into gear. But instead of heading straight for the edge of town, he circled the block and drove into the alley behind the bar.

Chapter Three

CLARENCE FOUND IT HARD to concentrate on work after Kelly left his office. As always when he had other things on his mind, the day seemed to drag on forever. He breathed a sigh of utmost relief when at last he was able to lock the front door behind him and walk the few blocks to his cozy cottage.

What am I to do with this unbelievable story? Mentally, he kicked himself and continued his internal discourse. That's not even a valid question. Kelly committed a crime of the most heinous variety. I have to involve the police.

Yet he had not gone straight to the sheriff's office today, as he knew he should have done. And he had not for one instant considered the story as a possibility for publication, even though it would certainly have been an exclusive for the Limelight. Something held him back.

First thing in the morning, though. I have no choice.

At home, he dined on a honeyed ham and cheese sandwich and three slices of fresh tomato, fresh from his garden and garnished with a generous sprinkling of salt.

Occasionally, he made a neat cut with his fork and brought a bite to his lips.

So absorbed was he in trying to puzzle out a solution to his dilemma that he stared down in surprise at the empty plate a few minutes later.

I don't remember eating. With a sigh, he carried his dish to the sink. *Oh, well. I trust it was good.*

Before crawling into bed, Clarence spent a long while on his knees, seeking direction from the only One with whom he was currently willing to share Jack Kelly's tale. Why was he so reluctant to turn the man in?

He had promised only to run some sort of ad, which in itself promised to be a problem. How, after all, does one discreetly run an ad in a newspaper asking for the return of a baby sold in the dead of night to a stranger with no name?

He had not promised Kelly any kind of secrecy or protection and did not intend to provide either. *So why didn't I go see the sheriff today?*

He stared into the darkness of his room long after he should have been asleep…because he knew why. He'd kept quiet because of the look in Kelly's eyes when he spoke of his wife. Never had he seen such a light of love. Annie Kelly seemed to be the only thing in life her husband held sacred.

He rolled over onto his other side, plumping his pillow a little harder than necessary.

Hmph! You don't rip a baby from the arms of a mother who loves it. Especially you don't do such a thing if you love that mother.

Yet, Kelly had done exactly that. Despite the lack of logic, Clarence knew in his soul the man cared deeply for his wife. How awfully sad that he loved alcohol more.

He drifted off in time to get a few hours' sleep before heading into the new day. He would drop in at Bonnie's first, then on to the office. But the moment Reta showed up to cover for him, Clarence planned to get himself on over to the sheriff's office.

Rounding the corner onto Main Street, he spotted a crowd of townsfolk milling around the railroad crossing at DiGiorgio and Main. Forgetting breakfast, he hurried to see what drew them.

A few ladies wept as he pushed his way through the crowd. Two men struggled through the press of bodies, all but carrying a rather large woman who appeared to have a bad case of the vapors. Even a few men looked a little green.

At the front of the gathering, a couple of deputies attempted to steer the ogling townspeople away from the scene.

"Go on home now, folks! There's nothing here anyone needs to see." The officer's bellowing voice stilled when he recognized Clarence. He eyed him warily before speaking in a resigned voice. "I don't suppose I can talk you into leaving, Mr. Camden."

"Afraid not."

"Well, don't touch anything."

Clarence nodded and continued, slowly making his way the few hundred yards down the railroad to inspect the accident scene.

The early morning cargo train passed through town at about six o'clock each morning. Whoever had been driving the vehicle Clarence saw up ahead—mangled beyond any hope of a happy outcome—had apparently not been aware of this schedule. From the condition of the ruined automobile, he guessed that it had plowed into the side of the freight train and been dragged to its current point of rest. Somehow, either upon impact or during the friction-filled journey down the tracks, a fire erupted.

He picked his way through the litter of metal and empty whiskey bottles. Some had obviously been thrown clear upon impact, as they were unbroken. One stood upright, as if it had been carefully placed in just that position.

The twist of melted and seared metal was burned beyond any possibility of identification. So were the various body parts being collected by a team of workers and placed in a pile.

Now he understood the sick faces in the crowd.

Swallowing a large lump in his throat, he approached the grisly mound of burned flesh, pulling a handkerchief from his pocket to cover his nose as he stood over it.

A withered and blackened chunk that had once been part of someone's leg appeared to be the largest piece the clean-up team had found so far. Beside the leg lay most of a foot, all but one toe completely burned away.

And snugged against that partial foot…a finger.

Clarence drew in a sharp breath, unable to look away from this last burnt offering. Kneeling beside the unsightly heap, he called out for a nearby deputy, who approached with obvious reluctance.

"Sam, I need to see the front side of that finger."

"You're a pain, Camden." Shooting Clarence a look of intense displeasure, Sam knelt beside the gruesome collection. Fumbling in the pocket of his overcoat, he pulled out a wrinkled white handkerchief and used it to nudge the blackened digit into a new position.

Clarence emitted a harsh, guttural sound, choking on the breath he had been holding.

"What?" The officer spoke through gritted teeth, making no effort to disguise his mounting irritation.

The ring was nearly hidden by the puffy, swollen flesh around it, but the three tiny blue stones were still intact.

"I know who this finger belongs to."

The rest of that day and most of the next were a blur of questions and answers.

Clarence managed, without revealing Jack Kelly's heinous crime, to provide the sheriff, the morgue, and a couple of insistent county employees with enough information for the remains to be disposed of in whatever manner they chose. The man's wife deserved to mourn his passing without the bitterness that would come from knowing what he had done.

What good could telling her possibly do now? Kelly had not known the name of the man who purchased the child. He had no idea where or even in which direction they had traveled. Even the make of their vehicle was a mystery. Chances of finding that baby were slim to none.

But he did have an opportunity to offer Kelly's wife the key to a brighter future. He could not place her baby in her arms. Nor could he give her back her husband, drunk or sober.

But he could let her know Kelly was dead. Something about the way the man had talked about his wife told Clarence she would never move on with her life as long as the slightest chance remained that her husband might return.

Sheriff Headley was reluctant to give him the permission he sought…to deliver the news to the widow himself. The finger bearing that distinctive wedding band was the only evidence connecting the driver of the demolished motor vehicle to Jack Kelly. The old lawman seemed worried about the potential for misidentification.

But Clarence was certain.

"Look, Sheriff, I saw that ring on his finger the day before the accident. I held it in my hand and examined it. That's Jack Kelly's ring."

"What makes you think it's one-of-a-kind?" Headley demanded. "I don't like identifying a body based strictly on a piece of jewelry."

"I don't like it, either, but in this case, what else do you have? I know that ring belonged to Kelly. He said it had been his wife's grandfather's. I doubt there's another one just like it anywhere…and certainly not around here."

The sheriff sighed. "I know you think you're right, Camden. I just wish I could be a little more sure myself!"

Clarence snapped his fingers. "I have an idea. Would you get the ring, please?"

Sheriff Headley pulled open the evidence drawer in a cabinet behind his desk. Removing the little item, he made as if to hand it over, but Clarence backed away.

"No, I don't want to look at it. I noticed something about Kelly's ring that morning while I held it in my hand. This is our chance to see if it's the same one."

"Spit it out then."

"There are three blue stones, one a little larger than the others. One of the small stones has a tiny chip, very slight, at the edge of the setting. It could almost be taken for a scratch."

Headley studied the ring in silence. After a moment, he reached into his desk and pulled out a magnifying glass.

Clarence watched, relaxing only slightly when the sheriff nodded, still studying the stones. At last he held out the wedding band, indicating with a nod that Clarence should take it.

"All right, Camden. Considering the condition of the…body, this is prob'ly as close to an I.D. as we're gonna get. But I can't for the life of me understand why you want to give the man's wife the news." He shook his head, eyeing

Clarence as if he had grown another head. "Tellin' a woman her husband is dead ain't fun, let me tell you. Why would you want to do it?"

Clarence drew a deep breath, letting it out slowly as he raised both eyebrows, meeting the sheriff's curious gaze. "I'm not sure. Something about the way Kelly talked about her. I want her to get the news from someone who had at the very least spoken to her husband before he died." He shrugged and shook his head. "Maybe I just want to break it to her in a less formal manner."

The sheriff cackled. "You got somethin' against uniforms and badges?"

"Not at all!" He smiled at the older man. "But I'm glad you're wearing them, and I don't have to."

"Fine then. Get on over there and tell the poor woman she's a widow."

Clarence picked up his hat and set it atop his head. He held out his hand, and the sheriff shook it.

"Thank you, Sheriff."

"I oughta be thankin' you. I shore don't wanta do it."

He was almost out the door when Sheriff Headley spoke again.

"Camden."

He turned, and the other man looked at him for a moment without speaking. At last he shook his head and offered half a grin.

"Someday I expect to hear whatever it is you're not tellin' me now."

"Someday," Clarence promised, "you will."

No one responded to his first two knocks, and Clarence heard no stirrings from within the house. Maybe she really wasn't home. Yet his gut told him the woman was there, ignoring his persistent tapping.

"Mrs. Kelly? Mrs. Kelly, are you there?" He landed three more solid raps against the splintered wooden door and turned to go, disappointed but not defeated. He would try again later.

Behind him, the door creaked open. He turned, and laid eyes on Annie Kelly for the first time.

She was the most beautiful mess he'd ever seen, or ever would again. He knew that without a shadow of a doubt.

Her silver-gold hair—not silver as in gray, but a beautiful silvery gold—had obviously not been brushed that day, nor possibly the day before. With the dimly lit room behind her, cornflower blue eyes seemed over-bright against the paleness of her skin. She wore a wrinkled, spotted gingham housecoat with all the buttons in the wrong holes.

She looked half dead, yet still gloriously gorgeous. He wanted nothing more than to pull her into his arms and make everything better.

Now that she'd opened the door, he couldn't find his voice.

Finally, the woman spoke, so softly he had to strain to hear. "Yes? I'm Mrs. Kelly."

He opened his mouth and for a moment feared he would never again be able to make a sound. He desperately cleared his throat and forced words from between numb lips, gratified to hear them vocalize, though he barely recognized his own voice.

"I'm sorry to disturb you, ma'am. I know you've been through a difficult time, and I apologize for dropping by like this."

She just stood there, her eyes lifeless and dull, clearly waiting for him to state his business and leave. He shifted weight from one foot to the other, uncomfortable under her detached gaze.

"Look, I…I really don't know how to say what I've come here to say. Perhaps I should start by telling you who I am." He attempted a small smile, which faded and disappeared when Annie did not offer one in return. "My name is Clarence Camden. The Lamont Limelight is my company…my…uh…my newspaper."

Still no response. He sighed and plowed ahead. "I'm afraid I have some bad news, Mrs. Kelly."

For the first time since she had opened the door, Annie appeared to hear what he was saying. Her chin lifted slightly, and her eyes widened.

"You've seen Jack." Again he almost missed the whispered statement. "Is my husband all right?"

"I've seen him." He hesitated. "May I come in, please? This could take a few minutes."

Turning, she walked away without a word. Since she did not close the door in his face, he followed. Motioning him toward a worn sofa, she perched on the edge of a straight-backed chair across the room and waited in dull silence.

Clarence spoke slowly, uncertain where to start. "I found your husband…uh, well, sleeping…in front of my office three days ago."

"He was drunk, of course." A touch of bitterness colored the widow's voice. "You don't have to be afraid to say it, Mr. Camden. I know all about Jack's drinking problem."

She closed her eyes briefly, with a sad little shake of her head. "Poor Jack. He took this whole thing much harder than I would have expected of him."

Suddenly those vivid blue eyes flew open and stared directly into his. "Did he tell you our baby girl was kidnapped five weeks ago?"

Clarence looked away. "Yes, he told me. I'm very sorry, Mrs. Kelly."

Annie shrugged. "Jack started drinking again that day." Clarence leaned forward, trying to hear her better. "He actually stopped for a while, you know, when we knew we were going to have a baby. He promised he wouldn't drink anymore."

She began to rock back and forth, twisting her hands together in her lap. "He didn't really want children, but he knew I did. And he seemed to be honestly trying to quit, right up until the baby disappeared."

"I'm sure it was most painful." Clarence thought his murmured response completely inadequate, but he hadn't the faintest idea what to say, in light of what he knew.

A shadow of emotion passed over her face as she nodded. "Yes, it was. It is. Even Jack took it hard. I knew he was drinking again. I smelled the whiskey on him that first day after …after she was taken."

She shook her head, and her puzzled eyes met Clarence's. "I don't know where he got the money to buy the nasty stuff. We've barely had enough to survive on. What little he brought in from working in the fields simply wasn't enough. It's hot out there, and that's hard work. But…well, I suppose things are tough for everyone. All over.'"

Again he avoided her eyes, and finally she moved on.

"So. He was passed out in front of your office. But I'm sure that's not why you're here. What happened?"

"Well…" Clarence half wished he had let Sheriff Headley do his job. "I tried to wake him and couldn't, so I…well, I dashed a pitcher of cold water in his face."

She chuckled, a bitter, hollow sound that hurt his ears. "I've done that a time or two myself."

He hurried on with his story. "I let him clean himself up

in my washroom. I'm afraid he was sorely in need of a bath. Then I fed him breakfast, and we talked."

She watched him, the deep, sad pools of her eyes watchful, more alive than they'd been. "Did he say where he's been for the past five weeks?"

"He said he was trying to find your baby for you."

"Of course. He'd do that. When he isn't drinking, Jack's a dear, kind man."

She was silent for a long time. When she spoke again, Annie Kelly's searching gaze reached right into Clarence's soul. "Where is my husband now, Mr. Camden?"

He stood and covered the distance between them in two steps. Annie's eyes widened with something like comprehension as he knelt and took one of her hands in his own.

"Mrs. Kelly…Annie…there's been an accident."

Every vestige of color drained from her cheeks, and Clarence understood she already knew what he had come here to tell her. She shook her head, her eyes pleading with him to leave it unsaid.

He heard a soft crunch as his teeth ground together. This dreadful errand must be seen through, as much as he'd love to grant the wish in Annie's eyes. Meeting that blue gaze with a steady one of his own, he picked up her other hand and held them both in a strong, comforting grip.

"I think your husband drank again after he left my office, but I can't say that for sure. I only know that he…well, he drove his vehicle into the side of a freight train two days ago."

Annie drew in a sharp breath and shook her head from side to side, silently begging him to take it back.

"I'm so sorry, ma'am. Your husband, he…well, I'm afraid he didn't make it."

She pulled her hands from his and covered her face. He

remained on his knees, silently offering his support. Finally she raised a tear-wet gaze to his.

"I want to see him."

Clarence had expected this. What he had not realized was how hard it would be to explain why her request was impossible.

"Mrs. Kelly, I'm sorry, I..." Clarence drew a deep breath. Just say it. "I'm afraid there is no...body for you to see. There was a fire, and—"

"No." Annie's chin shot up, and the first signs of life showed in her eyes as she glared at Clarence. "No! If there's no body, then it wasn't Jack."

"I wish I could say you're right, but...it was your husband, ma'am." Reaching into his pocket, he pulled out the wedding band Sheriff Headley had placed in his trust.

He took one of Annie's hands, noticing the matching ring she wore. Gently, he unfurled the cold fingers and pressed the tiny object into her palm.

Her eyes clashed with his for a long moment. He saw the sheer determination it took for her to lower her gaze and look at what he had given her.

Clarence wasn't sure what he expected. Sobs, screams, denial, even anger. What he did not expect was the sudden stillness that enveloped the two of them. They sat in utter silence as Jack Kelly's wife accepted yet another devastating blow to her heart.

She seemed to shrink before his eyes, to simply fold into herself. Tears raced each other down colorless cheeks, yet she made not a single sound for the longest time. Not even a whimper. Then she fixed Clarence beneath a dull blue gaze and spoke, chilling him to the bone.

"God has forsaken me."

Rising from her chair, Annie Kelly crossed the room and

pulled a family Bible and a fountain pen from a well-used, battered shelf. Clarence watched, at a loss. Returning to her chair, she placed the big book on her lap and flipped over a couple of pages, stopping at one titled, "Deaths." Annie's hand shook only a little as she penned her husband's name on the first line in a beautiful, flowing script.

"Did you say two days ago?"

He nodded and watched as she entered the date. That done, she closed the big book, stood and walked across the room to replace it on the shelf.

Turning back to Clarence, she spoke in an eerily calm voice for a woman who had just been informed of her husband's horrible, fiery death.

"Thank you, Mr. Camden, for bringing me the news. You're very kind. But now, I hope you'll excuse me. I need to be alone."

Clarence didn't like it. "Mrs. Kelly, I don't think I should—"

She raised one slender hand, silencing him. "Please."

Reluctantly, he left her to handle her sorrow in her own way. But he could not bring himself to walk completely out of her life. He might never be able to do that.

Because it was his business to know the business of others, Clarence was aware that Dale Corman—a well-recognized name in Lamont—owned the shanties in this particular farm labor camp.

He also knew that those living in these pitiful wooden shacks were the lucky ones. Many unfortunate people, after making the long, arduous trip to California in hopes of finding better lives than the ones they'd left behind, found themselves living in tents. In many cases, entire extended families existed under a single canvas shelter. Some actually made their homes in chicken coops and other outbuildings made available to them by various landowners.

Annie Kelly would not live in a chicken coop, not if Clarence could do anything about it.

He set off in search of Dale Corman.

By the time he left Corman's Camp and returned to his office, he owned the rickety little shack Annie called home.

Part Two

1959

Chapter Four

"JULIANA....JULIANA! I'M SORRY, darling. I'm so sorry!"

The tortured cry brought Juliana Camden rushing to the closed bedroom door. With her hand hovering above the glass doorknob, she debated the wisdom of entering the private sanctuary during one of her mother's "dark days."

She closed her eyes, and a tear dropped onto the front of her simple cotton blouse. She desperately wanted to help, but how? How often had she stood in this very spot, before this same door, listening to her mother's private torment? So many times she had worried and wondered about the horrible headaches that sent Mama to bed for days at a time, days when she moaned and cried in agony, often calling out to Juliana for unneeded forgiveness.

Juliana was strictly forbidden to enter the room during these attacks. Her mother insisted recovery came only through seclusion and silence in the pitch blackness of her bedroom, where the windows had been covered for many years with heavy dark fabric.

Yet there were times, like today, when Mama's pain was

so palpable as to be felt outside her door, and it was more than Juliana could stand to let her endure it alone. She drew a deep breath and lifted her chin, suddenly determined to go to her.

"Don't do it, child."

She whirled away from the door, stifling a startled cry. "Daddy!"

A sad smile passed briefly across her father face. Clarence Camden crossed the room and brushed a tear from her cheek with the pad of one big thumb. "You have to respect her wishes, Julie girl. I know you want to help, but, well, your mother has to deal with this in her own way."

Wrapping an arm around her, he led her away from the door.

"She's in so much pain." Juliana's whisper held a world of agony. "And why does she beg me to forgive her? Mama has never done anything but love me!"

"Shhh!" He drew her into his arms. "Of course she hasn't. It's just the illness. She'll be herself again soon."

"But for how long? She needs to see a doctor. Something is terribly wrong!"

"I've tried many times to get her to see Dr. Gossner, you know that. But she refuses, and I will not force her."

"It hurts to know she's in such pain, and I can't help her at all." Tears welled up yet again in Juliana's eyes.

"Yes. I know." Her father's voice broke, and he covered his face with one hand.

Stricken, she wrapped both arms around his waist, resting her head on his broad chest. "Dear Daddy! I know you wouldn't let Mama suffer like this, not if you could do anything to help her." Tiptoeing, she kissed his cheek. "What would I do without you? What would either of us do?"

"You'll never know, child. I'm here to stay."

Juliana clasped his big hands, smiling a little as she did so. Spending time with her father was one of the greatest joys in her life. He always made her happy, and the pleasure she derived from losing her small hands in his very large ones was an extra little blessing. He was a big man overall and well-known for having a heart just as oversized.

She guided him to the kitchen and gently pushed him toward a chair at the table. Placing a cup of hot coffee in front of him, she dropped down at his side.

"What is wrong with her, Daddy? Do you know?"

His handsome face clouded, and he shook his head. "Your mother has her own demons to fight, I suppose. I would give or do just about anything to free her from them." His voice roughened with an emotion too strong for mere words. "If I knew how to fix this, don't you know I would have done it by now?"

"Of course I know that! I just can't help feeling there's something tormenting her. She suffers so horribly with these…what does she call them? Sick headaches? Surely there's something that can be done."

"There's nothing you or I can do besides love her. Only God can help my beloved Annie, and even He can't unless she allows it."

"You can't believe she doesn't want help!"

He patted her on the shoulder as he set his empty cup on the table. "I didn't say that. But your mother seems to think she doesn't deserve help, that these attacks are some type of punishment. As long as she believes that she won't accept help from God or anyone else."

A tear streaked a path down Juliana's cheek, and she brushed it away impatiently. "Mama has never done anything to deserve this kind of punishment. She's good and kind and beautiful—inside and out!"

Her father chuckled. "You don't expect an argument from me, do you? My Annie is an amazing and wonderful woman. I'm just saying she doesn't seem to believe that herself. She magnifies her every human shortcoming. I think she feels she doesn't deserve you or me or any of the other good things in her life."

"Daddy, I can't believe there's nothing we can do!"

Her father got up and carried both of their cups to the sink then walked back to the table. Placing a finger under Juliana's chin, he forced her to look up at him. "We can pray, child. We can always pray."

Squaring his broad shoulders, he gently patted the top of her head and said good-bye. As publisher of the local newspaper with offices a mile north of their home in South Lamont, he left the house promptly at seven o'clock every weekday morning.

Juliana sighed and began washing the two cups they had used. Only when they were dried and put away did she go into her own bedroom and close the door.

The room reflected the immaculate condition her mother insisted on throughout the house. The only thing out of place was the envelope on her neatly made bed. She eyed it as if it were a coiled snake but picked it up after a moment to remove the single sheet of paper folded inside. For what must have been the hundredth time since its arrival the day before, her eyes skimmed over the words.

Dear Miss Camden,

Thank you for your recent submission to Voice of Hope. As always, we enjoyed your story and plan to use it in an upcoming issue of the magazine. Payment is enclosed with this letter.

In addition, I have an offer I hope you will consider. The

44

recent loss of one of our staff writers has created an opening I need to fill as soon as possible. Being familiar with and in admiration of your work and knowing you live within easy commute of our office, I was hoping you might join the staff.

Of course, it's possible you prefer working freelance. If, however, you are interested in this position, I would very much like to speak with you. Will you please call me as soon as possible at the number on this letterhead?

Sincerely,

Mr. Will Dawson

Editor

Voice of Hope Magazine

Juliana allowed the letter to drift onto the bed as she buried her face in her hands. Groaning, she sank to her knees.

Here was the opportunity she had been waiting—no, praying for, literally dropped into her lap. She had long dreamed of the chance to work on staff at one of the magazines for which she wrote freelance articles and stories. Yet now that the chance was offered her, she saw no possibility of accepting it.

With Daddy at the office every day, she could not think of leaving Mama. Although not allowed to actually tend to her through the excruciating episodes, she could not bear the thought of leaving her mother to endure them alone, without even a loved one nearby.

Kneeling beside her bed, she began to talk to her best Friend, as was her habit each day. This morning, she would pray for her mother, as always, but she would also talk to God about her own concerns and thank Him for the many blessings in her life.

With poor Mama suffering untold tortures, and Daddy bowed beneath the weight of his wife's physical and mental condition, God was her only confidante—and she desperately needed Him now.

"Julie girl! Wake up!"

Clarence shook Juliana, and she slowly opened her eyes, gasping and sobbing, still not fully awake.

"You're crying, sweetheart. Are you okay?" He knelt at the side of the bed and placed a gentle hand on his daughter's trembling shoulder. "What is it, child?"

She shuddered, her thin body wracked with sobs that wrenched at his heart. "Mother!" she cried out. "My little Mother!"

Clarence's hand paused in its gentle patting of her shoulder. *My little Mother?* He'd never heard Juliana refer to Annie in that manner. Besides, aside from only now getting over the terrible sick headache she'd been suffering for days, Annie was fine.

He switched on the bedside lamp and was shocked at Juliana's appearance. Tears streaked her colorless face. She had obviously been weeping long before he heard her frantic cries. Her long hair, black against that porcelain skin, was plastered to her head and soaked with tears and perspiration.

Clarence gently pried apart her hands, which were clenched together in her lap as she sat bolt upright on the bed.

Gripping them within his own, he vaguely registered their iciness. He had to do something. "Julie, wake up!" He raised his voice, hoping to break through the thick layers of sleep.

The girl started, and her gaze fell on him with slow but welcome recognition. "Daddy?"

"Yes, it's me. Everything's okay. Just relax, sweetheart."

Tears continued to fall down her face in a steady stream, but she was awake.

"I'll be right back." Clarence left the room but quickly returned to kneel beside the bed. Awkwardly, he wiped at his daughter's flushed cheeks with a damp washcloth.

She took it from him and squeezed his hand. "Thank you, Daddy."

She ran the cool cloth over her face, held it there for a moment before returning it to him with a shaky smile. Still sniffling quietly, she bent to remove a comb from a drawer beside the bed and drew it through her tangled hair.

"Are you all right?" Clarence hoped the girl didn't hear the shakiness in his voice.

Laying the comb aside, she smiled weakly and nodded. "I'm sorry. I don't know what that was all about."

"You must have been dreaming."

Juliana gave him a half nod, seeming a bit uncertain. "I guess so," she agreed, but Clarence heard a note of hesitation in her voice.

"But …?"

"It was just kind of strange. I must have been dreaming, but I don't remember any real particulars. I just know I had…" She choked on the words. "I had lost my mother."

"You worry about her a lot, sweetheart. Especially when she's ill."

"Yes, but it wasn't Mama I was crying for."

Clarence shook his head, confused. "You said you had lost your mother."

She nodded, obviously troubled. "I know. But –" Sighing, she looked up at him, and he found himself struck yet again, as he had been so often throughout the years, by her beautiful eyes. Right now they were the color of molten gold. "This will sound crazy, I know, but I wasn't me! I was someone else, and my little Mother was dying. I didn't think …." She paused, swallowing hard, and he knew she was recalling the intense sorrow she had felt. "I truly didn't think I could live without her. I felt so lost, and incredibly frightened of being alone."

He frowned. "You used those words earlier, Julie girl. 'My little Mother.' I've never heard you call her that before."

She tilted her head, nodding thoughtfully. "I didn't realize I'd said it. I never have called Mama 'my little Mother.' But, like I said, I wasn't crying for my mother. I was mourning…someone else's."

Clarence stood, then bent to kiss her cheek. "Dreams can be a little distorted sometimes, child. Just let it go, and try to get some sleep." He stood and pulled the covers up to Juliana's chin. "You sure you're okay now?"

"I'm fine, Daddy. Go to bed."

The door closed behind her father, and Juliana burrowed out from beneath the cocoon of cover he'd tucked around her. Smiling, she switched off the lamp and lay back against her pillow.

In the darkness, her smile disappeared. The overwhelming emotions that had tormented her dreams still lurked on the outskirts of her mind. Her heart felt raw and sore, and she resisted the possibility of returning to that dismal dreamworld.

Staring wide-eyed into the darkness, her mind ran in vicious circles, frantically avoiding sleep.

Awakened hours later by a light tap on her door, Juliana was instantly frightened for her mother. Her panic, always just below the surface, was stilled by a familiar voice from the hallway.

"Juliana? Are you awake?"

Annie Camden insisted on calling her daughter by her full name, and Juliana loved the sound of it on her lips, just as she adored the shortened version spoken by her father.

"Yes, Mama. Come in!" Already on her feet, she reached for the soft chenille robe draped across a chair near her bed, and quickly belted it around her waist.

"How are you feeling?" She anxiously searched her mother's face as the older woman stepped into the room.

Musical laughter soothed her heart like a salve as she allowed herself to be drawn into her mother's arms.

"I'm fine, darling, I really am!" Mama's voice was a gentle caress. "I wish you wouldn't worry so. You know, I always come through these annoying little headaches just fine!"

Clinging to the frail frame, she fought back tears that seemed always so ready to fall. "They're more than 'little headaches,' Mama. Something is not right. Please, please go see Dr. Gossner!"

"Now, why on earth would I do that? For a headache? I most certainly will not waste his time with such a thing! Dr. Gossner is a busy man."

Juliana pulled away, looking reproachfully into her mother's eyes. "I'm so frightened for you!"

"Honey, really, I'm fine. Don't worry about…"

She broke off as, in avoiding Juliana's pleading gaze, her eyes fell on the small table beside the bed. "What is this? You've sold another article, haven't you?" She swooped up the familiar letterhead from Voice of Hope.

"Mama, no! Don't …!"

But it was too late. Juliana always shared correspondence from various publishing companies with her mother, and that eager lady was already reading aloud the short letter from Voice of Hope. Pride and excitement brought beautiful color into her cheeks, which Juliana rejoiced about even in the grip of a clutching panic.

"'If, however, you are interested in a staff position, I would very much like to speak with you. Will you please call me as soon as possible at the number on this letterhead?'"

A delighted smile made Mama's delicate beauty almost breathtaking. She laughed in unfettered delight and tossed the letter into the air, clapping her hands like a child. Then she grabbed Juliana in a tight hug.

"When did this get here? Have you called him yet? Oh, this is wonderful, darling! I told you you were good!"

Juliana could not help laughing as her mother danced around the room.

"When do you start? Oh! We have to get you a car! How will you get to…?"

Laughing, Juliana pressed a gentle finger against her mother's lips. "Mama, calm down! You'll make yourself sick again."

"I will not be sick again!" Her mother's face wore a warm glow of pleasure. "This is…why, this is perfect! It's what you've always wanted!"

Suddenly, she stopped, her eyes fixed on Juliana's face. "What? I know that look. Don't tell me you're thinking of not taking this job."

"Please don't get so excited. You've been ill. Come on, Mama, let's go get some coffee."

She led the way to the kitchen. Her mother followed, but not before scooping the letter up off the floor where she'd dropped it in her excitement.

Acutely aware that Mama watched her every move, she filled the old coffee pot with water and measured out grounds.

She's going to insist on discussing that letter. Why on earth didn't I put it away?

"Come, dear. Sit. A watched pot never boils, you know."

She joined her mother at the table and sat silent, her eyes downcast.

With a hand still slightly shaky from her recent illness, Mama raised Juliana's chin, and she reluctantly met her questioning gaze. "What is it, darling? Tell me."

"I'm just not sure this is the right thing, you know? I'm a freelance writer. I love being at home with you."

Horrified enlightenment dawned in those beloved blue eyes. "That's it? That's it, isn't it? You're worried about leaving me here alone!"

Juliana never ceased to be amazed at her mother's insight, but this time it was so swift she was shocked into silence. Annie bounced up out of her chair and set about finishing the job Juliana had started.

"Well, I won't have it!" She jerked a can of cream out of the refrigerator and slammed the door hard enough to rattle its contents. "You have dreamed of working on the staff of a Christian magazine since you were just a little girl. Now here's the opportunity you've been waiting for, and it's so close to home. Why, Bakersfield is only thirty minutes away! Voice of Hope is a reputable magazine—a Christian magazine. And they've come seeking you out. You didn't even have to ask for the job!"

"Yes, Mama, I know." Juliana tried to break in, desperate to soothe her mother's obvious frustration. "Just listen—"

"No, Juliana. You listen to me." Annie Camden was a gentle woman, but when her mind was made up on any subject, both Juliana and her father knew there was no dissuading her. "You are not going to throw away this opportunity because you're worried about me."

"But Mama, I–"

"No! You will go—right now—and call this Mr. Dawson and arrange to meet him as soon as possible. There will be no further discussion as to my being here alone."

It can't be good for her to get this excited. Not this soon after being so ill...

Juliana spoke soothingly. "Mama, please. I only thought…"

A cup landed in front of her with such force that a good deal of the hot contents sloshed onto the tabletop. Dropping into a chair, her mother spooned sugar into her cup as she spoke.

"There is nothing to think about. How can you even consider throwing away this opportunity? This is the field you have worked so hard to be a part of!"

Juliana realized she would not be allowed to speak a word until her mother had her say. Sighing, she reached out and gently pried the spoon from her hand before she could dip it once more into the sugar bowl.

"You've got more sugar than coffee now, Mama," she said quietly.

Her mother made no response other than to pick up her coffee and sip at the black sweetness. Neither woman spoke until Mama lowered her cup to the table and gripped Juliana's hand in her own. Her soft voice vibrated with feeling.

"The work you do, darling…it's a God-given talent. You've always had a wisdom far beyond your years and a true understanding of people. You also have an amazing gift for communicating that wisdom in a way that touches your readers." She drew a shaky breath. "This job would make it possible to expand your outreach and touch more young women—some of whom are searching for answers to life-altering situations. Are you really going to throw away a chance like this?"

Juliana hadn't heard her mother make such a long speech in too long to remember. A beautiful light of passion shone in the dear eyes and brought delicate color to her face.

I wonder if Mama realizes she called it a "God-given" talent?

Although without question a gracious, kind woman, Juliana's mother had never attended a church service with her—at least, not within her recollection. Nor could she remember ever having heard her pray. Though she never put up a fuss when Juliana and her father attended church or said grace at the table, she never took part in their worship herself.

As a child, Juliana had once asked her father why her mommy did not go with them to church. He explained that she was once a very strong Christian but had been hurt a long time ago when she lost someone she loved.

"Her heart is bruised, Julie girl." She could still hear his gentle voice trying to make her understand. "I think she's a little angry at God right now."

"Well, we'll just pray for her, Daddy. Jesus will heal her heart, won't he?" Young Juliana had been confident of her heavenly Father's ability to fix any situation.

Now, she leaned close and kissed the older woman's cheek. "You're right, as always. I cannot say 'no' to God's calling. But I can't be unconcerned about leaving you here alone, either."

"I'll be just fine, darling. I always am, aren't I?"

She rose and began to putter about the kitchen. "I think I'll fix us some breakfast. How about some toast and maybe a couple of eggs? You go get dressed and freshen up; then you have a call to make."

"For such a sweet woman, my little Mother, you're quite

stubborn, you know!"

"Me?" Mama lifted an eyebrow in mock surprise then smiled and pointed at the door. "Go!"

She blew a kiss across the room and went, only vaguely aware she'd called her Mama "my little Mother."

Chapter Five

SHE DREW A SHAKY BREATH and stepped through one in a pair of big double glass doors. Large blue and white letters on the facing wall assured her she had arrived at Voice of Hope—Christian Magazine.

The receptionist looked up with a wide, open smile. The girl's eyes traveled the length of Juliana's dark blue two-piece outfit, and she found herself tugging at the hem of the tailored jacket.

Was the collar straight on the soft white blouse beneath? And her hair…! She had pulled her hair back into an attractive twist but, as usual, a discreet examination revealed that, as usual, a couple of unruly strands already trailed down each cheek.

"Good morning. May I help you?" The warm voice soothed her taut nerves.

"I'm Juliana Camden." She silently bemoaned the slight tremor in her voice. "I have an appointment with Will Dawson."

"Miss Camden! Oh, it is nice to meet you." The girl stood, extending her hand. Surprised, Juliana took it in a firm grasp. "I can't tell you how many times I've found just the answer I was praying for in one of your stories."

Warming to the friendly receptionist, she felt herself begin to relax. "You're very kind to say so."

"Not at all. It's the truth." The young lady returned to her seat. "Thank you for lending your talent to the Lord."

"Oh, I don't lend it!" She sent the other girl a gentle smile. "It's already His. I simply give it back."

The young receptionist nodded. "I guess that's true, Miss Camden, but if you didn't give it back, those wonderful stories wouldn't happen. Excuse me, please."

She picked up the telephone and used one manicured fingertip to punch a couple of buttons on the switchboard.

"Miss Camden is here. Yes, of course." Dropping the receiver back onto the telephone, she smiled. "He'll be right out."

"Thank you." Juliana tried to still the frantic beating of her heart as she waited. "I feel a little at a loss. You know my name, but I don't know yours"

"Claudia Poole." The girl emitted a shocking, most unrefined snort, forcing Juliana to hide a huge grin behind her hand. "Not that most people care about that. They just want me to do my job and get them in to see whoever they're here to see—and preferable without a wait, although I don't know how I could possibly change that." Her laughter held no ill will.

"Well, Claudia, I care about your name. Thank you for making this process a little easier for me."

"If I did that, then I'm doing my job right, Miss Camden."

"Juliana…please."

"Juliana it is." The girl smiled, a wonderful, quirky dance of her lips that Juliana found charming and irresistible.

"Miss Camden?"

Her heart responded to the deep, resonant voice by diving to her stomach and bouncing back up into her throat in the space of two seconds. Hardly daring to breathe, she turned to face Will Dawson.

Definitely easy to look at. Was he Italian? No…perhaps French, given the smooth olive complexion. Black hair swept back in crisp waves from a ruggedly handsome, aristocratic face. A strong jaw complemented the square chin beneath full, firm lips. In contrast to his otherwise European appearance, the man's eyes—almost translucent blue— seemed a stark but extremely attractive contrast. A slightly crooked smile, in Juliana's opinion, only added to his considerable charm.

In the instant it took her to assess his appearance, his eyes grew wide, and the crooked smile broadened into delighted laughter. In two giant strides, he was across the room, and Juliana was in his arms!

Too shocked to protest, she glanced frantically at Claudia, but the wide-eyed receptionist seemed frozen in place as her boss wrapped Juliana in a bear hug, lifting her off her feet to swing her around.

"Where did you come from, little one?" His voice rang with surprise and delight. "How long has it been? Five years? Six?"

He set her on her feet and tucked her hand under his arm. "Claudia, didn't you say Miss Camden is here? We may need to postpone our meeting half an hour or so." He glanced around the lobby, empty but for the three of them. "Where is she?"

Claudia grinned, sweeping an arm in Juliana's direction with exaggerated ceremony.

"Miss Camden, meet the esteemed editor and publisher of Voice of Hope, Mr. Will Dawson. Will, Miss Juliana

Camden."

Juliana knew by the annoying heat in her cheeks that embarrassment…and something else…had painted them a deep pink. She scolded herself, ashamed to have enjoyed that brief moment in the arms of the handsome stranger, who clearly thought she was someone else. How on earth would she overcome this awkward moment and carry on a successful interview?

But her potential employer only laughed. "Don't be silly, Claudia! Where is Miss Camden?"

Juliana disentangled her arm from his. "Mr. Dawson, I'm so sorry. You seem to have mistaken me for someone else. I am Juliana Camden. Perhaps I should come back at a better time?"

Will's clear blue eyes narrowed as they moved over her face. Finally he shook his head and offered a rueful smile.

"Miss Camden, what can I say? I am so sorry! You look very much like—" He paused, shaking his head. "No, no—you look *exactly* like my cousin. I suppose it's obvious I don't see her often, nor have I seen her recently."

Juliana managed to shape her trembling lips into a smile. "Well, they say we all have a double."

"Yes, they do say that, don't they?" he murmured.

She'd started to be a bit uncomfortable under his intense scrutiny when Will finally drew a deep breath and smiled.

"Well, shall we try this again?" His smile remained slightly bemused as he reached for her hand. "I'm so pleased to meet you, Miss Camden. Will you come with me to my office, or have you decided this is the last place you'd ever want to work?"

Juliana laughed, and the awkward moment passed. "I think I can risk it." She gently extricated the hand he still held.

At last he turned away, visibly forcing his gaze from her face, and opened the door he had come through. "Come with me, please."

She followed him down a long, narrow corridor and into a spacious office. By the time he motioned her inside, Juliana's heart threatened to explode inside her chest.

At twenty-three, she had met very few men who merited a second look. She had dated only a couple of times, never having desired to form anything beyond friendship with any of the young men who attempted to court her. "When Mr. Right comes along," she always told her friends, "I'll know him."

But she hadn't even dreamed she would know him instantly.

However, her heart seemed to be trying to tell her something—pounding thunderously one moment, fluttering like a thousand delicate wings the next.

Stop it! You're here to interview for a job—one you want very much. Don't mess it up by behaving like a lovesick schoolgirl.

"Miss Camden?" Mr. Dawson's questioning voice cut through her tumultuous thoughts, jerking her back into the moment.

"Oh! I'm...I'm sorry!" Her cheeks grew hot...again. How many times had he spoken her name? "I must have gone somewhere else for a moment."

He grinned, and her heart trip hammered. "Hey, don't worry about it. Not for a second. It's a long trek between here and the front door. I go a little blank on the journey myself sometimes."

She made a desperate attempt to gather her scattered thoughts and emotions. "I really am sorry. I don't know why I was so far away."

"It's perfectly all right." His lips twitched, but he spared her the humiliation of actually laughing. "Please have a seat. Heaven knows you must need it after the greeting I put you through."

Juliana sat in a comfortable wingback chair facing the big desk. To her surprise, instead of seating himself behind it, he dropped into the matching chair beside her.

"Look, do you think we can just start over? I'd hate to mess up what could be a good thing for Voice of Hope, and for you, because of a case of mistaken identity. What do you think? Can we get past this?"

"Past what?" She raised a blank gaze to his.

The man's laughter rang out, filling the room and sending its vibrations straight to Juliana's vulnerable heart. "Right! Okay, well, let's keep this really informal, shall we? It's not as if you're here to interview. We already know I want you on board. It's more like you're interviewing me, isn't it?"

"No, of course not! You're exactly what I've always wanted. Oh!" Her cheeks flooded with heat yet again, and she closed her eyes. "I mean, of course, that the magazine is everything… oh, dear! Mr. Dawson, forgive me." She drew a deep, steadying breath. "I'm sure you know what I meant."

He grinned, shooting her a teasing, inquisitive glance. But when Juliana squirmed uncomfortably, he made a gallant and obvious effort to hide his amusement.

"I am delighted to know you're considering my offer. However…"

His crooked grin tugged insistently at Juliana's heartstrings, which seemed to be set on high vibrato. "Since we have so effectively dispensed with any of the usual formalities, may I call you Juliana?"

She responded with a soft murmur of laughter. "Please do."

"Great. And I'm Will to everyone here."

Juliana nodded but chose to remain silent, not trusting herself to speak with any degree of intelligence.

"Well, it hasn't taken us long to decide you're part of the team, has it?" The twinkle in his blue eyes only added to their charisma. "The question is, are you willing to take on what I have in mind?"

Intrigued, she found herself able to speak without a noticeable tremor. "What do you have in mind?"

"Well, I want you to come aboard the writing staff, of course. Your stories have been a source of inspiration for our readers for as long as you've been contributing. Which has been…how long have you been blessing us with your work, Juliana?"

Will leaned over to pick up a folder off his desk but didn't open it, watching her face instead.

"I submitted my first work to Voice of Hope three years ago."

"That's about what I thought." He nodded, dropping his clear gaze to the file in his lap. "And during that time, we've come to look forward to your submissions. The response they draw from our young female readers is phenomenal. I hope you realize what a wonderful ministry you have."

Juliana tried to ignore the burst of pleasure his comment evoked. "I hope God can use my talent to help someone." She cringed at the prim note in her own voice.

He grinned. "Well, I know He can, and He does. I prayed long and hard before asking you to join us here at Voice of Hope. I want the right person for this position, someone who can minister to and inspire our readers. I believe that person is you. But there's something else."

His eyes searched Juliana's face. Finally, he leaned forward in his chair and let his hands fall between his knees as he met her nervous gaze head-on.

She caught her bottom lip between her teeth, certain Will Dawson could see into her soul, that he knew she was silly enough to believe herself completely, head-over-heels in love with him ten minutes after saying hello—however unprecedented that hello may have been.

"I want you to take on a…" Will broke off, his eyes probing hers. "Juliana, I'm sorry, but…what color are your eyes?"

Taken aback for a moment, she suddenly found herself laughing. "Last time I looked, I believe they were just brown."

"Oh, no!" He protested, shaking his head. "Those eyes are not 'just' anything. They're somewhere between amber and…what?"

He leaned in for a closer look. Discomfited, she dropped her gaze, the soft brush of lashes tickling her warm cheeks.

"Golden!" Triumphantly, he announced his decision. "You have the most unusual golden eyes. They're beautiful! I hope you don't mind my saying so."

Juliana was surprised to find she did not mind. Never had any man made such a forward statement within only moments of having met her. Indeed, she was certain she would not have welcomed such a comment from anyone else.

"Thank you." Pleased that her voice no longer trembled in sync with the ridiculous vibration of her heart, she nevertheless chided herself. *Could you be any more immature, Juliana Camden?*

Will appeared to also suffer a brief moment of self-consciousness. He cleared his throat, returning his attention to her file. "Well. Where were we?"

"I believe you were going to ask me to do something besides writing."

"Yes!" His contagious smile elicited one in return—though Juliana feared hers came off more expectant than contagious. "I was. Well, not really, no. I want you to take on an advice column."

"An advice column!" She was stunned. "I…I don't know if…that is, I hardly think I'm qualified…"

"Of course you are! The underlying counsel you provide in your stories alone is amazing. And your readers believe you have the answers they're looking for."

"You can't possibly know that." Juliana chuckled a little.

Nevertheless, a little tingle of excitement shivered its way down her spine as her prospective employer's enthusiasm became almost tangible in the small space they shared.

Will leaped up and hurried around behind his desk. Retrieving a large canvas bag off the floor, he returned to kneel beside her chair. When he spoke, his voice was a fervent whisper. "Everything in this bag is addressed to you, Juliana. Every…single…letter."

With that, he dumped the bag at her feet.

Juliana gasped, staring speechless at the pile of correspondence on the floor. Hundreds of letters, scrawled on plain white paper as well as pink, blue, yellow, and green. Beautifully written in scrolling calligraphy and painstakingly drawn in round, childish print.

Hardly aware of her own actions, Juliana slid off her chair and dropped to her knees beside the pile of paper. She sifted both hands through it, as if to convince herself the letters had actual substance. Wide-eyed, she skimmed a couple of short notes, then picked up a two-page missive, quickly scanning its contents.

When she looked up, her eyes swam with unshed tears, and her chin trembled with emotion.

"I don't know…" she choked and cleared her throat. "I

really don't know if I'm qualified to answer these questions. I have no training, no education as a counselor. This is a tremendous responsibility, not one to be taken lightly."

Still kneeling beside her, Will grasped both of her hands. "I don't take it lightly. That's why I've asked *you* to do it. You have tremendous insight into the specific problems and situations of impressionable girls just moving into womanhood, young ladies who, in all likelihood, do attend church—probably because their parents insist—but may or may not have a real relationship with God. They want to know the right and proper way to handle themselves in various situations."

He squeezed one of the hands he held and looked straight into her eyes. "Your talent is God-given, Juliana. What formal education could ever equal that? What could any professor teach you about right and wrong that would be better or more than what God Himself has instilled in your heart?"

Juliana shook her head. "Still…I feel as though it would be presumptuous to take on such a task."

A tiny smile lit up his fine features. "I had a feeling you would say that. Juliana, it is precisely that humbleness that these girls need—not lectures from someone who professes to have all the answers. They want to chat with Juliana Camden, the young writer who touches their hearts with her stories, makes them love her believable characters, stirs them with her godly wisdom. They want someone of their own generation, who can understand and relate to them and their very real problems."

He paused briefly but continued when she said nothing. "An older person would almost certainly underestimate the enormity of those problems. A trained counselor might very well consider them trivial or unimportant and churn out pat, unempathetic answers."

A striking nobility set Will's handsome face alight. Juliana's hands trembled in his.

"Think about it! For some of these situations, a pat, thoughtless answer could have catastrophic impact—literally life-changing results. I agree, it is a serious responsibility. But in your stories and articles, I sense a solid foundation of prayer and sincerity, a desire to guide your readers in the right direction—God's direction. What more could I, or anyone else, possibly ask for?"

Juliana could not find her voice. Will's passion touched her in the deepest part of her soul. She was suddenly every bit as certain as he seemed to be that God intended her to be here at Voice of Hope.

She was also absolutely sure she could not be an advice columnist. Not on her own. But with God's help, and with thought and prayer behind every answer, she might be able to make a difference in somebody's life.

"Okay." She finally managed to speak, smiling through the tears that poured in streams down her cheeks. "I'll try."

Will closed his eyes and released the breath he'd apparently been holding. Still on his knees in front of her, he gave her hands another gentle squeeze. "Yes!"

Juliana's pulse quickened when he opened those blazing blue orbs and smiled. Was that admiration in his eyes? Was it something more?

Her heart nearly stopped mid-beat when he spoke in a husky whisper. "Juliana Camden, I think I...I..."

He cleared his throat and abruptly released her hands. Rising from his position before her chair, he took a couple of steps backward. To Juliana, he appeared almost to be shrinking from her. But when he extended his right hand, she automatically placed hers in it.

His voice was that of the ultimate professional. "I think I'm going to like this arrangement!"

He moved to the door, and Juliana followed, dazed by his sudden change of demeanor. She still clutched a letter in one hand.

Will smiled politely. "Monday morning then, Juliana." The next moment, she was out on the street and back in the borrowed vehicle in which she had arrived.

Ten minutes into the half hour drive back home, she shook her head as if coming out of a daze and spoke aloud. "What just happened?"

Chapter Six

SPRINGVILLE, CALIFORNIA

"SIT DOWN NOW, MY LITTLE MOTHER. You're tired."

Gillian Parsons watched from the kitchen as her mother walked across the large living room. She dropped wearily into a big, worn recliner in her favorite spot beside the window. Her cheeks sported the first hint of pink Gillian had seen there in weeks.

Mary Helen Parsons' delicate beauty remained unmarred, despite the ravages of ill health on her frail body. Ever since her husband's death in a horrible machinery accident five years ago, she'd grown steadily weaker and weaker.

Oh, Papa, has it really been nearly five years?

Hanging a damp dish towel on a hook near the sink, Gillian sighed. Losing her beloved father had been hard. But watching her mother go so rapidly downhill afterward was, if anything, even more difficult.

Her parents' relationship had been a wonderful example of love as perfect as it gets. Even so, she could not help feeling something unusual prompted the severe bouts of depression her mother began to suffer following the accident. Then the headaches started, sending her to bed for days at a time, where she writhed in agony and cried out strange, nonsensical things Gillian did not understand.

But for right now, her little mother was better. She was tired but smiling, and she sported that tinge of healthy color in her cheeks.

"Thanks for helping with the kitchen, Danny." Gillian smiled at the handsome, copper-haired young man who stood almost a full foot taller than herself.

He grinned as he hung up his own soggy dish towel, and they wandered in to join the older lady in the living room. "I'll be happy to help with the kitchen any time you want to feed me another swell meal like that. It was superb!"

"The way to a man's heart..." She laughed, teasing her friend. "I can see how whoever wins your heart will do it."

To her surprise, Danny's ears turned a deep brick red, and he looked away. She frowned, confused. Did I actually manage to embarrass him? Had Danny found someone...?

Daniel Collins had been an honorary member of the Parsons family since the two of them were small children. In fact, he had been six and she just five when he bulldozed his way into a group of neighborhood kids who had provoked Gillian to miserable tears.

Always fiercely overprotective, Gillian's mother never allowed her only child to visit the homes of other children. She was welcome to invite friends to her home, but the other parents quickly noticed the complete lack of reciprocal visitation. Offended, they discouraged their little ones from forming friendships with the Parsons child. By the end of her first-grade year, Gillian was effectively alienated from her classmates.

On the day she met Danny, she had slipped off to the park without her mother's knowledge. That's where the little gang surrounded her, and their taunting got out of hand.

Until Danny saw what was happening. He crashed through the tight huddle of children and grabbed the sobbing little girl by the hand. Fuming, he turned to face her accusers. "Get outta the way, you buncha numbskulls! Can'tcha see you're scarin' 'er?"

He was taller and bigger than most of the other children. That, along with the thunderous frown on his freckled face, stopped them in their tracks.

He pulled Gillian away from the gang of little terrors then turned and shook a grimy finger in their direction. "And don'tcha ever let me see you pickin' on her again. Or I'll make ya sorry, ya hear?"

Nobody said a word as Danny, with Gillian in tow, stomped off toward her house. Safely away from her harassers, the young knight stopped and pulled off his dirty plaid shirt. Standing there in undershirt and patched jeans, he used the garment he had removed to clumsily wipe her drenched face. She was still crying quietly and hiccupping through her tears.

"Aww, don'tcha worry about that bunch." The boy's voice was a low growl as he attempted to soothe the little damsel in distress. "They don't know nothin'! Come on, I'll take ya home."

From that moment, he was her self-appointed bodyguard and best friend in the entire world. They played together, studied together, even accepted Christ together a few years later. He was like a brother to her, and Gillian could not imagine a life without Danny in it—even if he teased her to the point of distraction at times.

For once, though, it appeared she had somehow managed to embarrass him. *How odd! I didn't know he could be embarrassed— especially not by me. Hmmm.* She hid an impish grin. *This is ammunition!*

She was getting ready to leap on this unusual weakness when her mother came to Danny's rescue by expertly changing the subject.

"You know what sounds good to me, Gilly Bean?"

The grateful look Danny shot across the room did not miss Gillian's sharp eye. *What am I missing here? These two are up to something!*

"I can't believe anything sounds good after that huge meal."

She knelt beside her mother's chair and dropped a kiss on her cheek, willing herself not to go all weepy-eyed. Seeing her mother smile meant more than the world to her.

"I know, and I'm certainly not hungry!" Mary Helen rubbed a hand over her flat stomach. "But I keep thinking about that new ice cream we had last week. What was that flavor?"

"Rocky Road? You really liked it, didn't you?"

"I did like it. Do we have any left, darling?"

Gillian shook her head in disbelief. Her mother never had such a voracious appetite! But it was a welcome change, and she was more than willing to encourage it.

"No, it's all gone. But I'm sure McGillicutty's is still open. Shall I go get some?"

"Would you, dear? It just sounds so good."

She picked up her handbag, pulling out her car keys as she spoke. "Want to come along, Danny?"

Before he could respond, Mary Helen waved Gillian away. "Oh, let him stay here and babysit me." She tossed a fond smile at the young man. "Do you mind, Daniel, dear?"

Gillian's mouth dropped open. How odd! But then, perhaps it was a better idea for him to stay. Mother really shouldn't be left alone.

"Of course not, Mrs. P." Danny was quick to reply, but he was obviously every bit as surprised as Gillian by the request.

"Well…okay." She cast a narrow-eyed glance at her mother, but Mary Helen only smiled sweetly, and Gillian shrugged. "I'll be back as soon as I can."

She hurried out to her car, chiding herself for being so suspicious.

Danny loved Mrs. Parsons as if she were his own mother, but the woman had something up her sleeve. It was plain as the nose on his face, and he'd been told that was hard to miss.

She peeked through a crack in the curtains, watching as Gillian backed out of the driveway. The moment the little roadster roared off down the street, she was on her feet.

"Wait here!" She whispered, though they were completely alone in the house. "I have to get something from the bedroom."

He nodded, half grinning. Curiouser and curiouser. A moment later, she returned, clutching a thin book in one hand.

Dropping down beside him on the sofa, Gillian's mother laid a gentle hand on his arm. Her eyes, more blue than he ever remembered, met his directly. For one terrified moment, he thought she was going to cry.

"I must ask your confidence regarding what I'm about to show you."

He squirmed, uncomfortable with the deadly seriousness of her tone. But this was Mrs. P, after all. He would do whatever she asked.

"Yes, ma'am."

She smiled, reaching out to touch his cheek with soft, cool fingers. Too cool. Danny's heart contracted painfully. *What on earth will Gillian do if she loses her?*

"We only have a few moments, Daniel. Gilly will be back soon. Read this, please." She handed him the book.

He took it, glancing down at the title in consternation. "Mrs. P, it looks like your personal diary. I can't read this!"

She laughed, that trilling little bell-like sound that always made him feel warm and happy. "Of course you can. I've asked you to. Do it for me, dear. Please?"

He raked a hand through his hair. Reading a lady's diary seemed somehow akin to rifling through her dresser drawers, which he was sure he'd refuse to do even under gunpoint.

"Why would you want me to read your journal?"

"Well, I'm not asking you to read it all!" An impish smile erased ten years from her face as she curled up in her big chair. "I'm sure it would bore you to tears, but I need you to read the first entry."

Danny was not thrilled with her request. But he had never refused to do anything she asked before, and he was not about to start now. Hesitantly, he flipped open the cover, but she stopped him before he could read anything.

Her voice had lost all traces of merriment. "Daniel."

He looked up.

"You told me that you love her."

"With all my heart."

"I'm worried about Gillian if...well, you know. If something should happen to me."

"Nothing's going to—"

"Please. We don't have time for that. Something could happen to me. We both know I'm not well. I don't know

72

what's going on in my body, but something is. I need to know someone will be there for my daughter when I'm gone."

Danny swallowed hard, and his vision blurred with the tears he refused to let fall. Laying the troublesome book down on the sofa cushion, he walked across the room to kneel in front of his dear friend, taking one of her hands in both of his.

"Mrs. P, if Gillian will allow me, I promise you I will take care of her. Always."

"That's what I wanted to hear. Thank you, son. Now please read. We don't have much time."

Still he hesitated. "You're sure you want me to do this?"

"I'm begging you to."

He picked up the journal and read.

September 27, 1936

I suppose it's a little late in life to be starting a journal, but I'm so excited! I have been given a miracle, and I must start now to record its development. I know myself too well to say I'll write every day, but I intend to do so as often as I think of it.

God has not abandoned me, after all. He has answered my prayers, and I have a perfect baby girl!

Last year, when tiny Carissa was stillborn, I wanted to die too. I had waited for her, longed for her, carried her those nine long months. We had so many plans, such high hopes. Then she didn't live, and I felt as though my own heart would surely stop beating.

William was so patient and loving throughout that long ordeal. Had he not been there, I think I really would have gone to the grave with our baby. I lived only because he wouldn't let me die.

I hate to admit it, but I lost faith. Papa and Mama would

be ashamed of me. How can a woman raised by a preacher the likes of my Papa ever "lose faith"? But I did. I could not accept it. Why would a loving God allow me to lose the baby I wanted so desperately? And why, especially, would He then leave me unable to bear another child? Why?

Maybe Papa and Mama could have found a way to help me understand, but I didn't tell them what was happening. They were in Texas, after all...what could they have done? And Luanne...where is she? It's been almost five years now since she left us. Will I ever see my sister again?

Oh, yes, I lost faith. I decided if there was a God, as my parents believed, then He had abandoned William and me.

But He did not forget us. When I thought I would never be happy again, He delivered Gillian to our door and gave her to us.

Danny's breath caught in his throat, and he almost dropped the little book. He looked up at Mrs. P, but she only nodded a little and gave him a small, sad smile. Unable to speak, he returned to the journal.

Well, I guess He didn't actually give her to us. William paid her father nearly every penny we had at the time.

Should anyone ever read this journal (and I will take every precaution to make certain that doesn't happen, at least not until we find a way to tell Gillian the truth), what I've just written would be terribly confusing. I should explain:

We had only recently moved into a small farm labor camp right in the middle of California's booming agricultural belt. One end of Corman's Camp was made up of tiny, ramshackle houses like the one William and I lived in; the other end was known as the "tent city." Most of the tent dwellers were temporary, coming and going so often that it was impossible to know who would be living in each tent from day to day.

Even those of us in the wood shacks were migrants and wanderers. Most of us came to California looking for work when the horrible dust destroyed our lives back home. William and I came from Conlen, Texas, and there were immigrants in those camps from other mid-western states, as well. There was a lot of moving in and out, especially when work got slow and we heard there was more on down the road somewhere.

I kept to myself. I was bitter toward God and had no intention of attending church, even though there was one right there in the camp. Nor did I want to make friends. I went so far as to do our laundry in the evenings after the neighbors went to bed. That way, there was little chance of having to speak to anyone while hanging it out to dry.

Poor William! He worked in the hot fields all day then did any necessary shopping in the evenings. I refused to go to the market, which was within walking distance of our house. But my William never complained.

Looking back now, I am embarrassed and ashamed.

But God did not forget me, in spite of my behavior.

One night, exactly three months ago as I make this entry, we heard someone tapping on our door just before midnight. We were shocked and even a little hesitant to answer. William had a nodding acquaintance with a few people in the fields, but he didn't actually know them. Why would anyone be at our door, especially at such a late hour?

Still, we got up. William jumped into his trousers, and I threw on a housecoat. He told me to stay in bed, but I could not. I had the strangest feeling that I should be with him to greet this midnight caller.

"Who's there?" William called out.

"Name's Kelly." It was a man's voice.

"I think that's the fellow I worked with today." It was

plain William had no more idea what was going on than I did.

He opened the door, and a man stepped inside. He was tall and had to stoop a little to come through our door. In his arms he clutched a little bundle, wrapped snugly in a soft pink blanket that had obviously been hand-crocheted. (I must keep it for Gillian...) I was certain it was a baby, and I remember thinking that no man would be carrying an infant around the camp at midnight unless something was terribly wrong.

Something was.

Our visitor's gaze fell on me, and for a moment I thought he knew me, though I'm sure I'd never met him. I would have remembered. He was a handsome man, with a strong jaw and a cleft chin. His eyes, not really brown, but an unusual golden color, were truly beautiful.

That first moment when Gillian's father looked at me, those strange eyes glistened eerily. Under the light from the bare bulb overhead, they were almost wolfish. I remember shivering, as though caught in a cold draft.

"You told me yer woman wanted a child." He addressed William but kept that golden gaze on me. "I brung 'er one."

I gasped, and William stood in silence for at least a full minute. He was as shocked as I was. Finally, he said, "I'm afraid I don't understand."

Kelly thrust the baby at me. "Take her, ma'am. She's sleepin', but there ain't nothin' wrong with 'er. She's healthy."

He put that little pink bundle in my arms, and I pulled back a corner of the blanket to peek inside. I knew she couldn't be more than a few days old, and her father was right—she was perfect. I hugged her to my heart, already wanting to keep her forever.

William was worried. "Mary Helen, don't...."

I looked at my husband, and he broke off whatever it was he meant to say. He told me later that he knew right then it was too late for warnings. I had no intention of giving up that baby unless I was forced to.

I heard the anger in his voice when he spoke to Mr. Kelly, demanding to know the reason behind such an unheard of act.

"Just what I told'ja," that man said, with a little shrug of his shoulders. "I brung ya a lit'lun. Me and my wife, we didn't plan on havin' no young'uns. This one was an accident, and we can't afford to keep 'er, no how. You said your missus wants a baby. Well, my missus and me, we don't."

We were appalled, of course. But I hugged that beautiful baby close and felt little stirrings of life in a heart I had thought was dead.

William laughed, a strange bark that sounded not the least bit humorous. "Are you saying you're giving us your child?"

"I ain't zac'ly sayin' that. But maybe we could make a deal."

William snorted in derision, disgust written plain as day across his face. "I don't believe this! You want to sell us your daughter?"

He turned to me. "Mary Helen, give this crazy good-for-nothing his baby. And you, sir, I want you out of my house."

I shook my head and clutched the baby tighter. I could not let her go.

Kelly watched me. He shrugged, apparently nonchalant. "If you don't want her..."

"William!" I cried. "Please..."

I clearly heard the frustration in his voice. "Mary Helen, you don't buy children. It's not right!"

Kelly reached for the baby. "If you don't want 'er, I'll just find someone who does. I thought you wanted a baby, that's all."

William grabbed the man's arm. "You're going to go door to door to sell this child? Are you crazy, man?"

"Maybe I am." He stroked the baby's cheek with a long, tapered finger.

I clutched her to me, praying the man standing over us could not hear the loud pounding of my heart. I was terrified that he would tear her from my arms and leave.

"But it's true we got no money, and my wife and me, we don't want to be bothered nohow."

He raised those incredible eyes and fixed me under a golden gaze. "I thought you and your little woman here would love her." His next words were soft but curiously fervent, as though he were desperate for me to believe him. "I wouldn't let no one take her that wouldn't treat her real good, ma'am."

"You're a piece of work, Kelly!" William's fury chilled my blood. For a moment, I feared what he might do to the baby's father. "Fine, then. Supposing I agree to this insane scheme. You know I don't have any money. I'm a field worker, just like you. I live in a shack, just like you. What kind of deal did you hope to make with me?"

Kelly looked away, for the first time appearing somewhat ashamed. "You don't need much, man. Just enough for… for a little whiskey."

"Father God, help us all!" William rolled his eyes heavenward, white with rage. "You're selling that precious child to soothe an alcohol demon?"

Kelly's head drooped, and he shuffled his feet. "Guess you could say that."

William stomped into the bedroom. I heard a drawer open and knew he was getting what little money we had. A moment later he returned, a few bills and a handful of change clutched in one fist.

"This is every penny I have, Kelly. Twenty-five dollars. Oh, make that $25.73. Are you really going to sell your own flesh and blood for such a pitiful price?"

Kelly didn't take the money, and my heart quaked. It wasn't going to be enough!

"On one condition."

"What now?"

"You gotta get outta here. Tonight. We'll hafta say somebody stole her, ya know. I cain't zac'ly go sayin' I sold her to ya."

William didn't even blink. He continued to hold the money out to Kelly, and I've never—before or since—seen such contempt on his face. "We'll be gone by morning." His voice, so full of anger, so scornful, sounded completely unfamiliar.

Kelly bent and kissed the baby's forehead—clumsily, but with surprising tenderness, considering the awful circumstances. Then he looked at me. William still doesn't believe this, but I am convinced there were tears in those wolfish eyes of his.

"You look a lot like her Mama," he told me. "Ain't that somethin'?"

I nodded, unable to speak.

"You'll take good care of her, won'tcha, ma'am?" Again, I could only nod. Tears streamed down my cheeks, and my throat felt stuffed with something huge. I simply could not find my voice.

Taking the money William held out as if it were dirty, our midnight caller walked to the door and opened it, then paused. He didn't look back but spoke in a quiet voice I had to strain to catch. "Her name. It's Gillian Mary. She's five days old." Then he was gone.

We needed only about an hour to pack our few belongings into the car. We had no furniture to worry about—the house was furnished with a few cheap odds and ends. I packed our clothing and some groceries, and William loaded them into our car. By a little after two in the morning, we were on our way.

In the darkness, speeding down the road to I knew not where, I cuddled that baby girl close to my heart and could not have been happier.

My empty arms were filled.

Chapter Seven

DANIEL SLOWLY CLOSED THE JOURNAL and looked up, surprised to find tears on his face.

"It's all true, isn't it?"

Gillian's mother nodded. "Every word."

He shook his head, unsure what to say next. He was glad when Mrs. P's trembling voice filled the silence.

"I can't expect you to understand what drove us to commit such an awful crime."

Her face was white now, the earlier hint of pink just a memory. "But you have to know that William and I always loved Gillian. Both of us. We loved her as if she really were our own." She sobbed once, quietly. "She is our daughter, Daniel. She could not have been more ours if she had been born to us."

Once more, Danny found himself kneeling beside the frail woman he had loved since childhood. He wrapped both arms around her and pulled her head down onto his shoulder. "Hush, Mrs. P, it's okay. I understand. At least, well, I think I do."

After a moment, she eased back and patted his shoulder. "I'd love to just sit here and let you comfort me." She smiled even as a tear slid down one cheek. "But we don't have time."

"I still don't understand what it is you want me to do." Danny shook his head hopelessly.

"I need you to help me find her family. Her real family."

Danny rocked back on his heels, shocked. Bouncing to his feet, he strode off across the room but quickly paced back toward Mrs. P, only to repeat the jaunt again and again.

She remained silent while he mulled over what she had said. He felt her tension, but she wisely said nothing while he digested all that he had learned.

"Why now?"

"That's a fair question. William and I always intended to tell her when she turned twenty-one. But the Lord called him on before that happened and I…well, I couldn't do it. I was afraid of losing her, afraid she would hate me…hate us…for what we had done. I'm ashamed to admit it, but I just…could not…tell her."

"And now?"

"And now I'm ill. Because of the circumstances, we never really had much to do with other members of our family. Somewhere, I have a sister. I don't know if she's still married, and if she is, I don't know her last name. Never even met her husband. She eloped with one of our father's farm hands within a week or so of him coming to work on our farm. William's stepbrother lives about an hour away. We saw his family a few times over the years, but never really stayed in touch. In fact, I haven't seen Otis since William's funeral."

Looking up at Danny, she continued. "We knew that the less contact we had with our families, the less chance there would be of anyone ever discovering the truth. At the time

Gillian came to us, we were desperately trying to just survive. We hadn't seen any of them for a couple of years, and we barely communicated. No one had any reason to think she wasn't ours."

Danny nodded. "I understand. But what's different now?"

"Now I'm sick! Don't you see? Because we cut ourselves off from family, our daughter has no one to turn to when I'm gone. When William passed away, she had me. But when I'm gone…who will she have then?"

"What about Poppy and Grams?"

"My parents adore Gillian, you know that, but they're both old. How long can they be here for her? She will have no one then…no one!"

Taking her hand, he looked into her frantic blue eyes and made a promise. "She has me, Mrs. P. If she'll have me, I will always be there for her."

"Sweet Daniel!" Her tremulous smile broke his heart. "I know you will. But don't you think Gilly has a right to know the truth? Shouldn't she have an opportunity to know her true family?"

He shook his head, emphatic. "They didn't want her! Why should she have to know that? You and Mr. P—you're her true family."

She bit at her lip before answering. When she did speak, she lowered her gaze, refusing to meet his eyes. "You know what haunts me? It never occurred to me until after William died. I began to be concerned about what would become of Gillian when I die, too, and I realized that…" Her voice caught, and for endless seconds she seemed unable to speak.

Danny strode into the kitchen and returned with a glass of water. She sipped at it before continuing. "Because of our desperation, perhaps…or maybe because we were young and unlearned…or even just that we were so shocked when Kelly appeared at our door that way—who knows why? Our reasons aren't really important now, are they? What does matter is that we took the word of a man so addicted to alcohol that he was willing to do anything to get it."

Danny frowned. "Took his word for what?"

For a long moment, she said nothing. Finally though, Mary Helen Parsons met Danny's eyes and said, "First of all, that the baby was his own. I do believe that much was true, because…well, because Gillian looks like him. Those eyes…!"

She closed hers, sighing deeply, before continuing. "But we also believed him when he told us his wife did not want her. Suppose he was lying, Daniel. What if, somewhere, some mother is still grieving for her lost child?"

Danny stood stunned as the full implication of her words hit him hard. She wept quietly into her handkerchief. "Gillian may have a mother—another mother—somewhere out there. It's possible she even had other children. Gilly might have brothers and sisters. There may be no reason for my daughter to be alone after I'm gone. I need to know the truth before I die. Will you help me find it?"

Daniel lifted his chin, determined to bring her peace of mind if it was within his power to do so. "Of course I will, Mrs. P. Don't worry. I'll find them."

Standing, the small woman stood on her tiptoes and brushed Daniel's cheek with her lips. "Thank you. You're a good boy, Daniel. Gillian's lucky to have you."

She disappeared into the bathroom to erase the telltale signs of tears on her face just as Gillian's roadster pulled back into the driveway.

The darkness was heavy, smothering, and she struggled for air. How she hated the dark! It always frightened her, even though Papa said there was nothing in it to fear because he would never let anything harm her. But he is gone, isn't he? Yes, Papa's body lies stiff and cold in that ugly, dark hole in the ground. And Mother...where is my little Mother?

Her heart raced, and she panted in sheer terror. Mother was somewhere in the Stygian darkness, all alone and not well. She must find her! She had to take care of her, make her well again. She could not lose her, too. Oh, what would she do if both Papa and Mama were gone? No! She could not bear that possibility.

"Mama!" She tried to scream but produced only a tiny croak of sound.

Desperately she tried again. "My little Mother..." Again her voice eluded every effort to bring it forth, and tears spilled in steady streams down her face. She clenched both fists, sucked in much-needed air, and forced the elusive sound past her lips.

"Where are you, little Mother?"

A piercing shriek woke her as it tore past her lips, and she bolted upright, breathing hard. A quick rap on the door startled her and, before she could answer, it flew open, and a small figure rushed to her side.

"Gillian! Are you all right, sweetheart?"

Her mother flipped on the bedside lamp even as she placed a gentle hand on Gillian's damp cheek. She reached up to clutch at the ministering hand, and the tears came faster and harder.

"Mother! You're here. Dear little Mother, I thought you were gone. I was alone, and it was dark. I was afraid, I was so afraid!" She choked on the rush of words, and her fingernails dug into the soft skin of her mother's palm.

Though still in the clutches of uncontrollable panic, Gillian worried about passing along her fright. She opened her mouth to say she was fine, but instead a stream of hysterical words burst forth yet again. "It was dark. It was so dark! Oh, Mama, I was scared. It was dark!"

Making little shushing noises, her mother lay down beside her and pulled her into a soothing embrace. She stroked her hair with one hand and spoke softly. "Hush, my darling! I'm right here. It was just a dream, just a nasty old dream. I'm here, Silly Gilly Bean. Mother's here."

Gillian hadn't required this kind of attention for many years, but Mary Helen fell easily back into the role of comforter to a frightened child.

Eventually, the sobs quieted, Gillian's body stopped trembling, and she released the crushing hold on her mother's hand. Neither of them spoke for a long time. They lay quietly, Gillian relaxing under the familiar touch. She snuggled into her mother's warmth and nestled her head on the older woman's shoulder.

"I'm sorry, Mother…"

"Shhhh. There's nothing to be sorry for, Gilly Bean. You just had a nightmare, and I'm glad I was here."

"You're always here for me." Tears pooled in her eyes once more, trickling down her cheeks before she realized they were there. "You'll always be here, won't you?"

"I can't promise you that, my darling. I'd love to, and I would if I could, but I won't lie to you. I'm sick, Gilly, you know that. I don't know how much longer I can be here for you. But I know Someone who will be."

Impatience hovered just below the surface of her voice. "Yes, yes, I know God is with me, and I'm grateful. But I need you, too!"

"Well, for right now, you've got me. What do you say we

both call it a night? Shall I leave the light on for you?"

Gillian hesitated, feeling like a frightened child again. "Could you…? Would you mind…just sleeping here with me tonight? Would you be terribly uncomfortable?"

Her mother laughed softly and hugged her. "Just keeps me from having to get up and get chilly again. Good night, Gilly Bean."

"Good night, my little Mother. I love you."

"I love you back." A drowsy murmur.

Gillian slipped from the bed long enough to turn off the light. Back under the covers, her hand closed gently around her mother's, and she allowed sleep to claim her once more.

Juliana sat alone in the dimly lit kitchen, sipping at a cup of hot tea.

She had awakened struggling against a heavy, suffocating darkness, crying out in terror for a loved one she could not find. "My little Mother!" The frantic cry awakened her, and she sprang upright in bed, a ragged breath catching in her throat.

Unwilling to risk a return to the nightmare, she slipped into her robe and made her way to the kitchen for a soothing, hot drink.

On the table in front of her lay the letter she had unwittingly carried out of the office when she left her Voice of Hope interview. Without a single doubt, she knew the author was somehow connected to her nightmares.

"Who are you?" She ran her fingers over the neatly penned words, whispering into the silence. "And who invited you into my dreams?"

Juliana rubbed at her throbbing temple with one hand as she parked the brand-new blue-gray Volkswagen outside the office. Her father had insisted on buying it for her, stubbornly ignoring her insistence that she had enough money in savings to purchase a used vehicle herself.

"Not a chance, Julie girl! This is your first car. I know you never wanted one before, but you need it now. And this first one...well, it's a gift from your mother and me. End of discussion."

She had to admit she loved sporting the little bug around. The half-hour drive from South Lamont to Bakersfield seemed only an enjoyable outing, a few minutes in which to commune with God and reflect on all the new blessings in her life before plunging into each day's work.

In the three weeks since her interview at Voice of Hope, her unexpected attraction to her boss had not changed. Every glimpse of Will's face only further confirmed the sudden, unexpected love that had nearly swept her away that first day.

She was far too honest with herself to pretend it was anything else: God had brought her to her Mr. Right. The problem was he didn't seem to know it. Nevertheless, she was convinced she was exactly where she was meant to be.

Calling out a cheery good morning to Claudia as she rushed through the lobby, she hurried down the long hall to tap softly on Will's office door, peeking in at his bellowed invitation.

"Hi. Do you have a moment?"

"Of course." He still did an occasional double-take when he saw her, and she knew her resemblance to his cousin caught him unaware at times. At this moment, he actually appeared a little dazed.

"Will?"

He snapped to attention. "What's up?"

"Would you mind reading this? I'm having trouble coming up with an answer, and I can't get this girl off my mind." Juliana placed the slightly frayed letter on his desk and offered a half-embarrassed smile. "She even made her way into my dreams last night."

She had been working on replies to the pile of mail Will had dumped at her feet three weeks earlier—letters written before she even officially had an advice column. To her surprise, she received more every day. If the volume of mail was any indication, the "Just Ask Juliana" column might be an overwhelming success.

The responsibility of her role as advisor to these hurting, confused readers weighed heavily on her heart. Usually they were very young women, still coming into their own identities. More and more often though, she heard from young wives and mothers, as well. She felt some concern about her ability to handle the load when the advice column became official in the upcoming edition.

Motioning her into a chair, her boss picked up the letter, reading aloud.

Dear Juliana,

I guess you would probably call me a backslider. I once had a strong faith in God, but I have endured so much pain in the past few years that I wonder now if He even exists. Why would a loving Father allow awful things to happen to His children who try to do right—people who love Him?

I won't go into all that in this letter. Suffice it to say that I have not attended church in some time. But I still enjoy Voice of Hope, and, in particular, I love reading anything under your byline.

I do know you're not an advice columnist, but I'm curious what you would do in my situation and hope you'll take time to think about my letter.

You see, I'm trying to prepare myself for the loss of my little Mother.

Juliana had read and reread the letter over the past few days. Now, listening as Will read it aloud, she found herself once more recalling the vivid dream she'd had weeks ago when her father awakened her in the night. She had dreamed of losing a "little Mother" even before coming to work here at the magazine. Tears streaked down her cheeks as he continued.

(My mother is not quite five feet tall, delicate and petite. When I surpassed her height at a very young age, I started calling her "my little Mother.")

My beloved Papa, the love of her life and my greatest hero, was killed in an accident on his job five years ago. Mother has not been well since then. I am unspeakably frightened at the prospect of life with both of them gone. The world seems such a dark place—and I guess I'm something of a coward. I have always feared the darkness.

A couple of nights ago, Mother said some things I found confusing. She begged me to forgive her for keeping "the truth" from me, insisting she had done so only because she loved me. I have absolutely no idea what "truth" she was talking about.

She then showed me where she had hidden her journals—dated from the year I was born until shortly after Papa died, when she apparently quit writing in them.

"When I'm gone," she told me, "I want you to read them. But before you do, go to Corman's Camp. You will find yourself there."

Mother instructed me not to read the journals until I find what I'm looking for. When I do, she said, these books will help me understand everything.

I promised her, of course. But now I don't know what to do. I have no idea where this place is or even if it really exists. My little Mother was running a high fever at the time. It's possible she wasn't even coherent.

Even if I were to find a place called Corman's Camp, I don't know what I'm looking for. "Myself?" What on earth does that mean?

Should I just chalk it up to the product of a fevered mind? And if I do that, should I also pretend those diaries don't exist? I suppose there must be something in them that I need to know, since they are on my little Mother's mind even while she is so ill. And yet, I wish she'd never shown them to me. I'm tempted to burn them and never know... whatever it is.

I'm sorry this is such a long letter, but I really have no one else to turn to. I hope you can help me.

What would you do, Juliana?

The letter was signed, "Afraid of the Dark."

Chapter Eight

JULIANA WIPED AT HER TEARS as Will finished reading and handed the letter back. He remained silent for a moment, and she appreciated his thoughtfulness in not commenting on her emotional reaction.

She had been surprised by her ability to get into her readers' minds and know more than they actually said to her. With "Afraid of the Dark," she felt almost as though she had crawled beneath the poor girl's skin.

"Well, this is certainly a different kind of plea for advice, isn't it?" He casually pushed a box of tissue across the desk, and Juliana took the time to dry her eyes. She took a few deep, calming breaths before giving him a small smile.

He hiked an eyebrow. "What do you think?"

Juliana shook her head. "I have prayed and agonized over this one, but I cannot find an answer. I feel almost too close, even though I have no idea who she is. I know it sounds crazy, but…"

"No. There's something special about this one, even to me." His blue gaze rested on her face. "I will help you pray, but I'm afraid that's all I can offer at the moment. I don't know what you should tell her, but I'm certain you'll give her the right answer."

"Thank you." Juliana rose to go but paused and turned back. "Will, do you know where I live?"

"Lamont, of course."

"South Lamont, yes—more commonly known as Weedpatch, believe it or not. But within that small community is a neighborhood with a name all its own." She looked directly into his eyes, which were alight with interest. "Corman's Corner. That's where I live."

Will's body stiffened. He leaned forward, his brows drawn above those translucent blue eyes, wide now with disbelief.

"Corman's Corner?"

At her nod, he leaned back in his chair, stroking his chin with the long fingers of one hand. He appeared lost in thought.

"Why a separate name for part of a small, probably unincorporated town?" he finally asked. "I've heard of such things in large cities, but it hardly makes sense in a place like Lamont."

"It is strange, I know. It started back in the Dust Bowl days. A flood of migrant workers came here to the San Joaquin Valley looking for jobs—I'm sure you've heard the stories."

Will raised one hand and wiggled it back and forth, indicating he'd heard a little.

"Well, Dale Corman saw an opportunity for profit in that situation, and set up a farm labor camp—Corman's Camp."

He ran a hand through his dark waves, his eyes widening, but he motioned for her to continue.

"It consisted of a large number of tents—that area was called "tent city"—and several very small, hastily and cheaply-thrown-together houses. Corman ran it as a fairly lucrative business for a number of years. Eventually, though, as immigration from eastern states slowed a bit, the tent city ceased to exist.

"But Mr. Corman's houses remained, and that little neighborhood became known as Corman's Corner. It's nothing more than several acres of land on one corner of a fairly busy intersection in a tiny community, and it's not on any map."

Will listened closely. Watching him, she thought she knew exactly what he was thinking. What were the chances that this letter would have been received by someone who not only knew about, but lived in, the obscure location in question?

Finally he stood and came around the desk to sit beside her. "You need to focus on this. Go home. Take the letter with you, spend some time with it. Pray on it."

He sent her one of those crooked smiles that played utter havoc with her heart. "I should say "pray again," since I know you've already done so more than once. I don't want you to read or answer any other letters."

She was already shaking her head. "But…"

He held up a hand to silence her. "This did not come to you by chance, Juliana. Somebody needs help, and the sooner the better. I'm more concerned with the girl's underlying tone than her actual words. And something tells me you may be the only one who can help her."

She reluctantly agreed to go. *Not that I think I'm anybody's lifeline. But I won't be able to get my mind off this poor girl long enough to be of any further use here.* Besides, she still had a headache.

Sighing in resignation, she slipped the letter into her bag and walked out the door.

The telephone strident ring reached her even before she stepped into the house half an hour later. Dropping her handbag just inside the door, she rushed to answer it. *Mama's still in bed. That's not a good sign.* "Hello?"

"Julie girl! What are you doing home? Are you okay?"

"I'm fine. What's up?"

"I hate to ask, but I need you to do something for me, and it's rather important."

"Anything you need, Daddy."

"Thank you, my dear. Would you be kind enough to fetch some of my notebooks down from the attic? They're all dated, shouldn't be hard to find. I need all of last year's. There should be one from each quarter. I'll send someone by for them within half an hour or so."

Moments later, she stepped out of her bedroom dressed in a comfortable circle skirt and pale-yellow, button-down shirt, soft with age, that she loved too much to part with. Pushing open a narrow door in the hall, she peered up the dark stairway.

As a child, she had played in the large upper room occasionally but hadn't been there in years. She groaned, thinking of all the dust and cobwebs she would likely encounter. Nevertheless, she took to the stairs, resigned to the task.

The door creaked a little as she opened it, reaching around the edge to flip a light switch. "Good heavens!" Amazed, she allowed her eyes to roam the long, narrow room. "Who would have thought?"

The room did not lie beneath layers of dust. Like the rest of the house, it sparkled, and appeared neatly organized and carefully arranged. Juliana ran a finger over an old desk just inside the door. Not a speck.

She chuckled, amused at her mother's pristine housekeeping standards. *I wonder how many of our neighbors could boast such a spotless attic?* The chuckle became a gurgle of helpless laughter. *How many would even want to?*

The attic ran the entire length of the house—not exactly a small space, but her father had given her an approximate location. Now, seeing the pristine order of the roof space, she did not expect to have a problem finding his notebooks.

Touring the room slowly, she noticed an item here and there that stirred long-forgotten memories. Her old red bicycle, mounted on brackets on the wall. Somewhere around age fifteen, she had developed a sudden self-consciousness about being seen on a bike.

She shook her head, laughing a little. Maybe she should get it down and start riding again—a little exercise wouldn't hurt, especially since she spent so much time sitting at a desk these days.

A doll carriage with one wheel bent at an odd angle held a tattered rag doll. Juliana picked it up and hugged it to her heart.

"Hi, Jelly Bean! Are you lonely up here?" She replaced the doll in the carriage and gave it a gentle pat. Jelly Bean had been her best friend—indeed, her only friend—for many of her childhood years.

An ironing board leaned against one wall. Next to it hung an old scrub board. And there was the bookshelf Daddy mentioned. Familiar notebooks, all identical, were lined up on several shelves, neatly dated along the spines. This was proving even easier than she had anticipated.

Thinking she'd made short work of this little trip down Memory Lane, Juliana grasped the four books her father had specified and tugged. She was already anticipating a tall glass of something cold and carbonated before tackling that difficult letter again.

They were packed too tightly; she could not budge them. Annoyed, she jerked hard in an attempt to pull the books free, yelping in surprise as the entire shelf rocked forward.

"No!" She threw her body against it, heaving a sigh of relief when it slowly fell back into place—but not before several books crashed to the floor.

"No! Not now!"

She couldn't leave this kind of mess in Mama's spotless attic; it would be sacrilege. Chuckling softly at the thought, she dropped to her knees. But as she reached for the first notebook, which had fallen open, her eyes fell on words scrawled in her father's neat handwriting.

"His name was Jack Kelly, and he told me he sold his baby girl."

That story must have sold a lot of newspapers! Juliana tucked a finger into the page and turned the book over to read the date on the spine.

"Nineteen thirty-six. The year I was born." She opened the book, unable to resist reading more.

I found a drunken man blocking the door to the office this morning. His name was Jack Kelly, and he told me he sold his baby girl.

"Leave it to Daddy to get right to the point," Juliana murmured, smiling. "Typical newsman."

I arrived, as usual, about seven o'clock. He appeared to be passed out cold, lying squarely in front of the door.

He wasn't, not quite. I roused him enough to get him up and into the office. Not that I wanted to…he reeked of alcohol and filth. Once inside, he dug through his pockets and found a tattered piece of paper. His voice was weak, barely audible, and his hand trembled violently as he handed it to me.

Almost belligerently, he told me he didn't have any money but wanted to put an ad in the paper. I took the note and read it.

'Pleez bring her bak. Her mother greves.'

Then he told me what he had done. The man sold his infant daughter! What kind of monster could do a thing like that?

I wish I hadn't found him. I wish I hadn't read that pitiful note. Now I don't know what to do.

Juliana brushed at her damp eyes with the back of a hand. "Poor Daddy! What on earth did you do?"

She glanced at her wristwatch and gasped. "Oh, dear! The messenger will be here!"

Making up her mind to return later and find out how her father had handled his inebriated visitor, she found the notebooks he needed and rushed downstairs just in time to hear a soft tap on the door. Daddy must have told the man to be as quiet as possible, so as not to disturb Mama.

With the notebooks safely on their way, she stopped outside her mother's door and listened. No moaning or crying. That was good.

"Mama?" She called out softly, not wanting to wake her if she was sleeping. When there was no answer, she headed for the kitchen.

A few moments later, she was armed with a sandwich, a soft drink, and an aspirin for her aching head. Carrying a plate in one hand and her drink in the other, she retired to her own room to concentrate on the disturbing letter from "Afraid of the Dark."

Before long, her father's journals completely slipped her mind.

Danny knocked on the door and waited, nervously twirling his driving cap in his hands. Since reading Mrs. P's journal three days ago, he had wrestled with himself almost constantly. How could he find peace with being a part of something that would surely deal yet another blow to Gillian's precarious peace of mind?

She had taken her beloved Papa's death so hard. Even now, she grieved his passing. And Mrs. P's decline over the past few years was obvious to anyone who cared to notice. He knew Gillian lived in constant fear of losing her mother, as well.

Her grandparents lived in a small apartment behind the Parsons' home. Her father had built it after moving the elderly couple from Texas to be near their daughter. Grams and Poppy had been the lifeline that kept Gillian from sinking on numerous occasions since her father's untimely death.

What would finding out this family's long-hidden secret do to the woman he loved?

Danny longed to be there for her. While he could and did comfort her in the capacity of a dear friend, he longed to wrap her in his arms and soothe away her fears as only the person closest to her heart could do. He'd known she was the only girl in the world for him ever since the day when, as a tousle-haired boy, he had wiped away her tears with a dirty shirt.

The door opened, and there she stood, smiling out at him. For a moment, her beauty stole his breath away. From over his shoulder, the sunlight reflected on those eyes of hers, making them gleam like gold. His hand itched to smooth back the wayward strand of silky dark hair that had fallen across one cheek.

"Danny! What are you doing here?" He seemed unable to

push his voice past his throat, and she finally spoke again. "Well, are you coming in or what?"

His cheeks warmed, and he silently bemoaned the Irish lineage that made his embarrassment always so obvious.

"Sorry. Yes, for a moment."

"How come you're driving Rusty?" She had come up with the name for his dilapidated Ford sedan long ago. He had every intention of honoring the trusty car with a coat of paint one day, but as yet it hadn't happened. "Can't walk three blocks any more? You're getting soft!"

"Maybe. But I'm actually on my way out of town. I just wanted to stop and say good-bye, and make sure everything is okay over here before I leave."

"Everything's fine. Mother's sleeping now, but she's had a couple of really good days. You know, I think she's going to get well!"

He nodded, smiling at the eager hope in her voice and praying she was right. If she lost her mother any time soon, he feared the damage to her emotional well-being might be irreparable.

"That's great, Gillian. I will keep praying for her."

She said nothing, and Danny's heart ached. He had watched her slow, steady withdrawal from God since her father's death, and he prayed for her always. But nothing he said seemed to get through. She seemed unaware that she was walking away from her only Source of hope and healing. Nothing reached beyond her bitter pain.

"Where are you going? Do you have time to sit down? I just made some of that Texas tea you like so well."

"No, thanks. I really have to get on the road. I'm on my way to Woodlake. My friends there, Pastor Melvin Vaughn and his family, are expecting me in time for dinner."

"You'll make it. Rusty might be ugly, but he's got

moxie."

Danny laughed. "Rusty thanks you…I think."

Plopping down onto the sofa, she patted the seat beside her. "Well, sit for a moment and tell me what's going on in Woodlake. Are you preaching? You're becoming quite the evangelist, you know. I'm so proud of you!"

She smiled up at him with candid admiration, and Danny clenched his jaw hard, forcing himself not to sweep her into his arms and pour his heart out. He balanced uncomfortably on the edge of the sofa, not daring to get too close to her.

"Thank you!" he managed when he thought he could speak again. "You know that's my heart's greatest desire— to do something for God, to help lost souls find their way to Him."

"You will, Danny. I know you will."

He cleared his throat, looking away from the warmth in her golden eyes. How could she not know how he felt?

"I'm actually not going there to speak this time," he said, desperate to steer his mind from the route it was trying to take. "Pastor Mel has a guesthouse on his property, and I've asked him if I might use it for a few days. I need some time to pray and work through some things."

Gillian's expressive face immediately showed her concern. "Is everything all right? Can I help with anything?" She placed a delicate hand on his cheek, her expression questioning.

He pulled away, clenching his fists. "I'm fine, Gilly."

A shadow of hurt clouded her golden eyes, and he wanted to kick himself. "Okay," she said quietly. "But… have I told you lately that I love you?"

She had been saying those same words to him for years, but this time he was too vulnerable. He caught his breath and held it for a long moment then softly ran a finger down her cheek. When he spoke, his voice was husky, brimming with emotion.

"Gillian, Gillian!" he said, his voice catching on her name.

"Please don't say that anymore...not unless you mean it!"

She frowned, clearly puzzled. "Danny?"

He gripped her shoulders and desperately searched her eyes, looking for some reflection of the love he knew must be plainly written in his own.

"What is it? What's wrong?" Her voice trembled, and Danny forced himself to relax, aware that his unexpected overreaction had hurt and frightened her. Years of practice had made him an expert at reading her facial expressions.

Releasing her, he turned away, shoulders drooping. She waited in silence. *Well, no wonder, you big oaf! She's afraid to say anything.* He put forth an enormous effort to pull himself together before turning to take both her hands in his own.

"When I return from this trip, perhaps we can go somewhere together, just the two of us. I...I need to tell you something."

Again she nodded, obviously confused by his odd behavior. "Of course. You'll call me?"

Having regained his composure, he nodded and wrapped an arm around her shoulders, pulling her briefly to his side. He dropped a gentle kiss on top of her head and whispered against her hair. "I'll call you."

Rising swiftly, he stepped to the door and slipped outside, softly closing it behind him. But when he looked back at the house as he pulled away from the curb, the door hung open and Gillian stood there waving good-bye.

Chapter Nine

A TALL MAN WITH A SPATTERING of gray in his dark hair, Pastor Melvin Vaughn was a good many years Daniel's senior. The kind-hearted minister's family consisted of a lovely, fun-loving wife and a daughter only a few years younger than Daniel. Despite their age difference, the two men had bonded instantly when they met a few years earlier at a statewide ministers' retreat.

Daniel was fast becoming known in California's Christian community as a dynamic and anointed speaker. He spent a lot of time on the road, as invitations were extended from various churches throughout the state. One of his strongest supporters, Mel had also become his spiritual mentor.

Arriving in Woodlake just in time for dinner that evening, Daniel enjoyed the time spent with his friend's family. The Vaughns' obvious love for one another extended to him, making him feel one of them. Still, he was relieved when the pastor suggested they take their coffee and apple pie into his office.

Settled comfortably into matching armchairs, their

steaming coffee mugs resting on a small table between them, the two men were alone for the first time since Daniel's arrival. He sighed, resting his head against the high back of his chair as he closed his eyes.

Mel gave him only a few moments before speaking into the silence. "Something is heavy on your heart, my friend."

Daniel opened his eyes and managed a weak smile. "Yes." He reached for his dessert.

The older man's fork cut through the flaky crust of his wife's homemade pie, but he did not bring the bite to his lips. He focused his full attention on Daniel, and his kindly face wore an expression of gentle concern.

He finally allowed himself a taste of his pie when Daniel said nothing more. They sat in comfortable silence, simply enjoying each other's company—along with Noni Vaughn's luscious apple pastry.

Finally, Daniel placed his fork on his plate and set it aside. Only then did he look at his friend and speak what was on his heart.

"An old friend has asked a favor of me," he said. "I love this woman as if she were my own mother, Mel. But she's asked me to do something I'm not entirely comfortable with."

Mel raised an eyebrow. "Did she ask you to do something you think is wrong?"

Daniel shook his head. "No. Mrs. P would never do that. But the results of her request may be far from what she hopes. There's a high potential for hurt and disillusionment, not only for her but for…" He stopped abruptly and cleared his throat, unconsciously lowering his eyes from his friend's steady gaze. "For her daughter. Perhaps even for other people they've never met."

"I see." Mel nodded thoughtfully. "You could just say no, right?"

"I could, yes. But it's very important to her, and… well, she's ill. She seems all but certain she's dying, and she could very well be. If carrying out her request will bring her some sort of peace, then I feel I must do that."

"But that peace could be very costly for others."

"Yes."

"Then I'd say you have some praying to do, my young friend."

Mel's smile soothed Daniel's anxious heart, and he found an unexpected smile of his own. "That's why I'm here. I appreciate your allowing me to use the guesthouse. The plan is to closet myself there for the next few days, just me and God and His Word. Hopefully I can find some answers and a little guidance in this situation."

"You know I'll be praying with you, son. Do you wish to be left completely alone?"

"I'll be happy to see you any time."

"Well, I was thinking you might join me on my daily walk. It will do you good to get out and get some sunshine each day. If you want to talk while we walk, I'll be happy to listen. If not, we'll just walk."

"Sounds good."

"Then I'll be by at about six o'clock in the morning. I do my best walking before the world starts talking." Mel rose from his chair, and Daniel quickly followed suit. "The daughter, Daniel…what's her name?"

A rush of treacherous color made itself felt in his cheeks. "I, uh…I beg your pardon?"

Mel smiled. "I think you know what I'm asking, son. The moment you mentioned her, it was written all over your face. You love her, don't you?"

Daniel shook his head, chuckling despite his embarrassment and the aching throb of his heart. "How do you do that, Mel?"

The minister said nothing, simply raised an eyebrow and waited. Finally Daniel nodded. "Her name is Gillian. And yes, I've loved her almost as far back as I can remember—since we were kids."

The other man nodded. "Pretty name. Perhaps you'll tell me about her while we're walking tomorrow." He squeezed Daniel's shoulder affectionately. "Come on. I'll get your key and walk over with you."

Danny alternated between pacing the floor and kneeling beside his bed for hours that night, seeking God's direction regarding Mary Helen's request. What if he did find Gillian's family, and what if they were the terrible people they seemed to be? How could he look her biological father in the face and maintain a Christian attitude?

And if, as Mrs. P feared, there was a mother who loved Gillian and wanted her in her life, what would that knowledge do to her?

Groaning, he made one last plea for the night. "Father, I admit I'm at a loss. I don't know what to do. I don't know what's right. But You do! You know Gillian's family—both of them, the one she knows and loves and the one she was born into. You know their stories, and You understand them, even more than they do themselves.

"If it's Your will that she know about all this, then lead me to them. Help me find them, and above all, give me the wisdom to handle the situation in whatever way will be least hurtful to everyone involved."

Rising from his position on the floor, Danny sat for a moment on the edge of the bed, head bowed, eyes closed, still in a prayerful frame of mind. Because his actual prayer time was coming to an end, he was surprised to find himself all at once wrapped almost physically in a holy atmosphere. Filled with an overwhelming sense of God's presence, he went still, awed by this unexpected honor and waiting on the Father's next move.

"There were two of 'em, ya know."

Not at all what Danny expected. The audible—and very human—voice startled him, and he sprang to his feet.

Whirling toward the slow, drawling voice, he stared wide-eyed at a tall, thin man folded into a low chair across the room. He had no problem seeing his visitor, even in the dim light. The man wore a threadbare plaid shirt and khaki slacks. He bent forward, his elbows resting on bony knees as he bounced a worn brown hat from one hand to the other.

The intruder's eyes were fixed on Danny's face, and he found himself all but drawn into their liquid amber depths. More golden than brown, and fringed by thick dark lashes, they were hauntingly familiar.

Do I know him? He tried to recall the faces of Pastor Jones' small congregation but could not find this man in his memory.

Though he did not feel threatened, he was more than a little ill at ease with the idea of a stranger simply walking into his private quarters in the middle of the night. He distinctly remembered setting the lock on the door.

Is this guy real? If he is, why is he here? And who is he? Maybe he's lost or even not quite right in the head.

Swallowing nervously, he took a step across the room. He opened his mouth, half surprised to find he could speak.

"Who are you? How did you get in here?" He resisted a strong urge to reach out and touch the old fellow, to see if he were real.

The man smiled, accentuating the cleft chin and the single

dimple, just one, in his left cheek. Danny had often ribbed Gillian about the little dent in her chin but, truth to tell, he found it almost maddeningly attractive.

This man's undeniably handsome face must have drawn similar reactions from the opposite sex a few years back. In his younger days, he must have been quite the ladies' man.

"Oh, there ain't a lot o' doors that can stop me," the old fellow drawled. "But I ain't here ta hurt'cha. Just came by to tell ya somethin'."

"To…tell me what?"

"Do what the lady ast'cha for. It's time."

"I beg your pardon?" Danny thought he knew to whom his visitor referred, but how could this stranger possibly know anything about Mrs. P's request?

"Does it matter how I know?"

Did he just read my mind? He glanced back toward the bed. Maybe he was dreaming and would see his own sleeping body lying there. But the bed was empty, of course. He hadn't even crawled between the sheets yet.

"Who are you, sir?"

"Just someone who knows about yer problem, son. And I can help ya, if you'll listen to me. Why don't'cha just sit down fer a minute?"

Danny sidled toward a straight-backed chair, not taking his eyes off his guest, who didn't speak again until he was seated.

"There, that's better! Now you just listen, and I'll say what I got to say and be gone."

Still half convinced he was having the strangest dream of his lifetime, Danny nodded. The stranger hung his ragged hat on one knee and proceeded to stroke the cover of a worn black Bible that lay on his lap. Three gold crosses adorned its front cover, their once-bright gold worn dim and dull with age.

Where did the Bible come from? Was the old fellow holding it all along?

Danny fervently wished he could awaken. While he didn't sense any physical threat, he did feel decidedly odd about his current situation. He would be much more comfortable when he opened his eyes and found himself alone in the room.

His visitor chuckled. "You're a good man, Daniel Collins. Gillian could do worse."

He knows my name…and Gillian's!

Shaking his head, the old man rolled his hypnotic eyes and twisted his lips into a wry half-smile. "Oh, well, you'll understand later, I suppose. Do what the lady ast'cha to, lad. Do it for the girl and for…her mama. And since you're wonderin', it's the right thing for the lady that ast'cha, too."

Danny gave up on understanding how this mysterious old man knew so much about him. What mattered was that he apparently did. Maybe he really could help him know what to do.

"But, sir, I don't even know where to look for them. Corman's Camp? I've never heard of it. And I can't find it on any map I've looked at."

"Nope. It ain't on any map. But you'll find it. Just head south and listen for the voice of hope."

The uninvited guest placed his hat on his head, unfolded his impressive length from the low chair, then walked to the door and opened it.

"Wait!"

The old man stopped and turned. A beam of moonlight sliced through the window and across his face, and his eyes shone like bright gold in its glow. Little fingers of electricity shot down Danny's spine.

"Will she ever love me?" He blurted out the impulsive question even as he chided himself for doing so.

Fool! Why would this strange man know a thing like that?

"Love." The lines in the old man's face suddenly appeared countless and deeply grooved. Why hadn't he noticed them before? "Now, son, that ain't a subject I ever knew much about. But iffen you love her, don't let nothin' stop ya from tellin' her so. And if she chooses ta love ya back, don't never hurt 'er, ya hear? You treasure it, because we don't always get a second chance. Understand?"

A tear slipped from one eye, and even that tiny drop of moisture shone with an unearthly gold light as it trailed down the old fellow's thin, leathery cheek.

Danny averted his gaze, his visitor's unstated pain too powerful to witness. He heard the click of the latch and looked up to find his guest had gone.

Jumping up, he shot across the small room, calling out as he swung the door open. "Please, wait!"

But the old man was nowhere in sight. Danny rushed outside in his pajamas, hurriedly checking both ways down the short roadway in the light of the full moon.

A few streetlamps further illuminated the narrow street, but his strange caller was gone as surely as though he had never been there at all. Danny shook his head in disbelief and sighed, even now questioning the reality of what had just happened.

The old guy never even told him his name.

Pastor Vaughn stopped dead still in the middle of the tree-lined dirt road and turned to look at Daniel, his brown eyes wide and shocked.

"That could only be Ol' Travelin' Jack!"

"You know him?" Danny grinned, suddenly feeling a little foolish. "That's great, man! I thought I was hallucinating. Where does he live? Can you take me to him?"

The minister stared at him for a long time, finally nodding slowly. "Sure, I can do that. He's just around the corner here."

Why am I so excited by a second chance to meet a faded old codger who doesn't even have the manners to knock on a door before entering?

But he was. He desperately wanted to talk to this Travelin' Jack again. If God wanted to use the old guy to deliver a message, he wanted to hear it—all of it.

He was a little let down when his friend turned to walk through the gates of a small, beautifully maintained cemetery. He looked around for a caretaker's cottage. Perhaps that was how the old man made a living. But he saw only a small mausoleum.

"Mel. This is, uh…a graveyard."

No answer.

"I thought we were going to see Ol' Travelin' Jack."

Mel nodded, his lips curved in a small smile. "We are. Come on."

A few hundred yards into the cemetery, they turned and walked through a rusty gate leading into a fenced section.

"These are all county plots." The older man gestured toward row upon row of unpretentious gravestones. "Folks who left no money to pay for their burial and who had no known family to pick up the slack."

Danny saw that many of the graves had only numbered markers to designate the resting place of their occupants— not even the simplest of tombstones. On the few graves that did boast some sort of stone, many lacked even a name. The county had either been unable to identify the bodies or indisposed to spend further funds.

I guess the need for an I.D. doesn't extend past death.

"Interesting, my quirky preacher pal." He swallowed an annoying lump in his throat. "But a little depressing, wouldn't you say? I vote we go see Jack now."

Mel stopped and pointed down at a small headstone, about ten inches square, which bore only the words, "Travelin' Jack." No date of birth or death.

"The church paid for this little headstone. I wish we could have afforded more."

Shocked, Danny stared down at the tiny stone, feeling somehow deflated. When he could find his voice, he raised his eyes to his friend's. "I don't understand. Obviously this is not the man who visited me last night. What are you trying to prove?"

"Nothing, son. I couldn't prove it if I wanted to, but I think this is the man who visited you. He fit your description perfectly." The pastor knelt to brush away a bit of debris from the sad little stone.

"I knew Jack as well as anybody did. He lived in the guesthouse where you're staying now for the last couple years of his life and helped me out around the house, the church, the grounds—wherever I could use him—to earn his keep. The only problem is, Ol' Jack died about six, seven years ago."

Danny thought his own incredulous laughter sounded more like a bark than an expression of humor. "So…what are you saying? That I had a face-to-face conversation with a ghost? I wouldn't have taken you for someone who'd believe in such things."

"I don't."

"What then?"

The other man turned and began walking slowly toward

the gate, and Danny reluctantly followed. He almost felt the need to sit beside Jack's grave for a time.

"I don't believe in ghosts, but I do believe in angels."

"Angels!" Stunned, he stopped in his tracks and just stood there blinking at his friend. "You think I was visited by an angel?"

Mel nodded. "I do. You said the room took on a holy atmosphere just before you heard Jack's voice. And you told me you didn't feel threatened at all."

"No, I didn't. But I can't say I felt exactly comforted, either!"

The pastor laughed softly. "Well, I doubt most of us would in the physical presence of a heavenly being!" He touched Danny's arm and silently urged him on, continuing to talk as they walked.

"Here's what I think, son, for what it's worth." Mel paused, sending Danny a sideways glance. "Now don't ask me to give you book, chapter, and verse for what I'm going to say, because I can't do it. I'm just telling you what I think, after years of hearing folks tell me about their experiences. You understand?"

"I got it, Reverend. No scriptural back-up, just a godly man's hunch. I'll take it."

Chapter Ten

"OKAY, THEN, HERE IT IS." Mel paused, drawing several deep breaths before plowing into his take on Daniel's visitation. "God understands man's need to communicate with an entity he can relate to—in other words, a human being. We know, because it happened in the Bible, that angels can take on human forms. Well, I believe the Father might sometimes allow an angel to take on the form of a human who has passed on in order to get a message to someone connected to that person."

"But I'm not connected to Jack in any way."

"How do you know that? You were praying about a specific situation, as I recall—one with factors completely unknown to you. What if Ol' Jack was connected to someone in that set of circumstances? I'm not saying he was, you understand, because I never knew much about him. Nobody did. He drifted into Woodlake some years ago and wound up living in a cardboard box behind one of the beer joints, just a broken old alcoholic with nothing to live for. Some of our outreach people found him and brought him to the church."

They were walking slowly back down the same road they had already traveled. Danny was so wrapped up in Mel's theory that he hadn't even noticed when they departed the cemetery.

"Did he ever accept Christ?"

The pastor smiled, his dark eyes softening. "Yes, he did. And as far as I know, he never touched a drop of alcohol again."

"Praise God!" Danny wondered why he felt so relieved to hear this news about a man he did not know. "He never shared his past with you?"

Mel shook his head, cocking his head thoughtfully to the side. "No, not really. Every once in a blue moon, he'd say something that would almost give me an inkling what he was about, but no…he never really shared who he was, not with me. Not with anyone that I'm aware of."

The two men walked in companionable silence for awhile. Danny was trying desperately to make sense of the situation, and Mel graciously allowed him time to work things out in his mind.

"Mel, I have an idea, but it just seems too crazy."

"It's not exactly a normal situation, son. What are you thinking?"

Danny started to speak, but stopped and shook his head. "I don't know. It's probably ridiculous."

"Tell me."

He came to a decision just as they reached the guesthouse. "Come on in. I have a story to tell you, and I'll be interested in seeing whether you come to the same conclusion I think I'm reaching."

He used the key the Vaughns had given him to open the door, and the two of them entered. Somehow, the place felt different to Danny now, knowing a certain old man known only as Ol' Travelin' Jack had spent the last years of his life there.

He poured two glasses of iced tea from a pitcher in the small refrigerator then joined Mel at the dining table.

"What I'm going to tell you is in the strictest of confidence." He waited for the pastor's grave nod before continuing. "Gillian's mother asked me to read an entry in her journal—an entry from twenty-three years ago. I was uncomfortable even reading it, and I certainly wouldn't share it, except…well, I know I can trust you, and I need to know what you think about it, especially now that your old friend Jack has come into the picture."

Mel nodded, a warm smile conveying his complete understanding of Danny's awkward position. "Tell me only what you're comfortable with sharing, son."

Danny was silent for a long time. Finally, however, he drew a deep breath and began talking, relating the entire story from beginning to end. The minister did him the courtesy of not interrupting. When he finally stopped, the older man still did not immediately speak but brushed a hand across his eyes and cleared his throat several times.

"Well." He spoke so softly Danny had to strain to hear. "That sheds a whole new light on your angelic visitor." The pastor stood and turned to leave the room. "Follow me."

Puzzled, Danny trailed along behind, stepping across the small living room and into the cottage's single bedroom. Mel knelt to open a drawer in the bedside table and pulled out a worn Bible, its black leather cover— ragged and curled at the edges—adorned with three faded gold crosses.

Mel slowly fanned the pages, revealing margins riddled with scribbled notes. Verses and entire portions of scripture were highlighted and underlined. The Book had clearly been well used.

"This was Travelin' Jack's most prized possession." Mel squatted down beside the bed then twisted around to sit on the floor, his back against the bed. "Come on down and have a seat." He beckoned Danny to join him. "I want to show you something."

Lowering himself onto the floor beside his friend, Danny looked down at the Bible. Mel had opened it to one of the fill-in pages at the front.

"Read this."

As Danny looked down at the scratchy letters on the front page, he drew in a sharp breath, realizing his hazy idea had been right on target. "I was right!"

On the line under the words "This Bible Belongs To," Ol' Travelin' Jack had printed his name.

Kennith Jack Kelly.

"Juliana?"

Early Friday afternoon, and she was deeply into the first story she had written in a while. Will's voice did not register until he spoke her name again, more loudly.

"Hello? Anybody home?"

She looked up, a little dazed and preoccupied. It took her a moment to understand that he had been calling her name with no response.

"I'm sorry, I didn't hear you."

The twinkle in his blue eyes created an uncomfortable arrhythmia in the region of her heart. "That's an understatement! I'm not sure you were even in this realm."

She laughed a little sheepishly. "You could be right. I've been so wrapped up in getting the advice column going that I've neglected the other side of my job. This is the first story

I've written since I came to work at Voice of Hope."

"Oh." His disappointment was unmistakable.

The two of them had the copy room to themselves. It was one of those rare days when all of the staff writers were out on assignment at the same time.

"What? You don't want me to write now? Or I should have written more already?"

"Neither. I was just getting ready to go grab a bite to eat. I thought if you weren't too busy, you might want to come along. But if you're wrapped up in your story, of course, I understand."

Juliana ripped the sheet of paper out of the big, black Royal typewriter and fit the cover over the machine almost in one motion. Smiling, she pulled her handbag from a drawer and stood.

"Where to?"

They wound up at a small restaurant Will described as "a little hole-in-the-wall café." Apparently the owners agreed, for on the front window someone had painted the name Hank's Hole-in-the-Wall Café. Tucked into a jumble of commercial businesses on a side street a few blocks from the magazine's offices, the little restaurant held only six tables, each of which could seat up to four people. At the moment, they were all empty.

"It's usually packed out in here." Will looked around as they made their way to the back of the room. "But we are a bit past the lunch hour."

"Good!" Juliana grinned. "Maybe we'll have it all to ourselves the whole time."

He pulled out a chair for her then seated himself across the small table. "That would be nice, I agree, but I doubt Hank would!"

"We'll pray Hank up some business when we leave."

His laughter echoed in the empty room. "Deal!"

Just then, a man entered from a door Juliana assumed led to the kitchen. He trudged behind the counter, wiping his hands on a white dish towel. His booming voice filled the small room.

"Howdy, Will! Who's the dame?"

Will shook his head, coloring a little as he grinned at Juliana.

"Behave yourself, Hank. Meet Hank O'Hare, Juliana. He's the owner and resident rapscallion here at Hole-in-the-Wall. Hard to look at and not the most mannerly sort, but the man can cook like nobody's business."

Hank's steel gray eyes softened as he rounded the counter, offering his hand to Juliana. "Pleased to meet'cha, miss. How'd you come to be hangin' out with the preacher?"

"Preacher?" Juliana looked at Will in startled inquiry.

"Come off it, Hank. You know I'm not a preacher!" Her hands rested on the table's surface, and Will took both of them in his own. "Ol' Hank here thinks anybody who cares about his soul is a preacher."

"Hmpf!" Hank grunted. "You bein' worried about your own soul don't bother me none. The problem is you can't stop frettin' about mine!"

"Now, you know I only invite you to church because I love you, man!"

The café owner's ruddy cheeks flamed, and he deliberately turned his back on Will's broad grin. "Fiddle flakes!" He aimed an exaggerated grimace in Juliana's direction. "You need a menu, hon?"

Before she could reply, Will cut in. "By all means, take a menu if you want one. But let me just tell you, there's not another BLT in town like the one Hank makes. I'm going to have that and a bowl of macaroni and tomato soup."

She shrugged and smiled up at her red-faced host. "I'll have the same."

Hank rushed off into the kitchen, and Juliana, alone with Will, discovered she was at a loss for anything to say. She breathed a little sigh of relief when he took care of that problem with a simple question.

"How are you coming along with that letter? I haven't had a chance to check back in with you since I sent you home with it a couple of days ago."

"I took care of it."

Will raised his eyebrows. "Really? I thought you must have done something since you moved on to a story, but…'took care of it'? What does that mean?"

"I wrote a response." Juliana's lips curved into a sheepish smile. "A rather long response, actually—and mailed it. After you sent me home that day, I spent the entire night in prayer. You'll probably think I've gone over the edge, but I even went so far as to anoint that piece of paper with oil and hold it in my hands while I prayed."

Will shook his head from side to side, his clear blue eyes resting softly on Juliana's face. "You're incredible."

Something in his deep voice upped the tempo of her heart to what felt like a downright dangerous level.

She tried to produce a light laugh, but even in her own ears, the resulting sound was hollow. "Spoken by a man who hasn't the slightest idea what I said to that girl. How do you know it was even worth reading?"

"I just do. Because I know you care about her and because I know you."

She stared at the table, unable to meet his eyes. "You don't know me at all. Only what you see at work."

"I know all I need to know!" Gently, he squeezed the hands he still held atop the table. "I know how concerned you are about the folks who write those letters you answer every day. I can see without half trying that you're smarter, sweeter—and certainly easier to look at—than most women. And I know I'd like to know you better."

That last comment surprised Juliana into looking up and into his eyes. She opened her mouth to speak, not really knowing what she'd say, but was interrupted when Hank appeared with their drinks.

He left immediately, promising to bring their food before they could say 'Jack Sprat,' and she wasn't sure whether to be thrilled or chilled when Will picked up right where he had left off.

"So what do you think? Can we spend some time together…just the two of us? See what we really think about each other?"

Suddenly too shy to speak, Juliana cleared her throat and forced her voice past trembling lips. "We could do that, Will…I'd like to. But what about the office? What will everyone say?"

"They'll say exactly what they've already been saying."

She gasped. "What have they been saying?"

He chuckled, shaking his head in wonder. "You really haven't noticed, have you? Every time I stop by your desk, the entire copy room goes silent, and every head in the room turns our way. I don't know if they've read my mind or if theirs are just suspicious, but it's pretty clear everyone in that office thinks we're either already seeing each other or that it's about to happen."

Her cheeks burned. She had certainly not imagined herself the subject of the office rumor mill. "That can't be good!"

He shrugged. "They're going to talk about someone, you can count on it. I guess I don't mind if it's me…especially since they're almost right. I do think the new girl is something pretty special. But I promise not to tarnish your reputation by flaunting it."

In the silence following that statement, Hank plopped their plates down on the table. She didn't know whether to be disappointed or relieved when Will released her hands and reached for a napkin, which he unfolded with a grin and tucked into his collar like a bib.

"There ya go, preacher man." Hank wiped his hands on the ever-present white dish towel. "Miss Camden, I hope you like the BLT and soup. If you don't, blame the parson here. He recommended it."

"Mmmm, it smells delicious. And it's Juliana. Please."

Hank nodded and sauntered away, but not before she saw the pleased smile that creased his craggy face.

Reaching across the table, Will took her hand again while they bowed their heads and said grace. They filled the next few moments with light, comfortable conversation as they dove into the delicious meal.

Juliana was grateful for the reprieve. She needed a moment to gather her scattered thoughts.

Not given to playing silly mind games, she had known Will owned her heart from the first day she met him. And there had been a moment that day when she was certain he felt the attraction, as well. But he had so effectively doused that initial emotion that she wondered if it had existed only in her own imagination. Indeed, he seemed to go out of his way to keep their relationship on a professional level.

Until today. Today he wanted to get to know her better. She had hoped for that every moment for the past several weeks. So why couldn't she embrace the blessing instead of doubting it?

"I didn't mean to worry you, Juliana." His gentle voice

broke into her musings, and a wave of heat washed over her face.

"Oh, no, I wasn't—"

"Yes, you were." Will's lips curved into a lopsided smile, and her heart leapt and danced in ridiculous response. "Juliana, we shared something special the day I interviewed you. I know you felt it, too. At least, I thought you did, and I hope I was right." He chuckled sheepishly. "I came that close to telling you right then and there how I felt, but…"

In the sudden silence, Juliana watched a range of emotions chase one another across his expressive face. He was plainly struggling with something.

"Will? Is there something you want to tell me?" Juliana shoved her plate aside. This time it was she who placed her hand atop Will's on the table, gratified when he turned his over to take it in a firm grip.

He was silent for a moment, studying her face. She said nothing, simply waited.

"There are things about me you don't know…"

"I thought that's what this was all about…us taking time to find out more about each other."

He sighed and closed his eyes as a shadow of pain passed briefly over his handsome face. When he opened them to look at her, a familiar coolness had settled over their translucent blue depths.

"Listen, I'm…I'm sorry. This was probably a bad idea, after all."

A tight band wrapped itself around her heart, squeezing it in a painful grip. *No. This is not happening!*

When she spoke, her voice was every bit as chilly as Will's blue eyes.

"Let me just get this straight. Am I to understand now that you do not want to get to know me better? That everything you have just said to me is a lie? Because I think that's what I just heard."

Will frowned, shaking his head. "No. No! I would never lie to you. You can't believe that, Juliana. I do want to know you better. Nothing could make me happier. But …" He paused, drawing a shaky breath before going on. "There are things you don't know, things that might make you not want to know me at all. Please try to understand!"

She gathered up her purse and gloves, searching for a reason to look away from the stark pain in his expression. It was more than she could stand. *Why won't he allow me to be there for him?*

With a disappointed glance at his tortured face, she rose and stepped toward the door. "I'll meet you at the car. You'll need to pay Hank."

"Juliana, wait —!"

She stopped but did not turn. "Will, I won't play games. When you decide how you really feel, let me know. Until then, please…please just leave me be."

As the door swung shut behind her, she heard Hank's sarcastic drawl. "Nice goin', preacher man! I could'a handled that better myself."

Chapter Eleven

NEITHER OF THEM SPOKE UNTIL Will parked in the lot outside the office.

"Juliana, I'm sorry. I wish I could make you understand."

She made no effort to alleviate his guilt but met his gaze squarely and waited, hoping he would say something to make sense of what had just happened.

Disappointment shadowed his face when she failed to reply. "You're angry. I guess I don't blame you, but I need you to believe I meant what I said. Every word."

"Even the last ones, Will? The ones that made all the others a lie?"

His eyes, full of raw pain he made no attempt to hide, were fixed somewhere in the empty air just over her head. A muscle worked in his jaw, and he swallowed hard before speaking through thin white lips. "I'm so sorry."

"So am I—more than you know." She shut the door behind her with a soft click, marched across the lot to her own car, and drove away, not bothering to return to her desk.

Alone in her little beetle, she considered simply quitting her job. But she had never been a quitter, and she loved Voice of Hope and her "Just Ask Juliana" column. Already she had come to feel that some of her readers actually looked up to her, even depended on her for advice. She would not leave them unless she was asked to go.

But that disappointing lunch date made her seriously doubt her own heart. Perhaps she had been wrong about Will being "Mr. Right." What a ridiculous term that was, anyway! She supposed any man could be the right one if she tried hard enough to make him so.

On Sunday, Juliana and her father walked to the morning service. The small church they attended was just up the road a piece, and they always enjoyed the early morning trek together. But this time, the walk was too quiet, and he noticed her distraction.

"Are you going to tell me what's on your mind, Julie girl?"

Startled out of her slightly bitter musings, she smiled. "I'm sorry, Daddy. It's nothing, really."

"Oh, I think it is. You've not been yourself all week. I kept hoping you'd share whatever it is with me, but I guess you're not ready yet, huh?"

"I can't hide much from you, can I?" A little smile broke through her gloomy mood.

Her father took her hand and tucked it under his elbow, where he covered it with his own. "Now what kind of father would I be if I didn't notice when my little girl had something heavy on her heart?"

A soft gurgle of laughter escaped, even through the unexpected tears that suddenly spilled from her eyes. "You know you're the best daddy ever, don't you?" She leaned in and brushed his cheek with her lips.

"That's enough, young lady. You'll have my face all pink before we get to church, and Pastor Obie will think I've been dipping into your pretty-up stuff. We can't have that, now can we?"

Juliana laughed, the first genuine amusement she had felt since Friday. "Absolutely not!" She gave his arm an affectionate squeeze.

"Well?" He cocked an eyebrow.

"Promise not to laugh."

"Cross my heart."

"Daddy, do you believe in love at first sight?"

Her father was silent for a long time, and finally he stopped walking. Placing his hands on her shoulders, he turned her to face him.

"I've never told you about the day I met your mother, have I?"

"No, I don't think so."

He nodded, a faraway expression in his green eyes. "Someday I will."

She grinned. "I'm gonna hold you to that, you know!"

Her lighthearted banter failed to induce a reciprocal mood in her father. When he tipped her chin up and looked into her eyes, she was surprised to see a myriad of unexpected emotions chasing one another across his broad face.

"Whoever he is, sweetheart, I hope he deserves you."

She laughed softly. "Probably not in your opinion, Daddy. But he's a good man."

"There are a few of those left, I guess. But, daughter, does he love our heavenly Father?"

"Very much."

"That's good then."

He took her hand, and they continued walking toward the church. Almost there, he spoke again. "About that question you asked…that love at first sight thing?"

"Uh-huh."

"The answer is yes, Julie girl. Without a single doubt."

The tension between Will and herself must be as obvious as a neon sign. What else could account for the averted eyes and broken-off conversations whenever she passed by someone's desk? Juliana's suspicion was confirmed when Claudia stopped her one morning as she crossed through the lobby.

"Morning, Claudia!" She called her usual greeting to the receptionist. The other girl's kindness on the day of her initial interview had not been forgotten. And Claudia had proven herself a true friend and team player on more than one occasion since.

"Juliana, wait! Do you have a moment?"

Turning back, she suddenly noticed her friend's gloomy expression. "What's wrong?" She hurried across the empty lobby, pulling a chair along so she could sit next to her. "You look awful!"

"Thanks." Claudia's wan smile did nothing to improve her glum appearance. "Just what I needed to hear."

"Oh, stop it. You know I think you're beautiful! I just meant you look upset, or worried, or something. What is it?"

Claudia's brown eyes filled with tears, and she impatiently dashed them away as they spilled down her lightly freckled cheeks. "It's Will!"

Juliana's heart jumped in annoying response to his name. "What about Will?"

"I can't seem to please him anymore! Everything I do is wrong. And I'm not the only one…half the staff is walking on pins and needles." Jerking a tissue from a box on her desk, she blew her nose, and Juliana was surprised by the stormy expression on the girl's face.

"Whatever it is that's going on between you two, you've got to fix it!" Claudia burst out. "Will's going to drive us all completely away if you don't."

Juliana could not find her voice to reply.

Since their disastrous lunch date the previous week, she had not spoken to him at all—nor he to her. She was grateful her job was one she could do without a lot of contact with the boss and had dreaded the time when she must ask his advice about anything. Apparently, even with a total lack of contact, they could not avoid the office rumor mill.

"Claudia, I…" She tried to laugh, but the sound fell flat. "I don't know what to say. Whatever is going on with Will— and I am sorry if he's being unpleasant—but I'm sure it has nothing to do with me."

The other girl sniffed and brushed angrily at a new onslaught of tears. "Oh, yes, it does! Everyone knows it does. Did you two have a fight?"

Juliana eyed her warily. "Why would you think that?"

"Because…because Will won't go anywhere near your desk anymore, and yet he can't stand not knowing where you are." She spat the entire sentence out in an almost-but-not-quite-unintelligible burst.

"What?"

"It's true. He refuses to go by your desk or buzz you to see if you're there. Instead, he calls me twenty times a day." The receptionist's normally pleasant voice took on a sour, mimicking tone. "'Is Juliana here yet?' 'Has Juliana gone to lunch?' 'Did Juliana leave any messages?' I'm telling you, he's driving me crazy as a loon! You've got to fix it, whatever it is."

As Claudia gave vent to the resentment she had apparently been bottling up all week, Juliana's own indignation rose. By the time the girl finished, she was trembling with anger.

Patting her friend's hand, she stood and replaced the chair she had borrowed. "Don't worry, I'll take care of this!"

"You won't tell him I said anything…?"

Juliana blew a kiss across the room as she slipped into the long hall leading to the offices. "Not a word, don't worry."

A moment later, she rapped sharply at Will's door and stormed inside before he could answer.

"Will Dawson, what in the world are you thinking?" Outraged, she started speaking before the door even closed behind her. "You said you would protect my reputation, not bring it into question! How dare y…?" She broke off, mortified.

Oh, forevermore! There's someone with him.

Will had been seated in one of the guest chairs in front of his desk, but now stood facing her, his mouth hanging open, stunned eyes wide with disbelief.

The young man in the other chair stood to his feet as well. His copper-colored hair and rust-brown eyes were in stark contrast to the paleness of his face as he gawked at Juliana. Before Will could respond to her verbal attack, the visitor spoke.

"What are you doing here?" The words were barely more than a whisper.

Shocked and embarrassed, she couldn't get a sound past her frozen lips. As if in a dream, she watched the stranger whirl and grab Will by both lapels. He spoke through clenched teeth, his furious voice sending ice coursing through her veins.

"If you've done anything to tarnish her reputation, so help me, you'll be sorry!"

Will raised both hands in the age-old gesture of surrender.

"Easy, Danny…it's not what you think."

The temporary paralysis that had frozen Juliana in place relaxed its hold. She dashed across the room to squeeze between the two men.

"Stop it this instant! Leave him alone. What is wrong with you?" She glared at the angry stranger, who appeared set on ripping Will limb from limb.

The young man blinked, eyeing her as if he were seeing a ghost. Slowly, he released his grasp of Will's crumpled lapels.

"You're not… But you look like…!" He shook his head and brushed a hand over his eyes. "I'm sorry, ma'am, but…who are you?"

Will placed a hand on the distraught young man's shoulder. "I know what you're thinking, Danny. I had the same reaction when I first saw her."

He took Juliana's hand and drew her close to him, slipping an arm around her waist as if he had every right to put it there.

"Sweetheart, this is Daniel Collins. He's going to marry my cousin Gillian—although I don't think she knows it just yet."

He turned to his confused visitor. "Danny, meet Juliana Camden. She's one of the staff writers here at Voice of Hope. She's also the woman I intend to marry—if she'll have me. Although, judging by her entrance just now, I may have a little work to do."

The other man's face was a mask of disbelief. He seemed unable to pry his gaze from Juliana, who squirmed uncomfortably—not only under his stare, but against the firm circle of Will's unyielding arm.

"I'm sorry, I don't understand. What's going on here?" Danny eyed Will in hopeless confusion.

Juliana jerked free, angry at both men. "You can ask me, Mr. Collins. I'm right here. And you…" She glared at Will. "You've got more than a little work to do!"

"Look, let's all just take a deep breath and start over, shall we?" Will's calm voice was an obvious attempt to defuse the charged atmosphere. "I gather you're extremely angry with me—yet again. I don't know why, but I'm sure I deserve it. However, in light of the fact that I have a guest, might we talk about it later?"

Juliana hesitated but nodded her assent, only slightly mollified.

"Good. Now if you'll take a seat, I think it's time we talk about this look-alike situation."

She perched on the edge of the nearest chair as Will turned back to his visitor.

"Do you have a picture of Gillian? I'm afraid I don't, not here at the office."

The young man pulled a worn wallet from his pocket, his gaze still fixed on Juliana. She was relieved when he flipped open the billfold and lowered his eyes to the photo he pulled from it.

"It's unbelievable!" He passed the photo to Will, who studied the little snapshot first, then looked at Juliana.

She'd had quite enough. Bouncing up from her seat, she marched the three steps to his side and snatched it from his hand. "This is ridiculous!" she spat. "I seem to be the object of interest here, so it's only fair I get a look at—oh, good heavens above!"

For a moment she could not catch her breath. When she did, she was unable to raise her voice above a whisper. "Who…? How can this possibly be?"

She swayed, and Will caught her, lowering her gently onto the chair she had just vacated. "Easy, sweetie," he whispered, taking her hands in his. "Slow, deep breaths. You'll be okay."

Without being asked, the visitor crossed to a side table, poured a glass of water from a pitcher, and brought it back to Juliana.

She wanted to argue, to tell Will that she didn't want to take slow, deep breaths. What she wanted was to know why the girl in the picture looked just like the girl in her own mirror. Instead, she obediently sipped the water and breathed deeply. Otherwise, she knew she would pass out, and she had no intention of doing that.

Within a few moments, she felt better, and the three of them sat facing each other. She made no protest when Will took her hand.

"I know how adamant you are about protecting the privacy of your readers. But I'm going to ask you to trust me, Juliana. I need to see that letter again—the one from 'Afraid of the Dark.'"

She hesitated. What could her reader's private pain have to do with this situation? Nevertheless, she reluctantly excused herself and hurried to her own desk, where she retrieved the two-page missive from a file folder. By now, it bore obvious signs of constant handling. Hurrying back through the copy room, she avoided the curious stares and sidelong glances of her co-workers.

"Good, you're back. Just hold on to that for a moment, please." He turned to his visitor. "Danny, how is Mary Helen?"

Juliana understood the confusion on the young man's pleasant face. Why had Will changed the subject?

"She's not well." Danny's questioning gaze rested on Will's face. "I told you, that's why I'm here. I want to see your father."

"Yes, I remember. Perhaps you'll feel you can share Mary Helen's confidence with me later, after you talk to Dad. For now, though…Danny, exactly how ill is Gillian's mother? Pardon me if I sound harsh, but…is she dying?"

Juliana gasped. She had never heard Will be so rude. At her reaction, he colored a little, but held his visitor's gaze and did not retract the question.

With a sigh, the young man shook his head. "I hope not. I don't know what it would do to Gillian if she lost her. But since you ask…yes, I'm afraid that could very well be the case."

Will gazed off into a shadowy corner of the room, obviously deep in thought. When he asked his next question, Juliana drew in a sharp, quiet breath. This time she thought she knew what he was getting at, though poor Danny still looked thoroughly bewildered.

"How about Gillian's relationship with God?" Will looked the other man full in the face. "Have you noticed any changes in that part of her life?"

Angry color rose from Danny's neck up into his face. "Where are you going with this? You're asking some awfully personal questions for someone who hasn't even bothered to check in on Gillian and Mrs. P since Mr. Parsons died."

Will responded with an acquiescent nod of his head. "You're absolutely right. I have been remiss. In my defense, though, may I remind you that Gillian and I have seen each other perhaps three or four times our entire lives? It's not as if our families were ever close. And I believe my father has been in touch with Mary Helen several times since then."

Danny shrugged. "Maybe. But I don't see how Gillian's walk with the Lord could possibly be of any relevance in this conversation."

Will plucked the letter from Juliana's cold fingers.

"Didn't you tell me you're headed to Weedpatch to preach, Danny?"

At the other man's short nod, Juliana gave him a tentative smile. "Where are you speaking?"

"I was invited by an elderly pastor…a friend of a friend kind of thing. Actually, he called and said God had been urging him to have me speak at his church for some time now, though we've never met in person. His name is Coffman. Obie Coffman."

Shocked, Juliana sputtered, "But…but that's my pastor. You're preaching at my church?"

Even Will looked surprised. Danny, however, blushed to the roots of his hair. "Oh, no. How will you ever be able to listen to anything I have to say after my behavior earlier?"

Both Juliana and Will burst out laughing. "You mean your threat to do my boss severe bodily harm?" Juliana sent a weak glare in Will's direction. "Because I'm not sure but what that might have been a good idea, after all!"

Will narrowed his eyes in mock warning, but Danny still wore a crushed expression. "I owe you both an apology. When it comes to Gillian I…well, I need to pray a little harder, I guess. I really thought you were her, Juliana, though I couldn't for the life of me figure out why she would be here. And you were so angry at Will. I was confused and upset, and I just…"

He sighed heavily, running both hands through his thick hair as he shook his head in resignation.

"Don't give it another thought!" Will smiled kindly at the other man. "Had the tables been turned, I assure you my reaction would have been much the same."

"Still, I'm sincerely sorry. I hope you'll both forgive me."

"All right then. Back to where we were." Will's voice was too hearty. Juliana hid an amused grin behind her hand.

Dear Will, you don't deal well with apologies, do you?

"You're preaching in Weedpatch—in Juliana's church, no less. She lives there, Danny, but I want her to tell you specifically where in Weedpatch she lives. I have a feeling you've heard of it."

Chapter Twelve

SUDDENLY NERVOUS, JULIANA LOOKED AT their visitor. "I live in Corman's Corner."

Danny's face went white beneath the ruddiness of his cheeks, but something lent a powerful, glad light to his eyes. "Corman's Corner?" The words were a raspy whisper.

Will nodded but held up a hand when the other man opened his mouth.

"Read this before you say anything." He handed over the letter that had become so personal to Juliana. Danny took it with a curious glance and began to read.

Soon he looked up, his fine copper-toned eyes glistening with tears. "It's Gillian, of course. I would know that even if I didn't recognize her handwriting."

"That's what I thought."

When he finished reading, the young evangelist folded the dog-eared letter with its splotches of anointing oil and returned it to Juliana. He said nothing for awhile, just stared off into the distance. She could almost see him putting pieces together in his mind.

When at last he spoke, his soft voice rang with certainty.

"'There were two of them.' Those were the first words Ol' Travelin' Jack said to me, and I had completely forgotten them." His eyes blazed, fired from within by something Juliana could not fathom. "He sold the Parsonses one of his babies, but there were two of them. They were twins!"

His remark stunned Juliana to the bone. She shivered, unable to absorb the full meaning of Danny's excited statement. Still kneeling beside her chair, Will slipped an arm around her.

"I think you're going to have to back up a little. Who is Ol' Travelin' Jack? And did you say he sold a baby?"

"I'm sorry. I should have handled that better. I suppose I do need to fill in some pieces." Danny sighed and raked a hand through his unruly hair. "Please understand. This is all new to me, too. I'm still in a bit of shock myself. And the information I've been seeking has come to me in the most unusual ways!"

With a tremendous effort, Juliana focused her bewildered gaze on his face. "Travelin' Jack…his name is Jack Kelly, isn't it?"

"Why…why, yes, it is! Kennith Jack Kelly. How did you know that?"

"By accident, actually…but I'll tell you about it later. Go ahead, please. You were saying…?"

"I don't know where to start."

"The beginning is usually best." Will smiled his encouragement.

"The beginning." Danny hesitated. "Well, for me, I suppose that would be when I met Gillian Parsons."

He drew a deep breath and launched into an account of

finding the sobbing little girl in the park, surrounded by a gang of bullying children. Choosing which bits and pieces of a lifetime to encapsulate for Will's and Juliana's benefit couldn't have been easy. Juliana assumed his God-given gift of speaking served him well.

Over the next hour, interrupted only now and then by a question from one or the other of his audience of two, Danny introduced them to the woman he loved, as well as her ailing mother and her late father.

He tried to make Will and Juliana really *see* himself and Gillian at age thirteen, standing side by side as they gave their hearts to God at the front of the church both families attended.

When he told them about William Parsons' death five years earlier, Juliana wept into her handkerchief. Her obvious empathy with the sister she did not know was touching—and astounding. Was this girl's relationship with her father similar to the near hero-worship Gillian had harbored for Mr. Parsons?

"I've never witnessed another marriage quite like the Parsons'. Their relationship epitomized the term 'holy matrimony.' Everyone who came into contact with them was profoundly touched by their love for each other and for Gillian. Their family seemed to be ideal."

Sighing, he moved on. "When she lost him, Mrs. P pretty much stopped living. She's always been a bit delicate—so tiny you'd think a strong wind might blow her away. But up until her husband's death, that appearance was deceptive. She was always on the go—cooking and cleaning for her family, taking care of them, participating in volunteer activities. But it all stopped when she lost Mr. P."

Envisioning the dear lady's too-thin frame, he shook his head sadly. "She's lost weight she could not afford to lose.

Her spirit remains strong, however, and I think that's because she so desperately wants to be there for Gillian. But her heart is not in this world anymore. She truly believes she's dying, and unless she can pull herself out of this overwhelming sorrow, I fear she will."

"That's so sad!" Juliana dabbed at her eyes with a handkerchief. "She sounds a lot like my own mother, to be honest. Of course, we still have Daddy—thank God! I don't know what either of us would do without him. But Mama has suffered severe headaches and various other physical problems for years."

"I'm sincerely sorry. I know how difficult that can be. I've watched it happen in Gillian's family."

"Thank you. But please…do go on."

So he told them about his most recent conversation with Gillian's mother.

"I'm breaking Mrs. P's confidence for the second time now." He looked up, meeting each of their gazes. "Please understand. I would normally refuse to divulge her secret under any circumstances, but I feel strangely compelled now, as I did the first time, to share it."

He outlined the diary entry he had read, watching Juliana all the while, concerned for her emotional well-being. He had dropped a torrent of startling information on her already.

Juliana leaned forward, listening intently, as Danny recounted his prayer-time visit from Ol' Travelin' Jack. When he told them about his trip to the little graveyard with Pastor Vaughn, she couldn't hold back a quiet sob.

He hesitated, but she motioned for him to continue.

"Mel is convinced I spoke with an angel that night." He cautiously gauged hers and Will's expressions.

"That was my first instinct."

Juliana nodded her agreement with Will's comment.

"Mine, too." She spoke from behind a drenched handkerchief.

"How odd!" Their ready acceptance of the idea surprised Danny. "Such a thing never occurred to me until Mel suggested it." His voice took on a ruefully jesting tone. "I guess the good Lord knew it would have overwhelmed me at the time."

"You're probably right." Will smiled a little, his head tilted in thoughtful consideration. "Our Father always knows what He's doing, my friend. He had a message for you, and you needed to be able to communicate with the messenger." A rumbling chuckle shook his lean frame. "Being struck dumb in spiritual awe would have made it difficult, don't you think?"

Juliana turned to look at him in surprise. "Impressive, Mr. Dawson!" Her light, teasing tone most likely told Will that she wouldn't stay angry at him forever. Danny found himself oddly pleased by that bit of insight. "Just when I start to think you're totally hopeless, you come up with something wonderful like that."

Will colored under his olive skin. "Please continue, Danny."

Danny didn't even try to hide his grin.

"Well, there's not a lot more to tell. Oh, yes—the Bible!"

"Bible?" Juliana frowned, puzzled.

"That's how I found out his name." He shifted in his chair. "Mel actually gave me Travelin' Jack's Bible, said I would know what to do with it when the time came."

"I'd like to see it." Juliana smiled shyly, then covered the beautiful curve of her lips with a handkerchief, clearly having mentally honed in on the slightly strangled quality of Danny's breath. He still had trouble with how much she resembled Gillian.

"I'll, uh—I'll get it from my car in a moment. There's not a lot more to tell, anyway. Just that before Jack left that night, he told me to 'go south and listen for the voice of hope.' I had no idea what he was talking about." He drew a deep breath that calmed his nerves and quieted his spirit.

"I stayed in Mel's cabin a couple more days and was there, in fact, when Pastor Turk called to speak with him about another matter. When he found out I was there, he invited me to Weedpatch."

He forced himself to look at Juliana again. "I felt an instant connection with your pastor. He's so soft-spoken, and yet his voice is almost mesmerizing. I found myself hanging onto his every word on the telephone. I can only imagine what effect that voice must have in person!"

Juliana said nothing, but her eyes were soft, and a fond smile danced at the corners of her lips. Daniel took silent note of her apparent affection for Pastor Obie Turk. It spoke well for the minister.

He hurried on. "Because I wanted to continue the errand I had started for Mrs. P, I was hesitant to accept his invitation. But then Mel told me Weedpatch is located a few hours south of Woodlake."

He sipped from the glass of water Will gave him. "Considering Ol' Jack's instructions, I found it too much to consider a coincidence. It had to be God's direction—no pun intended. So I called Pastor Turk back, said I would come immediately, and started driving south."

"I think you did the right thing." Will said, and Juliana nodded.

"I know I did, though I'll admit I wasn't too certain until I got here." Danny laughed sheepishly. "I'm afraid I was a little drowsy coming into town. With everything that's been happening the past few days, I haven't slept well. But as I entered Bakersfield, I noticed your billboard and very nearly wrecked the car." He chuckled. "That big sign roused me in a flash, you'd have thought it was spelled out in flashing lights."

Will frowned. "What billboard?"

Juliana, too, looked confused. "I don't think I've seen it."

"Of course you have." Daniel chuckled and rolled his eyes. "It's huge! The one at the north end of town, facing incoming traffic. 'We are the Voice of Hope! Are you listening?' Under that is your address and telephone number. Anyway, that's when I remembered what Jack had said. 'Listen for the voice of hope.'"

Will's mouth hung open. Juliana reached out with one small hand and gently nudged upward on his chin.

Daniel grinned and continued.

"I knew, of course, that you have this magazine—Gillian reads every word of each edition. Your families may not be exactly close, but she's proud of you, Will. Anyway, it occurred to me that your father is Mr. Parsons' stepbrother. Mr. P could have, just possibly, shared some of this story with him. I thought I ought to look him up, see if he knows anything that might help me find Gillian's birth family."

He drew a deep breath and tossed a relieved, all-wrapped-up kind of grin toward the other two. "And that's it. That's why I'm here." His grin wavered and became an anxious frown as he took in the bemused expression on his host's face. "What? What's wrong?"

Will's eyes shone with a reverent awe. "I have news for you, my friend." The same wonder Danny saw in his eyes could be heard in his voice. "I don't have a billboard at the north end of town. I don't have any billboards in Bakersfield!"

Will insisted on driving Juliana home, though she argued that she was perfectly capable of driving herself. But once inside his car and away from the handsome young minister, she realized what a toll the last hour had taken on her, not only emotionally, but physically as well. She could barely keep her eyes open.

I think my mind wants to go into hiding.

But she could not escape the truth. Her adored Daddy was not her birth father. She knew it with every resistant fiber of her being. The man who had been her hero all her life…the mentor who instilled in her a love for the Lord and the written word just like his own…had come into her life after she was born. He had to have—she could think of no other explanation.

Her natural father was Kennith Jack Kelly, a man so enslaved to liquor that he sold her twin sister to obtain it, and then abandoned his wife and remaining infant daughter.

Unless he sold me, too. Maybe Mama's not really my mother, either.

Outside her home, Will's eyes moved over her face with obvious concern. "Are you going to be okay?"

"I'm fine."

"I won't come in, unless you think you'll need me. You and your parents have a lot to talk about."

She nodded and reached for the door handle. He caught her arm. "I'll call you later, okay?"

"If you'd like." *Why do I feel so disconnected?*

Shutting the car door firmly behind her, she squared her shoulders and forced reluctant feet to carry her into the only house she had ever called home.

"I'm in here, Juliana!" Her mother's lilting voice came

from the kitchen. Juliana shuffled toward it. "How was your day?"

When Juliana did not reply, the older woman turned to look at her. With a gasp, she turned off a burner on the stove and hurried forward.

"Darling, what is it?" Taking Juliana's elbow, she urged her further into the room. "Sit down!"

She meekly allowed herself to be led to a chair and lowered into it.

"Clarence!" Mama called, her voice frantic. "Come quickly!"

Juliana heard the commotion going on around her but felt detached from it all. Her mind seemed shrouded in some kind of protective cotton, and if it were removed, she might break. Annie placed a glass of water in her hand, and Juliana's fingers closed around it. Chalk one up for instinct.

Her father appeared in the doorway and quickly crossed the room to her side where he knelt and took her hand. She closed her eyes, cherishing the familiar feeling of safety as her smaller hand disappeared into his big one. A tear fell from beneath her closed eyelids.

"What is it, Julie girl? Tell me what's wrong."

Opening her eyes, she let them roam over the beloved face, taking in the green eyes so different from her own. She searched his features for a resemblance she did not find.

Tears rained down her cheeks, and her lips trembled. She felt like a lost child. "I want you to be my real Daddy!"

Her father looked as though he had been punched in the stomach.

Behind him, her mother dropped the glass she had taken from Juliana's unsteady hand. It landed with a loud thump but didn't break, just rolled across the floor, spilling its contents in a wet stream over the linoleum.

Annie did not seem to notice. She sank into the nearest chair, one hand over her mouth, her blue eyes—also unlike Juliana's—bright with unshed tears.

A muscle worked in Clarence's jaw. He pulled Juliana into his arms and held her for a long time, saying nothing. When he finally did speak, his voice was hushed and broken. "I will always be your Daddy, Julie girl!"

She clung to him, sobbing. He cradled her in his arms. "There, there. Shhh, little one, don't cry."

When she finally managed to pull herself together enough to make sense, they moved into the living room. Her mother wept quietly, unable to stop touching her—stroking her hair, patting her arm, cupping her cheek.

"My poor baby. I'm so sorry, darling!"

She repeated the same words until Juliana thought she would scream. "Please, Mama, stop it. This is not your fault. Please!"

Wearily closing her eyes against the sight of her mother's tears, she let her head relax briefly against the back of her chair. May as well take the bull by the horns and get this over with.

"Please tell me the truth about two things." She forced herself to sit up and face her parents. "Who is Jack Kelly? And do I have a twin sister?"

Her mother shook her head, her eyes pleading.

"Tell her, my love. It's time." Her father's ever-gentle voice held an unmistakable, seldom-heard note of command.

Face ashen, her mother nodded, resigned to the inevitable.

Juliana and her father waited while Annie gathered her thoughts and her courage. Finally, she spoke, though her voice trembled and broke every few words. Not bothering to dry the tears that flooded her eyes, Annie Kelly Camden finally revealed the secret she had guarded for twenty-three years.

"Jack Kelly was…my husband. He was your biological father, though I'm not sure he ever could have been a daddy."

Sweet relief flooded Juliana's mind. "Then you are my mother? My real mother?"

Mama's face blanched, and her eyes widened in horror. "Oh, Juliana, yes! Why would you question that? I am your mother!" Her swimming blue gaze caressed Juliana's face. "And yes, my darling. You did have a twin sister."

Daddy stood and quietly left the room. He probably wanted to give them a little privacy, but Juliana wished he would stay. His presence soothed her taut nerves.

Soon, however, she was drawn into her mother's heartbreaking story.

Chapter Thirteen

SHE WAS BARELY SEVENTEEN WHEN she met Jack Kelly.

Keeping house for the widow who owned the cattle ranch bordering her parents' little piece of Texas property was no easy task. Crotchety old Widow Humes' reputation as a hard taskmistress was not without basis.

But then a golden-eyed cattle rustler came to work on the ranch, and the young girl suddenly found it much easier to go there each day. The handsome cowhand took to showing up at the most unlikely times and unexpected places, always with a charming smile and flattering words that turned her head, despite being known for possessing wisdom beyond her years, and being unaware of her own beauty. Widow Humes wasn't the only female in that community to have a well-earned reputation.

Their brief courtship took place in secret. Her devoutly religious parents would not approve of Jack Kelly. A heavy drinker, he'd earned a reputation too—for fighting when he was intoxicated. Had the girl's dear minister father known she spent her days within a dozen feet of such a man, he'd have been scandalized, and imagining her hot-headed mother's reaction sent the young lady into a fair tizzy.

Had they known what was going on, she'd have been strictly forbidden to leave the house, much less to see her suitor. So for the first time in her life, she deliberately set out to deceive her beloved parents, as well as her only sibling, a sister she adored.

When he asked her to marry him, the girl knew without doubt that her parents would not give their blessing. So she agreed to run away with the handsome man whose golden eyes mesmerized her, and filled her dreams, both waking and sleeping. He wanted to head for California, away from the horrible dust that was becoming a major problem in the eastern states. Sunny California was a land of opportunity, and there were said to be jobs enough for everyone.

The couple made their marriage vows in the neighboring county courthouse and headed off to California in his rattletrap pickup, which wasn't even loaded with possessions—they had none. She walked away from her protective Christian home into a whole new life.

Jack's drinking problem proved far worse than she had realized, and his fervent promises to stop lasted exactly one week. By the time the couple reached California, she was already an emotionally beaten woman. Her husband pressed her to forget her old life with her God-fearing family. In the spirit of that goal, he even gave her a new name, insisting on calling her Annie. Oh, well, what did it matter? By then, she had bigger problems than the name folks called her by.

Her parents would have welcomed her back home, but she was too ashamed to contact them. Besides, her father preached that a marriage was meant to last a lifetime, through good or bad, rich or poor, in sickness and in health. She had not made a bed of roses for herself, but she would lie in that bed if it killed her.

When she realized she was expecting a baby a couple of very hard years later, Annie was happier than she had been since her marriage. At her insistence, Jack once again promised to stop drinking, even though it was she, not he, who wanted children.

Things seemed to be looking up. He worked in the fields, whichever of them were harvesting crops at any given time. Though he wasn't what Annie would call ambitious, neither was he a lazy man. Money was scarce, but they got by, and they loved each other in spite of their differences.

She considered it a double blessing when she delivered twin girls so identical that even she could not tell them apart. In order to know which twin was which, she tied pieces of colored yarn around their tiny wrists— one pink, one a soft, minty green.

The babies slept together in a single crib, under blankets she had crocheted while waiting for them to be born…from the same yarn she tied around their wrists afterward.

"On that last night you were together, Gillian was under the pink blanket, with the matching yarn on her little wrist." Annie's voice was barely more than a whisper. "You had the green blanket and yarn bracelet. I looked down at the two of you before I went to bed, and I remember thinking how I wished Papa and Mama could see you and how sad that they didn't even know they had grandchildren."

Smiling a little through persistent tears, Annie reached out to stroke Juliana's cheek. "I even thought perhaps I would finally write, let them know I was okay and tell them about my beautiful girls."

Nestling close, her daughter rested her head, with its

mane of dark curls, on Annie's shoulder, and she smiled. Juliana needed her at this moment as badly as she ever had as an infant. Her fingers slid into the silky tresses, and she stroked them as she spoke.

"Jack was still awake when I went to bed that night. Lots of times he stayed up late, pacing the floor and just…brooding, I guess. We didn't have any money, so he couldn't drink, and besides, he had promised me he wouldn't." She sighed. "Whatever the reason, he was up for a while, but later he told me he came to bed sometime around midnight. You and Gillian slept well that night for the first time, and I didn't wake up until after four in the morning."

Annie choked but forced herself to continue. Now that she had started telling her daughter the truth, she wanted her to know everything. It would not be fair to fold under the pressure. So she continued.

"I awakened in a panic, my breasts swollen and heavy with milk, and knowing you both had to be hungry and wet. Already I was angry at myself for sleeping so long without checking on you. So I jumped out of bed…"

Her breath came in hitching gasps. gaze fixed itself on the wall across the room, but what she saw was a past she had hidden for far too long. Once again, she stood peering into a double-duty crib, where two infant girls should have been sleeping.

"I looked down into that little shared bed, and I thought surely— please, God! Surely I was dreaming. Only one baby lay there. But it was dark outside; the sun wasn't up yet. My heart pounded s– so h– hard against my chest, I…I thought I might faint, but I told myself not to p– panic."

When her daughter's hand covered both of hers, she realized they were clenched into tight fists on her lap, and she was rocking back and forth in unconscious panic.

Stop it! Juliana is upset enough already. With an enormous effort, she unfurled her fists and forced her body to stop its seesaw motion.

"I slipped around to the other side of our bed, thinking maybe…just maybe…Jack had brought one of you into bed with us. Perhaps you had cried, and I hadn't heard." A hoarse sob tore from her throat. "But there was no baby in our bed either.

"I turned the light on so I could see and walked back across the room to look down—oh, it was such a long ways down into that crib! And there you were, darling—all alone, still sound asleep. But Gillian was g– gone, and her little pink blanket was gone with her."

She drew a long, shaky breath then looked at Juliana. "I…I don't remember much else for quite a while."

Neither of them spoke for a long time.

Juliana finally broke the silence. "What happened to my…to Jack Kelly?"

Just then, her father stepped back into the room. He carried a notebook, which she recognized as one of those from the attic. Dropping it onto a nearby tabletop, he sat beside her.

"This book might help you understand some things." His gentle voice was a salve to her overwrought nerves. "You can read it later, at your leisure if you choose to. For now, though, I will answer your question to the best of my memory."

He told her then about his sole encounter with Jack Kelly and about the subsequent freight train collision. Choosing his words with care, leaving out the most grisly details, he recounted finding the ring that helped identify the man killed in that accident.

Juliana remembered the snippet she had read in her father's notebook. "So that's how you met Mama?"

He nodded, his eyes softening as they rested on her mother's face. "Yes. I talked the sheriff into allowing me to bring her the news because I thought it might be less cold and formal coming from someone who had actually spoken to Jack. To be honest, Julie girl, I met your father only a day before he died, and I'm afraid he didn't make a great first impression. His one redeeming quality was his obvious love for your mother. In a roundabout way, I owe him a world of gratitude because he gave me the most wonderful gift of my entire life. Had I never met Jack Kelly, I would not have come to Corman's Camp looking for his widow. But I did, and I met an angel and fell in love."

Mama laughed softly. "I wasn't very nice to you, either." She looked at Juliana, shaking her head in rueful recollection. "I can't imagine what he found to like about me."

Clarence smiled, and his warm gaze once again caressed her mother's face. Juliana wanted to burst into tears. This wonderful man that she adored…he was not her father. *Oh, Daddy, my wonderful Daddy! How am I supposed to deal with that?*

His gaze remained fixed on Mama, his adoration plainly written on his broad face. "I loved everything about you, sweetheart—from your tangled, uncombed hair to the mismatched slippers on your feet. From the moment I saw you, I knew my heart would never be my own again."

"Now you just stop that, Clarence Camden. You're making me blush!" Indeed, Mama's cheeks pinked to a lovely rosy shade.

Juliana smiled a little sadly. "I haven't seen the two of you play like this in a long time. It's nice. You should do it more often."

Her mother's eyes immediately filled with guilty tears. "Oh, darling, it's my fault. I have hidden from life behind my bedroom door. It hasn't been fair to you or your fath…to Clarence."

"It's all right, Mama. I might have done the same in your shoes. And I think I understand something else a little better now, too. All those times I heard you call out my name and beg for forgiveness…it wasn't my name at all, was it? You were calling for Gillian."

"Yes." Tears slipped from Mama's eyes to trail down her cheeks. "I failed her. How can a mother lie three feet away and…and *sleep* while somebody steals her baby? What kind of mother am I?"

"The very best kind." Joining her on the sofa, Juliana stroked her mother's hand gently as she talked. "What happened wasn't your fault, Mama. You have to stop blaming yourself now."

She raised her eyes to meet those of her father, who watched them from across the room. Locking her eyes onto his, she spoke to her mother. "I know it wasn't your fault."

Her father's face lost all color. "What are you saying, Julie girl?" His hoarse voice broke her heart. "What haven't you told us?"

Her eyes moved over the familiar lines of his face, searching for answers she could not find. Finally, she posed the question that burned in her mind.

"Daddy, why didn't you ever tell her the truth? You knew what my f…what Jack Kelly did."

Mama gasped, her confused gaze moving back and forth between them.

"Clarence?" Her trembling voice, barely audible, held a note of something that made Juliana suspect a part of her mother knew the truth already.

"Annie, I..." Clarence's shoulders sagged in defeat. "I wanted to leave you something to believe in. Your husband was dead. I saw no reason to defile what few good memories you had."

Juliana watched her mother shake her head in futile denial. "No. Please don't say it!"

He took her hand. "I have to, beloved. Juliana knows now, and I think you do, too, somewhere in your heart." He drew in a lungful of air before finally voicing the secret he had kept through all the years. "Gillian wasn't kidnapped, sweetheart. Jack took her. He...well, he sold her, Annie."

"No!" She was on her feet in an instant, a bright spot on each cheek providing the only color in her face other than the vivid blue of her angry eyes. "Don't you say that! He wouldn't have done it. Jack was weak, and he could be cold and unloving, but he would not sell a baby. Not his own flesh and blood. He wouldn't!"

Her father refused to look away from those accusing eyes, although his hands tightened into large fists as he faced Mama. A familiar pulse beat in his right temple. Juliana had seen it before, but not often...only when he was frustrated or upset almost beyond endurance.

"It's true, Annie. I'm so sorry! I should have told you long ago. I wanted to protect you, but I was wrong. If I had told you the truth from the beginning, you wouldn't have blamed yourself all these years."

Tears trickled down his cheeks, and the raw pain in his gentle voice ripped at Juliana's bruised heart.

"I truly did not realize that's what you were doing, sweetheart. I thought it was your grief that caused the headaches and the illness. If only I had known what was going on in your mind!"

Mama sank into a chair, shaking her head. Juliana moved

close and took her hand, stroking it once again, offer what comfort she could. In a moment, the full implication of what she had been told seemed to register, and her mother's eyes blazed into her own.

"If this is true, then Gillian must be alive. Somewhere out there, my baby is alive!"

Clarence knelt and pulled his wife into his arms. "We don't know that, my love. Please don't get your hopes up! I've been running an ad in the Limelight once every quarter ever since I met you, with no valid response whatsoever. Jack didn't even know the names of the people who bought her. We have no way of finding her now."

"We will find her!" Annie pounded his broad chest with her fists, sobbing brokenly. "We will!"

Juliana watched in silence for a moment. *Now. I have to tell her now.* She lifted her chin in sudden determination. "Mama!"

Cradled in Daddy's supporting arms, her mother stiffened before slowly turning to face her. Staring back into those tormented eyes, Juliana trembled from head to toe. Her voice, however, was clear and steady.

"I know where my sister is."

Gillian missed Danny. He had been gone longer than she expected. The least he could do would be to place a simple phone call. Restlessly, she wandered out the front door and strolled across the lawn to the mailbox. Perhaps he had written.

She found only a few pieces of mail and needed only a glance to see that none bore Danny's distinctive scrawl. Her interest waning, she half-heartedly sifted through the other envelopes.

One of them bore a familiar logo on its professional letterhead. She slipped it into one of the deep pockets in her full skirt before going back into the house.

"Do you feel like coming with me to check on Grams and Poppy?" She questioned her mother as she stepped into the house.

Curled up in a cozy chair near the front window, Mary Helen's head bent over the pillowcase she was embroidering. "Oh, I don't know, darling. Why don't you go on without me." Not a question, but a gentle command.

Gillian sighed, disappointed. "Come on, little Mother! It will do you good. Besides, you know Grams will worry if you don't come."

The older woman laid aside her embroidery, a tiny crease furrowing her smooth brow as she looked up. "You're probably right. I really don't want to worry her."

"Then come with me. You need a change of scenery."

With a heavy sigh, her mother looked away. "Okay, I'll come. But first, Gillian…remember that conversation we had, the one about my journals?"

"Yes, Mama, I remember." The subject irritated her, and she heard the tinge of impatience in her own voice. "And I don't want to talk about them again."

"I know you don't, Gilly. But I have another request. Will you bear with me for just one moment? Please?"

Gillian perched on the edge of the sofa. "Okay. What is it? But just so you know, I think this is ridiculous. You're not going anywhere!"

Her mother laughed softly. "Okay. We can hope. But just in case…Gillian, I need you to make me one more promise. I need to know that, whatever you find out in those journals, and however you feel about it, you will not abandon your grandparents. Not ever."

She jumped to her feet, shocked at the suggestion. "Mother! I love Poppy and Grams. I would never abandon them!"

Standing, Mary Helen crossed to her side and tiptoed to kiss her cheek. "I know you love them, silly Gilly Bean. But I still need to hear the words. I need you to promise me, no matter what, you will always love them and be there for them."

"I promise, my little Mother. I promise, okay? Now can we go?"

Mary Helen smiled, her blue eyes slightly misty as she stroked a strand of Gillian's dark hair. "Now we can go."

Chapter Fourteen

GILLIAN UNZIPPED THE LAVENDER-AND-white-striped skirt and stepped out of it. One of her favorites, the garment sported big purple buttons down the length of the faux opening in front. She laid it atop her bed and smoothed the fabric in preparation to draping it over a padded hanger. A crisp rustle from the pocket reminded her of the letter she had not yet had a chance to read.

Eager to see what Juliana had written, she rushed through her bedtime routine. With her mind on things far beyond facial cleansing, pure memory motion carried her through the little ritual. First, the creamy cleanser she used faithfully, no matter how tired, frustrated, or even sick she might be. Warm water to remove it, then a splash of cold to close the pores. Even as her thoughts took her down a dozen paths, she somehow remembered to pat her face dry gently, rather than using the towel to rub the moisture off with rough strokes.

She had almost forgotten about writing to Juliana Camden, an author of inspirational fiction whose stories she so enjoyed reading in her cousin Will's magazine, Voice of Hope. Of course, her letter to Juliana had not mentioned that

Will was her cousin. Indeed, she had not so much as provided her own name.

In all honesty, she had doubted her silly letter would ever reach its intended recipient. After all, the woman had not been an advice columnist at the time. Gillian was surprised to find the "Just Ask Juliana" column in the magazine only a month later, with a couple of letters from readers and Juliana's clearly prayerful replies.

Thank God she didn't print mine!

Mother occasionally thumbed through Gillian's Voice of Hope magazines. She would've identified "Afraid of the Dark" in half a heartbeat.

She pulled a soft nightgown over her head, still mulling over the possibilities within the envelope that rested on the center of her bed. It looked rather like an odd square in the lovely quilt Grams had made especially for Gillian.

Juliana had not put the letter into print, but perhaps she had replied to it. Or…the envelope might hold nothing more than a polite thank you for writing, along with an apologetic explanation that not every letter could appear in the column and an invitation to try again another month.

But somehow she didn't think so.

Finally climbing into bed, she stacked a couple of pillows against the headboard and leaned against them, then picked up the envelope with the swirly VOH logo in the top left corner. At last she tore it open, revealing more than one page of typed print. Smiling, she read:

Dear Afraid of the Dark:

Thank you for your letter. I am honored you would share such a private, personal matter with me. Sorry it has taken me so long to reply, but I did not want to respond until I could do so at God's direction. I want you to know that my answer is not given lightly but after a great deal of thought and even more prayer.

First of all, let me just say how sorry I am that you lost your father. I can tell by the tone of your letter that you harbor some bitterness regarding that loss, and I can certainly understand why.

My own father is my hero and my best friend. I would be devastated should something happen to him. My mother has debilitating physical frailties, as well...so I can certainly relate to your fear of losing your "little Mother."

But never forget this, my friend—no matter how lonely you feel, you are never alone. Even when you can't feel God's presence, He is with you. He loves you, and He will take care of you. His reasons for taking people we love are His own and not to be questioned right now, but someday we'll be able to ask Him why.

Try to remember that there is nothing in the darkness to fear—not if Christ dwells in your heart, for HE IS THE LIGHT!

John 8:12: Then spake Jesus again unto them, saying, I am the light of the world: he that followeth me shall not walk in darkness, but shall have the light of life.

He is the light. He is also love, and "perfect love casteth out fear." A wise man once said, "There is nothing to fear but fear itself." I consider that true, though perhaps for reasons different from that author's. You should fear your fear, because it is a symptom—a manifestation of not walking close enough to perfect love: God! When you've made peace with Him and walk alongside Him, you won't fear the darkness, because there will be none—you will be in the presence of the Light of the world!

When darkness threatens to overwhelm you, and fear becomes a monster in your closet, try reading the 23rd

Psalm...nothing, to me, is more comforting than that familiar, truly beautiful passage of scripture.

Now...as to your mother's journals, I must again take my reply from the Word of God.

Matthew 6:34: Take therefore no thought for the morrow: for the morrow shall take thought for the things of itself. Sufficient unto the day is the evil thereof.

My humble translation: Don't worry about tomorrow, it will worry about itself. Each day has enough trouble of its own.

It makes perfect sense when you think about it. Do not "borrow" trouble or worry. Today, your little Mother is still with you. Enjoy every single moment of today, and let tomorrow bring what it will. Deal with the future when it gets here. Until then, don't allow its possibilities to steal a single second of joy from today.

You have made a promise to your mother, my friend. It is to be hoped that promise will provide her a little peace of mind while she lives. When the Father does call her home, whether it happens tomorrow or twenty years from now, then you most certainly should fulfill any promise you made to her. But know this, dear one...when that time comes, no matter what secret is revealed within those pages, God will give you sufficient grace for that day and that situation.

It's all about trust—trust in God. I know you know Him. Now it is up to you to walk with Him and trust Him to be the Light that dispels the dreaded darkness.

If you feel you would like to, please let me hear from you again. I would be genuinely interested in knowing how both you and your mother are doing.

You will remain in my prayers.

Your Sister (in Christ),

Juliana Camden

Tears dropped off Gillian's chin, leaving inky splotches on the papers she clutched in her hands. Sniffling, she hugged the sincere letter to her heart for a long time. Finally she smiled mistily, and still grasping Juliana's wonderful words between her fingers, she slid out of bed and onto her knees, already feeling the comforting warmth of a long-neglected Light.

Gillian awakened feeling refreshed, as though a load had been lifted from her heart. Her eyes fell on the Voice of Hope envelope, and she tucked it into her pocket as she left her room, looking forward to reading it again when she could find a moment. How sweet of Juliana Camden to send a personal reply.

She had never done much writing herself; her talent lay in art. In the long hallway from her bedroom to the kitchen, her mother had lined the walls with her drawings and oil paintings, ranging in ability from her first attempt to her latest. She grinned, noticing a few of her early efforts as she headed for breakfast. *Some of those are not worth displaying, little Mother!*

To her surprise, Mary Helen was up and puttering about in the kitchen. She was fully dressed, every shiny silver-blond hair in place, and she was humming a familiar tune. When was the last time her mother had prepared a meal, much less dressed up as if she might go out at any moment?

From the doorway, Gillian drank in the unexpected sight, until the older woman caught sight of her.

"Good morning, darling! Why don't you get the juice glasses down? Our omelets are almost ready."

Gillian felt as though she floated across the room to wrap

her mother in a huge hug. She opened her lips to say something funny and lighthearted but discovered an enormous lump in her throat and could not say a word. Unexpected tears overflowed her eyes to streak their way down her cheeks.

For a moment, her little Mother looked as if she might join her and just have a good cry. Instead, she laughed lightly, and the musical trill warmed Gillian's heart. She hadn't realized how much she missed that bell-like laughter.

"Silly Gilly!" With the hand that wasn't clutching a spatula, Mary Helen gently patted her damp cheek. "Are my omelets really so bad?"

Laughing through her ridiculous tears, Gillian released her mother and reached for a couple of juice glasses. "Well, I'm not sure. It's been a while since I've had one of them, you know!"

Her mother clucked reprovingly, shaking a finger in her direction. "This can still be called off, you know. I'm sure Poppy would be happy to eat yours."

The first steaming egg and ham creation slid onto a plate and, before her mother knew what she was up to, Gillian snatched it off the countertop. "He'll have to catch me first!" A playful grin lit her face as she dashed off to her place at the table.

Within a few moments, they joined hands, thanking God for their food and for each other. Even as she acknowledged the improvement might be only temporary, Gillian rejoiced to see her mother acting more like her old self. A couple of times during the meal, she found herself swallowing another irksome lump in her throat as they talked.

"You seem to be feeling better." Tentatively, she broached the subject.

"You know, I really do feel almost like old times today."

Mary Helen smiled, spreading a thin layer of grape jelly on her toast. "The moment I opened my eyes this morning, something felt different. I don't know how to explain it."

Gillian placed her fork on her plate and pushed it back. "I think I do."

"You do? Then, by all means, do tell me!"

She hesitated, searching for the right words. "Mother, I know you've noticed my spiritual condition these past few years. I've felt alienated from God ever since we lost Papa."

"Yes, I noticed. But I've been praying for you all along, and I knew that He was still very near you. Sometimes we build up walls of our own making, and we just leave Him on the other side."

"Yes! That's exactly what I did. I was so devastated when Papa died. And then you started to get ill, and I was terrified of losing you, too." She choked up and reached over to take her mother's hand. "I just couldn't understand what was happening. I kept questioning why, if God truly loved me, He would leave me so alone!"

The older woman brushed at the mist in her vivid blue eyes. She nodded encouragement, and Gillian continued. "Danny tried to talk to me a few times, but I'm afraid I was rather rude." She blushed, even as her concern regarding his long absence resurfaced in her mind. "He's always so sweet, Mama. I don't know how he stands me sometimes."

"That's part of loving someone, Gilly Bean. You take them as they are. You love the good in them, even when you see the not-so-good."

"Yes, but there is no bad in Danny."

Now her mother's laughter rang out in the small room. "You think not?"

"There really isn't!" Gillian was insistent. "I've known him for years and years, Mother. He's truly good."

"You know, darling, I agree. But I'm thinking that perhaps even if there were some tiny bit of bad in Daniel, you wouldn't see it."

"Well, of course I would!"

Her mother raised a finely shaped eyebrow. "Would you? They do say love is blind, you know."

"Love? You think I love…?" Gillian stopped and sat staring across the table, wide-eyed. She felt the color drain from her face as she realized the truth in her mother's words. "Oh, my goodness gracious alive! I love him!"

Mother stood and began scraping bits of food from their plates, a pleased smile curving her lips. "My lands, child, I thought you'd never see it!"

"You knew?" Stunned, she sat unmoving in her chair while her mother worked around her.

"Of course I knew, darling! I'm your mother."

She bounced up, sending her chair rocking backwards. As she rushed to set it upright, her heart threatened to explode inside her chest.

"Danny! Oh, no…does Danny know?"

"Calm down, dear. I'm quite sure Daniel hasn't a clue."

With a moan, Gillian buried her face in both hands. "Oh, how will I ever face him again? How could I go and fall in love with my best friend? I'm such a fool!"

Her mother ran a gentle hand through her hair. "I think you'll find you're not the only fool who's ever fallen in love with a friend." The dry comment seemed to hint at more than it actually said.

She peeked through her fingers, her voice muffled. "What are you saying?"

Her mother hesitated. "Never mind. Just be yourself around him, dear. If it's meant to be, it will be."

"Oh!" Gillian suddenly tugged on her mother's hand,

drawing her down into the chair next to her. "You're right. I was almost ready to panic, but you reminded me." She pulled Juliana's letter from her pocket. "I have something I want to read to you. This letter came yesterday in answer to one I wrote some time ago."

Smoothing the neatly typed pages on the tabletop, she looked up. "After reading it last night, I had a long conversation with God and tore down the wall I had built between us. But, Mother, I think there's something in it for you, too."

"Well, if it helped you find your way back to God then I must hear it. I am so happy for you, darling! And Daniel will be thrilled."

Not quite ready to discuss Danny again, she chose not to respond.

She was also a little hesitant to share the whole story her mother was waiting to hear. "In order for you to understand what I'm going to read, you have to know about the letter I wrote to Juliana."

"Who's Juliana?"

"She's a writer who works at Cousin Will's magazine."

"I see." She plainly did not, so Gillian hurried on.

"Like I said, things began to grow dark around me when Papa died. Then you got sick. When you made me promise to read your journals, I knew that you really believe you aren't going to live."

A tear slipped from her eye and trailed down her cheek. "The thought of losing you was simply more than I could face. So I wrote to Juliana. I don't know quite why, except…well, I so needed to confide in someone, and every time I read something she's written, I get this wonderful feeling."

She looked away, then back at her mother, a little

embarrassed. "She seems so wise, Mother, as if she would know what to do in any situation. For whatever reason, she was the only person I felt I could talk to at the time." Her head drooped momentarily then she lifted her gaze to meet her mother's. "Forgive me for sharing something so personal with a stranger."

"There's nothing to forgive, Gilly. And if her answer has helped you at all then I'm very happy you did it." A sweet smile lit her mother's face as she pulled a handkerchief from her apron pocket and held it out to Gillian. "Now...I'm dying to hear what this young lady has to say."

Gillian blinked. Was Juliana a young lady? She really had no idea, did she? And it didn't matter. To her, Juliana Camden would be an angel at any age.

She read the letter aloud. Mother listened, nodding here and there, brushing tears at one point.

"How very beautiful!" The murmured comment when Gillian reached the end of the missive obviously came from her heart. "What a wonderful gift she has."

"Yes."

She waited, and after a moment, her mother's blue gaze met her own. She smiled through a mist of tears.

"You're right, darling. There's something in it for me, too. I've been trying to fix things for you myself, trying to take care of tomorrow today. By this time in my life, you'd think I would have learned to leave it all in the hands of our Father, wouldn't you?" She reached across the table to squeeze Gillian's hand. "I must trust Him to care for you when I'm gone."

Gillian hesitated. "Yes, that's true, though I love you for always wanting to take care of me. But it's more than that, little Mother. You're living your life as though you don't really have one because you're so certain you're dying. You need to start living again! Make every moment count, whether you have ten days or twenty years, just as Juliana said."

A long silence followed her words, and she began to fear she had said too much. But then her little mother looked up with a shaky smile.

"When did you become so wise, little girl? You're absolutely right. I have been living as if I'm already dead. It's not fair to you or to your Papa. I don't think he would have liked the person I've become."

"God must have been preparing you for a new start already, Mother. Didn't you say you woke up knowing something was different?"

"Indeed I did!" She started clearing the table again, and this time Gillian rushed to help her. "Well, in light of my new and improved attitude, why don't we go get Poppy and Grams and take a ride in your fancy little car? I think I'd like to see the sunshine!"

Gillian almost dropped the glass she was drying. "Really? You want to go for a drive?"

Answering laughter was interrupted by a knock on the front door. "Go on, Gilly. You get that. I'll finish up in here."

Hanging her damp dish towel on a hook, she hurried to the door. Who on earth could it be? Neither of them was expecting company. She swung it open, fully prepared to send the uninvited caller—probably a salesman of some kind—on down the road.

Her heart nearly stopped beating at sight of the young man on the front porch.

"Danny!" His name burst from her lips, and before he could reply she threw herself into his arms. "Where have you been? I was so worried about you!"

She hadn't meant to behave in such a forward manner.

But then, Danny was her best friend. Embracing him after long absences wasn't unusual for her. Maybe he wouldn't notice a difference in her response this time.

But she noticed his. Danny's arms closed around her, and he groaned.

"My sweet love!" His lips caressed her hair and trailed softly down her tingling cheek. "I never want to go anywhere without you again."

With that, Daniel Collins tilted Gillian's chin up and kissed her full on the lips, and she completely forgot to scold him for not calling.

Chapter Fifteen

JULIANA TOLD HER PARENTS EVERYTHING she knew, starting with the letter from "Afraid of the Dark" and ending with Daniel Collins' visit to Voice of Hope. Clarence tried to break in a couple of times with questions, but her mother hushed him, drinking in every word.

When the narrative ended, silence fell in the cozy living room. Her father's face was pale, his green eyes stunned. However solid his reason, he had misidentified the victim of a train crash over two decades ago.

Annie drew a sharp breath, her eyes blazing with more life than Juliana ever remembered seeing in them.

"You're sure it's her? I'm afraid to hope."

"It's her, Mama. Look." From her purse she pulled out the photo of Gillian that Danny had left with her.

Her mother's trembling fingers closed around it, and she clutched it to her heart. "I can't look." The agonized whisper pinched Juliana's heart.

Clarence made an obvious effort to pull his own emotions together and moved close, slipping an arm around his wife's shoulders. "Look at it, Annie. I'm right here. We'll do it together."

Slowly, her gaze dropped to the little photograph. She gasped, clutching at Clarence's big hand.

"Juliana, I…I would have thought it was you!"

"I know. It's kind of a strange feeling, actually, seeing a face that looks exactly like mine, yet knowing it isn't."

Her father's gaze moved over her face, clearly concerned. "How do you feel about all of this, Julie girl? Are you okay?"

"I'm fine, Daddy. It doesn't seem real to me yet. I mean…a sister. A twin sister! It's so strange, and yet…I think a part of me always knew she was out there."

Her mother nodded. "Yes, dear, I think you did. Some rather odd things happened when you were a child. I'm not sure if you'll remember them, and they may have nothing to do with Gillian, but …"

She paused, and Clarence cut in. "I think I know what you're talking about, Annie. Why didn't you tell me what you were thinking then?"

Annie shook her head. "I was a bit embarrassed. It seemed so far-fetched!"

"What are the two of you talking about?" Juliana was tired of people talking "around" her.

Her mother answered. "Do you remember the time you had to wear that sling on your arm for several weeks, even though you hadn't injured that arm in any way?"

"Of course I remember. I couldn't use my arm. It just hung limp, and the pain was awful!" She frowned. "But I don't see what that has to do with Gillian."

"Maybe nothing." That was her father's soft, calming voice. "But what if your sister hurt her arm? Broke it for instance. What if you were feeling her pain?"

Juliana gawked at her parents, completely speechless. Nevertheless, her mind instantly flooded with similar incidents. Surely such a phenomenon was impossible, and yet...could it be true?

"All of those times I had unexplained...things happening. Remember when I got that nasty rash, and the doctor insisted it was from poison oak? He refused to believe I had been nowhere around the horrible stuff. I've still never seen poison oak!"

At Annie's request, Clarence made another trip to the attic. This time he brought down his wife's journals, along with an inexpensive family Bible and a dust cloth, with which he proceeded to remove layers of dust from each item. Watching him, Juliana bit back a grin. Mama must have hidden these things away so deeply that even her stringent cleaning efforts couldn't reach them.

"I don't expect you to read all of these." Mama took Juliana's hand. "But there are a couple of entries that...well, they might help you understand the kind of man Jack Kelly was." Her lips twisted into a bitter smile. "And perhaps even the girl I once was."

"Mama, are you sure?"

"Yes, very sure. I have nothing to hide anymore."

Clarence groaned, reaching up to massage his temples with his fingertips. "I feel like such a fool! But it was Jack's ring on that driver's finger. I brought it to you, Annie, remember?"

She nodded, sending him a tender smile as she patted his big hand. "Yes, it was Jack's ring, my love. And I'm sure you jumped to the very conclusion he intended you to."

"Thank you for understanding, beloved. I would never have deliberately misidentified a body."

"Well, of course not! It never even entered my mind."

Juliana tucked a hand through her father's arm, resting her head briefly against his shoulder. "Both of us know better than that, Daddy." Sitting up, she shook her head. "That does bring up a question, though."

"Yes, it does." His voice was grave. "Who was wearing that ring?"

But Mama only shrugged. "Jack hung out among the dregs of humanity. There were many nights when he didn't come home, and I would hear about him having slept in an alley or holed up in some empty building. We will probably never know who that man was, Clarence, but my guess is that Jack found a body somewhere. It offered him an opportunity, and he took it."

"Perhaps you're right. Now that you mention it, I remember a lot of men, and women, for that matter, riding the freight trains during that time. Hobos and tramps, people called them. Truth is, most were just folks who were down on their luck and had nothing and no one to keep them in one place."

Juliana frowned, listening to her parents' conversation. "How sad!"

"Yes, it is—it was sad to watch, even then. But I don't think Jack wanted to 'die' so he could become a drifter, Julie girl. I believe he wanted to find the baby he sold and bring her back to Annie. And he wanted Annie to be free of him, in case he didn't come back."

"Well, whether or not that was his intention, he did help us find her," Juliana offered. "Just not during his lifetime."

"That's an incredible story Mr. Collins told you, Juliana." Her mother's eyes shone with unshed tears. "Who would ever think God would allow Jack to be a part of reuniting our family, even in a supernatural role? He was, after all, the reason we were separated in the first place."

Juliana's startled gaze met her father's. That sounded a lot like Mama giving God the glory!

Picking up his wife's hand, Clarence gave it a gentle pat. "I believe it, Annie. Young Collins said Jack made his peace with God before he died. If that's true, then his sin, no matter how horrible, was forgiven and forgotten. Forever."

"Amen." Juliana was deeply moved by her father's profound statement.

Another thoughtful silence fell, each member of the Camden family deep in thought. At last, Juliana stirred a bit. "Mother, Gillian doesn't know any of this yet. Danny wanted to break the news to her and her mother. He's gone back to Springville to do that. But he will be here again soon to minister to our church. Pastor Obie agreed to the delay—Danny was supposed to have started speaking tomorrow night."

Annie's face blanched. "Are you saying I can't see her? She's alive, I know she's alive, and I can't see my daughter?"

"No, Mama, that's not what I'm saying. It's just…well, you can't see her *yet*. This isn't something we can just drop in her lap and expect her to feel exactly as we do. Remember, Gillian has a family, one she loves and who loves her. We may have to give her some time."

For a moment she thought her mother would make a fuss. Her small hands clenched into tight little fists, and her lovely face wore that obstinate look she could get when her mind was set. But after a moment or two, she relaxed against the back of her chair.

"She's alive." A beautiful smile danced on her lips. "That's the most important thing. And she will want to meet us…if not now, then someday. I know she will. That's good enough. For now."

Mary Helen had slipped out the back door and gone to visit

Poppy and Grams, giving Daniel and Gillian a few moments of privacy. When she returned, she found them in the kitchen. Gilly had stirred up another omelet, and they were talking quietly as Daniel ate. She smiled as she opened the back door. *Will they even notice if I speak to them?*

"Daniel!" She greeted the young man as she stepped into the room. "We've missed you, son."

"I missed you, too, Mrs. P." He stood to give her a hug. "Both of you."

Gillian also rose from her chair and slid an arm around his waist. The girl looked happier than she had since her father's death.

"He loves me, Mother!"

Daniel blushed to the roots of his hair, and Mary Helen laughed softly. "Yes, darling. You were the one holding things up, you know."

"You knew? Mom!" Whirling, she shook a finger in Daniel's face. "You told my mother before you told me?"

He slipped an arm around her waist and drew her close to him. "She was my accomplice. Someone had to get you to see me as something besides a brother."

Gillian shook her head, her face drawn into a frown of mocking displeasure. "You two are not to be trusted!"

"But we did such a good job, Gilly Bean! I'm thinking Daniel and I might partner up and start some kind of matchmaking business. Is there such a thing?"

The young man laughed, shaking his head firmly. "Count me out, Mrs. P! I had a hard enough time getting my own date. I sure don't want to worry about anyone else's."

They moved into the living room as they talked, and Mary Helen sank into her favorite chair near the window. Reaching for her embroidery hoop, she sent up a silent prayer of gratitude. What a joy to feel well enough to be a part of the banter.

A short time later, she looked up to find Daniel watching her. Gillian flipped casually through the latest copy of Voice of Hope, which Daniel had found somewhere and brought home to her.

Mary Helen smiled, pleased as always by the lad's quiet thoughtfulness. She could not have found a better husband for her daughter had she been allowed to choose him herself.

Daniel cocked his head toward Gillian, one eyebrow parked high on his forehead. Pretending to scratch his head, he jerked a thumb in the direction of the kitchen.

He's found something already!

Mary Helen bent and began to push things around in her sewing basket, deliberately making a show of it. Finally she sighed. "Gilly, would you mind dashing over to Grams' place for me? I seem to be out of my royal blue thread."

Gillian jumped to her feet. "Sure, Mother. I'll be right back."

Just as she reached the back door, Mary Helen called to her. "Oh, and darling…ask Grams if she still has that chess pie recipe, okay? I want to see if I still remember how to bake."

The girl disappeared, her laughter echoing back to them. Mary Helen dropped the pillowcase into her basket. "You've found someone?"

Daniel nodded. He pulled in a lungful of air, releasing it slowly as he observed Mary Helen's anxious face. "I need to talk fast. She'll be back soon."

She perched on the edge of her seat, hands clenched together in her lap. "Tell me."

"Mrs. P, I prayed long and hard about what you asked me to do. I have to admit I wasn't comfortable with the idea. But God has been bringing things together in a way that is nothing short of miraculous. I want you to know the entire story, but I'm asking you to let me tell it to both of you."

Mary Helen shook her head in firm negation. When she could breathe again, she protested. "No! Gillian can't know. Not yet. Not until I'm gone."

"She needs to know, Mrs. P. There are things…well, she just needs to know." He sighed, continuing. "The man who sold her to you…her father…he's dead, and yet he kind of helped me find her birth family."

"I don't understand."

"I'm not sure I do, just yet. The point is you were right. He lied to you. Gillian has a mother who loves her. She thought Gillian was kidnapped—all these years, she's grieved for her lost child."

Mary Helen's heart quailed within her, and a pitiful whimper escaped her tight throat. Daniel's words brought her worst fears to reality. *Oh, God! Can even You forgive what we did?*

"Oh, no…that poor woman!" The moan came from some painful place deep inside her. "I am so sorry for her, for what I did to her. And Gillian!" Her frantic gaze flew to Daniel's face. "She will never forgive me."

She lowered her head into her hands as hot, salty tears streamed down her face. In an instant, she felt Daniel's arms encircle her. Gently, he pressed her head onto his shoulder, murmuring softly.

"Yes, she will. She'll be shocked, maybe even hurt at first. There's bound to be lots of adjustment. But she loves you, Mrs. P. Gillian will understand. You didn't know what you were doing."

She fought to control her tears. "I don't know if I can stand for her to find out."

Daniel opened his mouth to reply, but a small sound

behind them startled them both. He turned, releasing Mary Helen as he did so.

Gillian stood in the doorway, white-faced. A skein of blue embroidery thread hung from one hand. She clutched a recipe card in the other. Beside her, one arm wrapped around her trembling shoulders, stood an elderly woman with a roadmap of wrinkles lining her leathery face. Both women pinned Daniel and Mary Helen under piercing gazes—one a startling blue, the other gleaming golden.

Gillian's dainty chin lifted, a sign Mary Helen recognized as preparation for battle. Nevertheless, her daughter's voice trembled when she spoke.

"Find out what, Mother?"

"Oh, Gillian!" No wonder God had allowed the first part of her day to be good. She would need extra strength to finish it.

Grams kept an arm around Gillian as they crossed the room. She gently urged her granddaughter onto the sofa then turned, her lined features uncertain. Daniel shoved another chair close to Mrs. P's and hurried to Gillian's side.

"I've got her, Grams. Go to Mrs. P."

Mary Helen gave her mother a tentative smile as the older woman picked up one of her hands, patting it with her own little calloused one. She cast a grateful glance at her but spoke to Daniel.

"I think you've earned the right to call me by my first name, son."

His attempt at a smile fell noticeably shy of successful. "You know I can't do that. Would you settle for Mom?"

"I like it even better."

"Will you two please tell me whatever it is you don't want me to know?"

Gillian was curled up on the sofa, her feet pulled up under

her full skirt. She'd made herself as small as possible, just as she always did when trouble threatened her sunshiny world. In that moment, she looked like a frightened little girl. Her beautiful eyes were bright with the tears she refused to let fall, as well as anger and a terrible, tangible dread that broke Mary Helen's heart.

Daniel tried to place an arm around the girl's rigid shoulders, but she pulled away. He sighed and reclaimed his arm but stayed close to her on the sofa.

Already a wedge comes between them...and it's my fault.

Mary Helen lifted her chin in sudden determination. Daniel was right. The secrecy had gone on long enough.

"Gillian, Daniel is not to blame for any of this. I asked him to help me with something, and he gallantly agreed to do so—against his better judgment. I've been afraid to share it with you, but I can see that it's time."

"Share what with me, Mother?" Gillian's patience, never her strong suit, had reached the breaking point.

Unbidden tears blurred Mary Helen's vision as she drank in the sight of her beautiful daughter. Telling Gillian about the great sin of her parents would be far and away the hardest thing she'd ever had to do. Especially since she'd been the one who insisted on it, against William's will.

But tell her she must.

"Darling, I am so ashamed. Your Papa and I, we did something many years ago, something that was more wrong than we even knew. I'm going to tell you about it, and I pray you won't hate me when I'm done."

Gillian gasped. "Hate you? Mother, I could never hate you! You and Papa couldn't have done anything that bad. I won't believe it."

Mary Helen sighed, nodding ruefully. "Yes, we did. At the time, we didn't think of it as doing something 'bad...'"

Honesty demanded a pause. "At least, I didn't. But innocent people were hurt by our actions and have suffered all through the years because of it."

Grams fidgeted, her troubled gaze moving back and forth between her daughter and granddaughter.

"Mama, are you okay?" Mary Helen turned to look at her mother. "If this is too much for you, please don't feel you have to stay. I'll fill you in later."

"No, I want to stay. I was just thinkin' I should get your Papa. He should probably hear this, too…whatever it is."

Mary Helen's face crumpled. Her parents had suffered so much already. But they both had a right to know the entire story. They loved Gillian as much as she did.

"Yes, Mama, you're right. Go ahead, if you want to. I'll wait."

Daniel jumped up, already moving to the door. "I'll get him, Grams. You stay where you are."

While they waited for the men to return, Mary Helen excused herself and went to get her journals. Gillian should have them now. Their contents might help her piece together a few things in her mind.

Back in the living room, she placed the little stack of books on a low table beside Gillian. "These are the diaries I asked you to read when I'm gone. After today, there'll be no need to wait."

Even Grams looked puzzled. Gillian opened her mouth, ready to argue, but Mary Helen silenced her with a look.

Chapter Sixteen

"WE'RE HERE." DANIEL HELD THE door open for Poppy.

Ben Dorton's skin was sun-darkened and leathery, just like his wife's. Behind thick bifocals, his blue eyes, a shade darker than Grams', were accentuated by that dark skin and thick, snow-white hair. Having shared a lifetime together, the old couple had come to resemble one another, even in appearance.

Up until his son-in-law moved him to California some ten years or so back, Ben had been a minister—one of the old-fashioned, fire-and-brimstone preachers who served up the Word of God strong and undiluted. But away from the pulpit, his phenomenal sense of humor and obvious love for his parishioners earned him a reputation as a loving, wise, and generous man, and every child in his congregation called him Poppy.

He entered the room with a merry grin on his lined face. "Young Daniel tells me ya'll are blowin' up a tornada over here." Ten years in California had not robbed the old Texan of his twang. "I've come to help board up the winders."

"Here you go, Poppy." Daniel removed a couple of throw pillows from one end of the sofa. "Come sit with Gillian and me."

The old man bent to kiss his granddaughter's cheek, and then Mary Helen's, before folding his long length down onto the sofa. He reached over to place a comforting hand atop Gillian's.

When no one spoke, he glanced around the little circle of tense faces and heaved a sigh of resignation. "All right, folks, if it's a battle we're goin' into, let's do it right. Why don't we all just bow our heads and ask God to take the front line, shall we?"

Mary Helen felt her own tension ease under her father's powerful influence. No matter how bad the situation, he always seemed to make it better. She did as he suggested, and with her eyes closed, his gentle voice wash over her, soothing her frayed nerves. With his way of talking to the good Lord as if he were looking Him in the face, Papa's prayers always reminded her that God was, indeed, right there.

"Dear Heavenly Father, we come to You in a dark time of crisis, and we need Your light to lead us through it. I don't know what my daughter needs to tell us, Lord, but You know all about it. Whatever the situation, we trust You to handle it in a way that's best for ever'body. Bring peace to each heart in this room. Help us to be very aware of Your love and Your grace. Whatever winds blow against us today, help us to remember that You are the Master of the wind, and we have nothin' to fear. Thank you for the love we have for each other, Lord, and thank You for Your love for us. Direct our conversation, keep our spirits sweet. I ask these things in Your precious name. Amen."

Mary Helen raised her lashes, grateful for the sweet flood of peace in her heart. Through the mist in her eyes, she noted that each of the others brushed away tears, as well.

"Thank you, Papa." She sent him a shaky smile. "I feel better already."

Opening the little book on her lap, she drew a deep breath. "The best way I can think of to tell you all what happened is to simply read it to you from my journal. You're going to have questions—I know that, and I'll try to answer them all. But please...don't start asking them until I'm finished reading. If I stop, I'm not sure I can start again."

She pulled a handkerchief from her pocket and dabbed at the moisture on her cheeks.

"I started writing in these books three months after Gillian was born." With no further preliminary, she began to read.

Juliana's parents retired early to their room. Her mother was exhausted after the emotion-filled day, but Juliana could not remember ever seeing such peace on her face.

She picked up one of the journals Mama had given her but did not open it. Curling up on the sofa, she tucked her feet under her skirt and rested her head against the high back. Her fingers absently stroked the cover of the diary on her lap.

"God, give me strength."

Will had said he'd be in touch after she had a chance to talk with her parents. She would read a bit after he called.

Half an hour later, she sat up, startled, and rushed to answer a knock at the front door. She hadn't planned on falling asleep.

"Will! What are you doing here?" She stepped back, holding the door open. "Come in."

"I had to see you, Juliana." Will's blue eyes were shadowed with concern. "I've been so worried. How did it go?"

She motioned him into a chair, but he seemed unwilling to sit. He paced from one side of the room to the other.

She tossed him a tired smile. "I have to admit it wasn't easy, but I'm fine."

In two long strides, he covered the distance between them and pull her into his arms. She rested her head against his chest, grateful for his solid strength.

"I'm so sorry you had to go through this, sweetheart. How can I help?"

"You're doing it," she whispered. "You're here."

A muscle worked in Will's jaw, and he tightened his arms around her. "I want to always be here for you, Juliana. Always." He groaned, lowering his head to place a soft kiss on her forehead. "You know I love you, don't you?"

"I thought you might." She surprised him with a playful smile, and he chuckled as he pulled her closer. Snuggling into his arms, she murmured, "Say it again."

"I love you, my beautiful Juliana." His lips against her hair sent little lightning bolts of excitement through her body. "Forever and always."

Frowning, she pulled back and slapped gently at his broad chest. "Well, you have a strange way of showing it, Will Dawson! What has been going on in your mind? I actually decided a couple of times that you didn't even like me."

He led her to the sofa and sat beside her. "I'm sorry, my love." He took her hand in his. "You're right; I swing back and forth like a pendulum. I want so badly to just hold onto you forever, and never let another man anywhere near you. But…" He paused, and Juliana's heart thudded painfully.

"But what?" she demanded into the silence. "Will, please don't do this again!"

His jaw clenched, and his tormented gaze ripped at her

already flailing heart. "I'm trying to find a way to tell you why—Juliana, I can't expect you or any other woman to marry me. Ever."

Her breath caught in her throat, and for a moment she could not find her voice. Will's pain was etched into his face, his clear blue eyes like windows into a tortured soul. For his sake, she forced herself to smile, though her trembling lips betrayed her.

"I think you'd better tell me what this is about."

He made a couple of false starts, but she waited patiently, forcing herself not to urge him on. She felt his frustration and knew a war raged within his mind. Finally he drew a deep breath and made a visible effort to relax against the back of the sofa, still holding her hand in a tight grip.

"You've never met my parents." He spoke softly, and she leaned closer in order to hear. "I've wanted to introduce you to my Dad, but…well, that would have meant you also had to meet my mother, and I…I couldn't face that." He took out his wallet and pulled a photo from it.

"This is Mom," he said, smiling wistfully at the lovely face in the picture. "Ellie Dawson. Before."

Large and mischievous, Ellie's gray eyes twinkled up at Juliana. Even from the confines of a photograph, they glowed with life and happiness. Her hair, as raven dark as Juliana's own, fell in soft waves around a pixie-like face.

"Why, she's lovely, Will!"

"She was absolutely stunning. Before."

Pulling another photo from his wallet, he handed it to Juliana. "This is my mother now."

Juliana gasped, unable to prevent the involuntary reaction. This heavily lined face couldn't possibly belong to the same woman.

Ellie's lips twisted to one side in an unnatural grimace.

Hair that had flowed in soft, smooth waves in the first picture now lay flat and thin against her head. Juliana assumed the new style—a short bob—was easier for whomever had the duty of caring for Ellie. The woman's gray eyes were recognizable, though dull and lifeless in the new photograph.

"Oh, Will! What happened?"

He gazed off into the distance. "She started tearing her hair out several years ago. She would fly into rages for no apparent reason, and just rip it out by the roots, screaming and cursing—using language I wouldn't have thought she knew. She lost all control over her own emotions and behaviors."

He recalled an incident in which Ellie became furious at a woman in a department store for stepping into line in front of her. "This was before Mother became totally secluded. Before we had a diagnosis. I wasn't there, but I knew a young woman who was working in the store that day."

Lowering his head, he paused to swallow hard before continuing his story. "She said Mom behaved like a child having a tantrum, only…well, only it was worse because she's not a child. Juliana, my mother—my gentle, loving, Christian mother—shoved that woman onto the floor and kicked her, screaming and cursing, then proceeded to throw things at her…anything she could get her hands on. She grabbed packages out of peoples' hands and jerked merchandise off the shelves to hurl at the poor lady, who cowered on the floor in terror."

His voice broke, and Juliana sat quietly, stroking his hand, loving him, willing him to feel it though she didn't say a word. He had worked hard to make it this far. The slightest distraction might crumble his shaky resolve.

"She won't live much longer now. We have to force her to eat and when she does, she chokes on the food. Someone has to monitor every bite. My father is looking for help now. He had someone who came in a few hours a day, but she couldn't take it. She quit. Dad has reached the point of not being able to handle Mom on his own."

He looked up, and the sorrow in the blue depths of his eyes stole her breath away.

"To be honest, the quality of her life has so degenerated in the past few years that I can't even imagine her condition if she did live a long time. I try to remember her before the illness changed her, but…it's hard."

He paused again, and a wave of dull red crept up his neck and into his face. "I ask God's forgiveness every day for being such a horrible son. I know I should be concerned only for my mother's welfare, but I find myself living in dread of the day I see the first symptom in myself."

A single tear made its slow way through the five o'clock shadow on Will's cheek. Now he avoided looking at Juliana, and she sniffled quietly as great drops fell off her chin, forming a wet circle on her blouse.

"Not much is known about her condition yet. It's called Huntington's disease, and it's cruel." He choked but managed to add, "It's also hereditary. While it doesn't always pass down from parent to child, so far there's no way of knowing whether it has—at least, not until you start seeing the signs."

Juliana hurt for him as he explained the symptoms of the horrible disease. About ten years earlier, his mother, always the picture of style and grace, started falling over things, walking into walls—being, in general, uncharacteristically clumsy. Shortly thereafter, she began to experience involuntary body movements.

"It was awful to watch then, and it's unbearable now," Will choked out. "She has no control—none—over her own muscles. They twitch and jerk and contort…" he stopped, brushing a trembling hand across his face. "She's had a number of minor strokes, and each one leaves her a little more disconnected with reality."

"You don't have to do this, Will." Juliana spoke softly, gently kneading one well-muscled shoulder.

"Yes, I do." He sat up straighter, obviously determined to tell her everything. Raising his eyes to hold her gaze with his own, he placed a hand on each side of her face, tilting her chin up with his thumbs.

"You're young. You'll want children, Juliana. It's only natural." He shook his head, clenching his jaw against the emotional pain. "But I can't give them to you. I won't sentence a child to what I've watched my mother endure. It wouldn't be fair."

Will's pain cut like a knife through Juliana's soul. She raised a hand to stroke his cheek, every cell in her body aching to bring him comfort.

"I don't care, darling." In the strangled whisper, she tried to convey the depth of her feelings and her absolute willingness to make whatever sacrifice was necessary to be with him. "It doesn't matter."

"Ah, my sweet love!" Will gathered her into his arms. His gaze traveled hungrily over her face, as though attempting to commit every tiny detail to his memory. Slowly, he lowered his head until his lips touched hers. Juliana returned his gentle kiss, certain her heart had found those elusive wings.

But her joy was brief. Will abruptly pulled back and gently set her away from him.

"No!" It was a fierce growl, and before Juliana realized his intentions, he was across the room, his hand on the doorknob. "No, Juliana! I won't let you love me. Because you will care…there will come a time when you'll care desperately, and I won't be able to change a thing."

Her world spun in dizzy circles. She sat frozen, watching in helpless dismay as Will opened the door and turned back to blow a kiss across the room.

"I love you, sweetheart…enough to let you go. I'm sorry I let things get this far because now I've hurt you. But someday…someday I pray to God you'll forgive me for that. Good-bye, sweet Juliana."

She ordered her legs to move, to get her up off the couch and cross the room. She had to stop him—needed him to understand that she would have no problem loving an adopted child if ever she desperately wanted a baby. They had to be together. That was what was important.

But the emotional day had taken its toll, leaving her disconnected, as though she watched the heartbreaking scene through a thick, murky fog. By the time she found the strength to stumble across the room, throw open the door and call out his name, Juliana saw only the twinkle of red taillights.

Chapter Seventeen

MRS. P STOPPED READING, closed the diary, and laid it aside. Silence reigned. Pale and gaunt, she lifted a haggard gaze to her audience of four.

Danny's heart pinched. *God, help her! She looks like a woman awaiting a death sentence.*

Then Gillian spoke, and fear gripped his entire soul. Her voice emerged…tiny. Like a frightened, abandoned child. She seemed to have somehow reverted ten years in age while the woman she'd believed had carried her in her body and given her birth read that damning journal entry.

"No, Gilly Bean. I couldn't love you any more if you had been born to me, but you weren't, darling." Tears raced down the sweet mother's cheeks. "I'm so…very…sorry."

A myriad of emotions chased across the girl's face. "My own father just handed me to a couple of strangers, took money from them, and…left me there?"

The older woman nodded, catching her breath on a silent sob.

"Oh." The pathos in that one word touched Danny far more deeply than the expected tears or even hysteria would have. "Who ever heard of such a thing?"

"It's nothin' new, little one." The answer came in the old Texan's gentle drawl. "Been goin' on since Old Testament times." He picked a Bible up off a nearby table and flipped through the pages. "Right here. Joel 3:3 says, 'And they have cast lots for my people; and have given a boy for an harlot, and sold a girl for wine, that they might drink.'"

Another silence fell over the room. Everyone seemed lost in shock and confusion. Danny slid off the sofa where he sat next to Gillian. Kneeling on the floor, he turned to take her hand.

"Gillian—"

"Stop!" She jerked her hand away. "Just…just stop."

He ignored the wounded command. "Nothing has changed, sweetheart. You're still the same person you've always been."

"That's right, Gilly." Poppy took his granddaughter's hand and gave it a gentle pat. "This doesn't change a thing."

A tear fell off the tip of Gillian's long eyelashes. It seemed to Danny that the little drop hung suspended in midair for a full second before splashing down onto her cheek—a cheek as white as those of the porcelain dolls that used to line the shelves of her room.

"Oh, Poppy! You're wrong this time. It changes… ev–" Her voice hitched. "*Everything*!"

She jumped up, almost tripping over Danny's foot as she rushed to the door. He half rose to follow her, but she turned and raised a hand to stop him.

"I need to be alone. Please. I'm going for a walk by myself. I'll be okay." Her attempt at a smile broke his heart. "I promise."

The door shut behind her without a sound, and no one said a word until Mary Helen stood up and moved toward the kitchen. "I'll make coffee."

"I'll help." Grams wrapped an arm around her daughter's waist as they left the room together.

Danny looked at Gillian's grandfather. The lines in his face seemed more deeply etched than they had a bare thirty minutes earlier.

"What now, Poppy?"

The old preacher sighed. "Well, son, here's what I used to say to the church folks back home. When you reach the end of your rope—"

"Tie a knot and hang on." Danny finished for him, a little disappointed at such a pat answer. But to his surprise, Poppy shook his head.

"Nope. Why hang on to what's already givin' ya trouble? When you reach the end of your rope, just let 'er go."

Shocked, he eyed the old man. Surely he hadn't heard correctly.

"Sir?"

"You heard me. Just let go and let yourself fall…right into the hands of the only One who knows what's comin' up next. He'll put'cha back on your feet in a safe place."

Gillian had no idea where she was going. Her feet carried her swiftly down the street, away from the house. She needed to think, to process everything she had learned, but her mind felt overloaded, and she found herself incapable of lucid thought.

"Oh, Papa!" Hot tears streaked her face, and she walked faster, as though she might outrun the awful truth. "How can I live with knowing you weren't my father?"

No, my natural father was a man so despicable he could sell his own child for a bottle of whiskey—an evil man!

"Gillian Kelly." She whispered the name, and it tasted

bitter on her tongue, curdling like sour milk on her lips. Unbidden, a harsh sob rocked her body, and all at once, a wave of dizziness weakened her legs and tumbled her tummy. A mailbox provided welcome support while she sucked air into her lungs, making a desperate effort to calm nerves gone ragged. When at last the episode abated, she raised her head to look around.

She stood across the street from the park that had always been her haven when she needed one. Apparently her feet had known exactly where she needed to go.

Grateful to find herself alone, she crossed the road. A short walk into the lush, green acreage, she sank onto a bench facing a small pond in the center of the park. A couple of swans glided gracefully across the water, and she half smiled, appreciating the serenity of the setting.

But the smile melted into bitter tears, and she buried her face in her hands, sobbing her sorrow into the silence. She had been so happy when she awakened this morning, thrilled about her mended relationship with God. Then Danny showed up and said he loved her. For a brief moment, her life had been perfect.

How could things go so wrong so fast?

"Some folks'd be right proud to have a mother like your'n. She loves you more'n some folks ever get loved in a lifetime. But you now, you're poutin' 'cause ya weren't born to 'er. 'Magine that!"

Gillian gasped, lifting her tear-drenched gaze to the old man on the opposite end of the bench. She had not heard him approach, nor known when he sat down. *Where did he come from? And how long has he been there?*

She was startled, but somehow not frightened by the strange old fellow.

He sat up straight on the bench, long legs stretched out

and crossed at the ankles above a pair of shoes that had seen better days. He wore threadbare khaki trousers with a plaid shirt, and a battered hat rested on his lap.

"Wh– who are you?" Gillian's voice trembled as she struggled to contain her raw emotions. "How do you know about that?"

He smiled, turning on the bench to face her, and for the first time in her life, she found herself staring into a pair of eyes as golden as her own.

"Oh, I think you'll figger that out on yer own in due time. For right now, though, who I am ain't no matter. Who you are is." Gillian's uninvited bench partner seemed disinclined to part with his name.

"I don't know who I am." She choked back a sob.

The old man chuckled. "Now that is a fine pickle! Who were ya yesterday?"

"Gillian Parsons," she murmured. She looked away from the stranger's face to stare out across the pond. "Daughter of William and Mary Helen Parsons, granddaughter of Poppy and Grams, best friend to Danny Collins."

"Uh-huh, and now? All those folks done disowned ya since yesterday?"

"No, of course not." What a nosy old gentleman.

"Well, then?"

"Now I know they're not my real family."

"Families ain't always made outta blood, Gillian." The old man's gentle voice soothed like Grams' sweet Texas tea on a hot summer day. "Don'tcha know that by now? Love is what makes a family family. You still love 'em—those folks you mentioned?"

"With all my heart! That's why this hurts so badly."

"And they love you?"

"Yes." The word leaned a long ways in on sheepish, and

her cheeks warmed in reaction.

"Well, then, why all the tears? You mighta been give to folks who didn't think of ya as their own, folks not quite s'kind as the Parsonses." The old fellow nodded sagely. "Yep, you coulda had things a whole peck worse!"

She sighed. "I know, I know. I am grateful, but—"

"Don't see no room for no buts, Gillian. What's done is done, young'un, can't be changed." The old man reached out as if to touch her hand but did not. He smiled, and Gillian drew in a tiny, surprised breath. The smile revealed traces of what, in decades past, must have been a rare and unusual handsomeness. "Yesterday is gone—plumb outta sight. But tomorrow…now, you have a choice about that, little one. I wouldn't wanna throw it away 'cause things ain't 'zackly what you thought they were."

"But—"

The stranger raised a hand. "No buts."

As if a window had been opened in her mind, she saw the truth in his simple words.

"Who are you?" She studied the old fellow's strangely familiar face. "How do you know so much about me?"

"Oh, I ain't nobody special." His lips twisted into a crooked smile as he unfolded his lanky frame from the bench. "Just an ol' bum. Folks call me Travelin' Jack when they call me anything."

Gillian laughed softly, basking in the sudden wave of peace that washed over her sore spirit. How like God to send a "Jack" to help her sort out the mess another Jack had created. She favored the stranger with a misty smile. "Well, Travelin' Jack, today you've been somebody special. I don't know how you know so much about me but thank you for helping me see things in a different light."

"It's the least I could do, little one." When he looked

down at her, she noticed again his eyes, so similar in color to her own. "I'm glad you've had a good life, Gillian."

What a strange thing to say.

She stood, too, suddenly realizing how long she had been in the park. "Well…good-bye, Travelin' Jack. I've got to go. My family will be worried."

He nodded. "That they will."

She left him there beside the park bench and hurried away, all at once eager to get back home. At the corner, she turned to wave at her strange visitor, but he was nowhere to be seen.

"Thank you, Travelin' Jack," she whispered then turned to hurry back the way she had come. Back to her family. Back to Danny.

He met her halfway, and the moment he saw her, he knew she had found peace. Without a word, Danny opened his arms, and Gillian walked into them. He held her for a long time, loving the nearness of her, the silky softness of her hair against his cheek.

Still not having spoken, the two of them turned toward her home, walking the rest of the way arm in arm. When they stepped up onto the Parsons' porch, he stopped and turned her to face him. Lifting her chin with one finger, he captured her gaze with his own.

"Are you ready for this?"

She drew a deep breath and lifted her chin. "I'm ready."

They entered the house together, and Mrs. P looked up from her seat next to the window. Red rims around vivid blue eyes made them almost startling in her white face. She twisted a handkerchief in her hands and pinched her lower lip between her teeth.

Gillian flew across the room and pulled the older woman into her arms. "Oh, my little Mother! Please don't cry. Everything's going to be all right."

Danny stood back while she calmed her mother and hugged both grandparents. He had more news for them, but wanted their full attention. Only when they were all seated again did he speak.

"Mom, if you'll allow me, I'd like to share what I've learned with all of you."

She nodded, though Danny could see the fearful reluctance in her eyes.

"Don't worry." He spoke softly. "Trust me."

Gillian moved from her position on the sofa to sit at her mother's feet. Taking one delicate hand in a gentle grasp, she looked up. "Go ahead, Danny. Tell us."

No one said a word while he spoke. He started with his trip to Woodlake, though Gillian choked and had a coughing fit when he told them about Ol' Travelin' Jack's visit to his cottage. He moved on to his visit with Will at Voice of Hope, not forgetting to include the message on the billboard as he drove into Bakersfield.

"This is where things got downright unbelievable. Will and I were talking in his office. I went there hoping to see his Dad because I thought Mr. P might have shared something with his stepbrother about Gillian's birth family. But while we were talking, the door burst open and in walked…"

He paused, not quite sure how to tell them the rest.

"In walked who?" Gillian's impatience was barely contained.

Danny raised an eyebrow, shaking his head slowly from side to side. "Well, when she first came in, I was sure it was you, Gillian."

"Me?" Gillian was merely puzzled, but her mother

gasped.

Danny had a feeling she knew what he was going to say.

"Yes. I was certain it was you."

He pulled his wallet out and removed the photo Juliana had traded him for one of Gillian.

"This is Juliana Camden. She's a nice gal and very pretty, as you'll see. Your Cousin Will wants to marry her." He grinned a little, remembering, then plowed on, hoping for the best as he handed the picture to Gillian. "She's your twin sister."

Juliana made a decision as she lay sleepless in her bed. She had prayed a long time before crawling wearily between the sheets, and when she finally drifted off to sleep, it was with a sense of peace that God would lead her in the right direction.

"You need to meet her, Juliana."

She bolted upright and switched on the lamp beside her bed.

He sat in the chair next to her writing desk, a long-legged old man twirling a battered hat between the fingers of both hands. The desk lamp was unlit, yet a soft golden glow bathed the lined face of her uninvited guest.

"Who are you?" Briefly, she wondered why she felt no fear.

He didn't bother to answer her question. "Ellie Dawson. You have to meet 'er."

Juliana shivered and drew the sheets firmly up around her neck. "I don't understand. Who are you?"

"That's not important. What matters is that you meet Will's mother. She needs you."

"That's ridiculous. She doesn't even know me."

"Not yet, but she will. She needs you now."

The stranger stood, smiling in Juliana's direction, and her heartbeat quickened. *Those eyes...!*

"Who are you?" Hardly daring to breathe, she repeated the question she had already asked.

"I think you know who I once was, Juliana." The old man's wistful smile tugged at her heartstrings. "But I've been Travelin' Jack—just Ol' Travelin' Jack—for a long time now."

"Your eyes!" Juliana ignored the tears that blurred her vision. Her voice was a mere whisper, yet she knew the stranger heard every word. "They're like mine. You're my father, aren't you?"

Travelin' Jack reached out as if to touch her but never quite made contact. "I wish I had been. I just didn't know how."

Turning, he shuffled to the door, placing one gnarled hand on the doorknob before looking back at her. "Go to Ellie Dawson. And Juliana...." His eyes suddenly glowed like amber lights in the dimly lit room. Mesmerized, Juliana watched a single, shimmering tear leave a golden trail of moisture down one leathery cheek. "Be happy, child!"

He slid out into the dark hallway, closing the door behind him. With the soft click of the latch, she snapped alert and realized she had been in something like a trance state. She threw the covers back and swung her feet to the floor. *I have to stop him!*

"Please wait!" She jerked the door open, nearly slamming it into her own face as she rushed to catch up with Ol' Travelin' Jack. "Please!" The hallway was dark and empty.

"No, don't go, not yet!" Broken sobs tore at her throat and left a hollow ache in her chest. She sank to her knees on the cold floor and knelt there, sobbing.

"Wake up, Juliana! You're dreaming."

Mama?

She forced her eyes open. Her mother sat on the edge of the bed, concern etched into the lines of her face. "Hush, darling!" Her cool hands caressed Juliana's wet cheeks. "It's only a dream."

A dream. She shook her head, relaxing back against her pillow as she came fully awake. "But it was so real! He was right here in my room."

"Who was here?" A worried frown creased Mama's smooth forehead.

"My father. I think I just met my father."

Chapter Eighteen

"COME ON IN."

Will looked up from his desk in response to the soft tap on his office door, surprised when Juliana entered. She had avoided him for days, and he had tried to accommodate her by staying out of her way. No point in making things more difficult than they already were.

"Juliana! Is everything all right?" He motioned toward a chair and watched her perch self-consciously on its edge.

"Everything's fine." Her pallid cheeks negated the calm assurance in her voice. Will instinctively moved to go to her but firmly tightened his wavering resolve.

"What can I do for you?" He hated the detached, professional tone of his own voice and found himself transfixed by the cleft in her chin as she lifted it a bit higher.

"I know you're busy. I'll make this quick."

"No, I'm not. I…"

You're sputtering like a love-struck teenager. Sighing, he slumped against the back of his chair. "Yes?"

She leaned forward and slid a single, typewritten sheet of

paper toward him.

"What's this?" But he already knew.

"It's my resignation. Effective immediately."

"Juliana, there's no need—"

"Yes, there is. I'd like to start freelancing again, if you don't mind. It's not working out for me, being on staff."

Will bit down hard on the desperate plea that sprang to his lips. Wanting her to stay was selfish on his part, and he knew it. He had to let her do what was easiest for her.

"If that's what you want, then I suppose there's nothing I can do to stop you. But I don't want you to go. You're good at what you do—the best."

"Thank you." She lowered those long lashes over her eyes. "I've learned a lot, and I appreciate the opportunity you gave me. But it's time for me to go."

He nodded, drawing a deep breath and holding it for a moment. "As you wish, of course. But if you change your mind—"

"I won't."

She stood and walked to the door, looking back only when she had one hand firmly on the handle. "Good-bye, Will." The sadness in her eyes nearly undid him. When the door shut behind her, he realized his knuckles were white and aching on the armrests of his chair.

He folded his arms on his desk and buried his head in them, glad no one was there to hear the tremor in his hoarse whisper.

"Good-bye, my sweet love!"

Gillian closed her mother's journal, sighing as she rested her head against the high back of the chair and closed her eyes. Much of what she had read made sense only because she knew that long-held secret.

She still had trouble wrapping her mind around the fact that Juliana Camden was her sister. It seemed surreal in light of the emotional connection she had felt to the author from the first time she read one of her stories.

How odd that she had sought out Juliana for advice when she thought her mother was dying, rather than confiding in someone she knew—someone like Danny, who had been her best friend long before she realized she loved him in any other way.

She smiled a little, recalling the response to that letter. It had made a profound impact on her life, as though her sister had taken her by the hand and led her back to God. She was beyond grateful for that reconciliation and doubtful whether she could emotionally have handled the past few days without Him.

And her little Mother…a smile flitted across her face as she reflected on the change in her. Could holding onto that secret have been making Mama ill? She thought it entirely possible. Ever since Mama had shared the truth with the family, her health had steadily improved. Her appetite was back, healthy color tinged her cheeks, and her eyes sparkled with life. She seemed happy again for the first time since Papa's death.

Thrilled to see these positive changes, Gillian hesitated to bring up her desire to meet Juliana and her birth mother.

When Danny told them about his mysterious late-night visitor, she had felt an electric shock course through her body. Before her new fiancé ever revealed the old man's name, she had known his identity. It was Ol' Travelin' Jack, the same strange old guy she'd met in the park.

They had all been astounded at Danny's account of the apparently non-existent billboard he had seen in Bakersfield.

Given all that had taken place in recent weeks…Somebody was trying to bring her family together.

She tried to imagine Danny's shock upon meeting Juliana at Voice of Hope and giggled aloud, picturing brown eyes as big as dinner plates under his ever-tousled hair. "What's so funny?"

Her eyes snapped open. Her mother stood watching her from a bare three feet away, a mischievous twinkle lighting her eyes.

"How long have you been there?" Grinning, Gillian sat up, feeling a bit sheepish. "And why are you sneaking up on me like that? What kind of little Mother are you?"

The older woman seated herself nearby, still smiling. "I wasn't sneaking. You were just miles away, and I thought if you were having such a nice trip, I might like to come along. Now what's so funny?"

She hesitated, not sure it was okay to discuss her birth family. The subject had not been mentioned again since the day her mother's secret came to light.

"Tell me!" Mary Helen was insistent. "Laughter is twice as much fun when it's shared. Spill it, Gilly Bean!"

"Okay, okay. I was imagining Danny's face when Juliana burst into that office. He must have looked like a frightened child."

To her relief, the admission brought only an amused chuckle from her mother. "I'm sure he did. But in his defense, I'm fairly certain any one of us would have been just as shocked."

For a moment, neither of them spoke. Gillian was relieved her mother had reacted favorably to knowing where her thoughts were, but now she didn't know what else to say. "You want to meet them, don't you?"

I should have known I couldn't get around that eerie

insight of hers. How does she do that?

She raised guilty eyes. "There's no hurry." The response was too quick, she knew it immediately.

"No, but there's no need to wait, either—not if you're ready."

She stood and crossed the room to kneel beside her mother's chair, looking up to search the beloved face. "Are you sure, Mother? I don't want you to be uncomfortable with any of this, and I certainly don't want to hurt you."

"You are not to worry about that, darling." The older woman reached for Gillian's hand and gave it a warm squeeze. "It is I who have hurt you! I just pray you know me well enough to know any pain I have caused has been unintentional."

"I do know that, Mama. You did what you did with the purest of intentions. And you and Papa have always been the best parents I could have asked for." She hesitated then reached up to place a gentle hand on her mother's soft cheek. "You'll always be my little Mother. No matter what. I am blessed to have had you and Papa as parents."

"No, dear. We were the ones with the blessing." Mother's eyes moved lovingly over Gillian's face. "But now it's time, I think, for you to meet the family you were born to. I want you to do that, just as soon as you're ready."

Gillian smiled through the tears that misted her vision. "You're the best little Mother in the world!"

A playful smile lit her mother's face. "Was there ever any doubt?"

Laughing, Gillian bent to kiss her cheek. "I'll call Danny. He'll arrange it for us."

At the doorway leading into the kitchen and the telephone, she turned. Already, Mother's head was bent over her embroidery, a private little smile lighting her face. A long finger of sunshine reached through the nearby window, turning her neatly coiffed silvery blond hair into a shining crown.

"I love you, little Mother." She spoke too quietly for her mother to hear the words, but Gillian had never meant them more.

Juliana took a deep breath, straightened her shoulders, and rang the doorbell. Her stomach seemed to have a million fluttering wings. She was certain she had never done anything quite so bold in her life.

The door swung open, and an older gentleman peered out at her with an inquisitive smile.

"Yes? Can I help you?"

Her heartbeat thundered in her own ears, and she wondered if others could hear it as clearly. Her host, however, appeared to notice nothing out of the ordinary, so she took a deep breath and plunged ahead.

"Are you Mr. Otis Dawson?"

"I am. And who might you be, young lady?"

"I'm Julie Kelly." She felt a little guilty about using the unfamiliar name, but she wasn't really lying, she reasoned.

Daddy calls me Julie, and Kelly really is my name—or it would have been if Daddy hadn't adopted me. "I heard you were looking for someone to help with your wife."

Mr. Dawson appeared taken aback for a moment, but he swung the door open and beckoned her to enter. "Well, I have been thinking about it. I can't imagine where you heard that, but come on in and sit down. Let's talk."

Juliana seated herself on the edge of a graceful easy chair. It was upholstered in soft peach and yellow and blended beautifully with the muted tones in the rest of the room. The

Dawson home resonated with warmth and welcome.

Ellie probably did all this before she became ill.

"So, Miss…Kelly, isn't it?"

"Yes, sir. Julie Kelly."

"Miss Kelly. I'd introduce myself, but you seem to know who I am already." He shook his head, a puzzled expression in his translucent blue eyes—so much like Will's that Juliana found it hard not to stare. "You look familiar. I know I haven't met you, because I'm sure I would remember your name. I'm pretty good with names, if I do say so myself."

Juliana's heart almost stopped. Of course she looked familiar! How could she have forgotten that this man was Gillian's uncle? But then, it had been several years since he'd seen her sister. She'd just have to hope he didn't make the connection anytime soon.

"I wouldn't worry too much about that, sir." She forced a light-hearted little burst of laughter, hoping it sounded more natural to him than it did to her. "Folks always seem to think they should know me. I guess I just have one of those faces that looks like everyone else."

A familiar crooked smile curved her host's lips. "Your face is anything but common, Miss Kelly. But I guess I'm not going to figure it out today. I'm too old to think that fast!" He laughed easily. "So you think you can help me with Ellie, do you?"

"Yes, sir, I do." Drawing a deep breath, she told him the truth. "I don't know how you feel about such things, but I believe God sent me to help you with her."

Otis Dawson's brows shot upward. "Well, that's refreshing, coming from someone of your generation. Tell me, what makes you think such a thing?"

Juliana lowered her eyes, suddenly embarrassed. She certainly didn't want to tell this man about her dream. He would think she was insane, and she'd never get within a country mile of his wife. And she had hoped to make this happen without bringing up Will's name. Oh, well, so much for that. *I guess it's time for a little truth.*

"Mr. Dawson, I—"

A loud crash, followed immediately by an angry yell brought them both to their feet. Will's father was on his feet instantly. He tore out of the room, apparently forgetting he had a guest. Juliana followed close on his heels without a thought to the appropriateness of such an action.

Sitting up in a four-poster bed so huge it made her look like a child, Ellie Dawson sobbed into her hands. The pink satin bed jacket she wore seemed out of place on the skeletal lines of her body, which jerked with random, spasmodic movements.

Mr. Dawson rushed to her, weaving his way around an overturned bedside table and several books, which had obviously been flung across the polished wood floor. Behind him, Juliana heaved a silent sigh of relief.

From the sound of that crash, she'd half expected to find Ellie on the floor.

"There, there! What is it, my love? You didn't like any of those books?" Keeping his voice soft, he sat on the edge of the bed and drew the thin form into his arms. Rocking his wife like a child, he tried to soothe her obvious agitation. "Hush, dear…we'll find some you like better."

Juliana stood uncertainly in the doorway, wondering what on earth had possessed her to invade the privacy of this woman's bedroom. She turned, intending to slip away unnoticed, but it was too late.

"Otis, look, it's an angel! Please come closer, pretty angel…let me touch you."

The hoarse voice stopped her in her tracks. With a

thundering heart, she turned. The woman's bony, trembling fingers reached out to her. Her beautiful gray eyes shone with recent tears and new excitement. On the side of her face that wasn't paralyzed, her lips curved upward in a welcoming smile.

Juliana dared not meet Mr. Dawson's eyes, though his scrutiny tingled her skin. Instead, she lifted her chin and crossed the room to stand beside the bed. Taking the sick woman's hand, she smiled down into her pitiful, twisted face.

"Hello, Ellie." She kept her voice soft, silently praying for the right words. "My name is Julie. I'm here to help you feel better."

"Julie!" Ellie focused on Juliana. "Your eyes are golden, aren't they? Only an angel would have eyes like that."

"I'm no angel." Juliana smiled and gave the hand she held a gentle squeeze. "Just someone who wants to help you."

"I'm not supposed to know, am I?" For a moment, Juliana caught a glimpse of the same spark of life that had twinkled from her eyes in Will's picture. "Well, that's okay. I'll just call you Julie." She lowered her voice to a hoarse whisper. "It'll be our little secret."

She moved over in the bed, patting the space beside her.

"Otis, get up now, dear. Let the angel sit here."

Juliana squashed a giggle. Apparently she's already forgotten that's supposed to be a secret.

She finally dared to look at Will's father, dreading the anger she expected to see on his face. She had, after all, invited herself into his wife's private chambers. But Otis Dawson's face wore only an expression of disbelief as he obediently stood to make room on the bed.

"She doesn't like strangers!" His stunned whisper was not quiet enough. Ellie might have lost a good deal of hair and more than she could afford of her body weight, but her hearing had not suffered.

"Oh, go on now, Otis! This sweet girl's not a stranger. She's an angel!"

Mr. Dawson shrugged and motioned Juliana onto the bed. She perched on the edge, suddenly shy and unsure what to say.

But Will's mother had no such qualms.

"May I touch your hair?"

"Of course!" She removed the clip that bound her dark tresses at the nape of her neck. Freed from its binding, her hair fell down around her shoulders.

"Oh!" For a moment, Ellie seemed almost to stop breathing as her wide-eyed gaze explored the thick mane. Slowly, she extended one hand but stopped short of touching the luxuriant strands.

Juliana took the other woman's hand, bringing it gently to her hair. Ellie closed her eyes, and for several moments she gently slid the silky tresses through her fingers. Watching her, Juliana was dismayed to see a tear slide from beneath the closed lashes.

"What is it, dear? Why are you crying?"

"I used to have hair," Ellie murmured. "Just like yours. But now it's all gone." Her face crumpled. "I'm just an ugly, sick old woman."

"Oh, sweetie, no!" Juliana fought back burning tears. "You're not ugly at all. Beauty isn't in your hair, or your skin, or your eyes, you know." She gently unwound the other woman's fingers from her hair, a little surprised when the invalid made no protest. Ellie meekly allowed her frail hand to be pressed against her chest.

"Real prettiness is here…in your heart. That's the beauty that matters…not what you see in the mirror."

The misshapen smile tore at her heart, and she couldn't

help remembering the vivacious face in the photo Will had shown her. It must hurt, during this woman's decreasing moments of lucidity, to know that her physical beauty was a thing of the past.

"Thank you." It was a sad little whisper, but Ellie's eyes clung to Juliana's with something like hope. "I'm tired now, Julie-Angel. Will you read to me, please?"

Juliana glanced around the room, not even bothering to check the titles the woman had so vehemently discarded. Those were not on Ellie's list of favorites right now. Her eyes fell on a bookshelf laden with reading material. Atop the shelf was a Bible. That's what she reached for.

While she read aloud from the book of Psalms, Will's father quietly tidied the mess his wife had made. He watched Juliana closely as he worked. She felt it but concentrated only on the words she was reading and on the face of the woman in the bed, whose body visibly relaxed under the sound of her voice. By the time she finished the twenty-third Psalm, Ellie was sound asleep.

She tiptoed across the room to replace the Bible where she had found it then followed Mr. Dawson back to the living room.

"Well." He sagged wearily into a chair and motioned Juliana into another. "Young lady, I don't know how you did it. My wife almost always flies into a rage if a stranger enters her room. I'm tempted to believe she's right, and you are an angel!"

She averted her gaze from the question in his eyes. Mr. Dawson might not understand the instant connection between her and his wife, but she did. God had a hand in it. That's the only thing that made any sense at all.

With a tired sigh, Will's father continued. "Look, I know I should ask a hundred questions, find out how you knew I needed help, ask about your experience—all the things I would normally do before hiring someone to help in my home. But my wife likes you. That's half the battle already won."

He stared at Juliana for a moment before finally flashing her a tired smile. "If you still want the job, it's yours. How soon can you start?"

Chapter Nineteen

The trip to Corman's Corner somehow became a family affair with even Gillian's grandparents going along.

Gillian praised God for Danny's help. He made arrangements for them to meet the Parsons family and booked rooms in the hotel he had stayed in on his earlier trip to Bakersfield. Coincidentally or not, it somehow also worked out that they would be there during the same time he was preaching for Pastor Obie Coffman's congregation.

In the two weeks since her mother had given her the go-ahead to meet her natural family, Gillian had grown increasingly nervous about the upcoming reunion.

The night before they were to leave, she admitted her doubts to Danny. "I don't know what I was thinking! I'm not ready for this. Can you just…maybe put them off for a while? A month or maybe a year or two?"

He laughed and draped an arm over her shoulder, pulling her close to his side. "It's going to be all right, sweetheart. You can't get cold feet now."

Burying her face in his shoulder, she clutched at the front

of his shirt. "You don't understand, Danny. I really don't think I can do it!"

He hooked a finger under her chin, tilting her face up so he could look into her terrified eyes. "Yes, you can. You're stronger than you know you are. And it's not like you'll be alone. Your family will be there with you, and so will I. Trust me. You're going to love the Camdens."

"Okay, if you say so. But couldn't I love them later—like in my next lifetime, maybe?"

Danny chuckled. "It would disappoint Mrs. Camden terribly if you backed out. Juliana, too."

She groaned. "That's it…make me feel guilty!"

"Whatever it takes." He grinned and dropped a kiss on the tip of her nose.

Gillian pounded his chest playfully. "You're supposed to be on my side, Daniel Collins!"

"I'm always on your side." He grabbed her flailing fists and held them against his heart. "That's why I want you to meet them. You need to do this, Gillian."

"Oh, really?" She raised her brows in mocking sarcasm. "And since when do you get to decide what's best for me?"

"Since I got you to admit you love me. That gives me a right to care."

She narrowed her eyes in mocking speculation. "Please tell me you're not going to be one of those insufferably bossy husbands! Because I can still change my mind, you know."

"I could try to be." Danny's voice was teasing. "But I have a feeling you'll have the last word every time."

She snuggled close to his side, a contented smile tugging at her lips. "You're such a smart man, Danny dear!"

Sitting on the porch swing her Papa had installed shortly before his death, they both fell silent. She felt safe and protected at Danny's side, with her hand tucked into his.

Still, she found it quite disconcerting to know that, within a couple of days, she would have a whole new set of family members. A mother she never knew she had, who apparently had been grieving her loss all these years, and a sister...a twin!

Overwhelmed, she shrank from everything she thought she'd wanted so desperately. She whispered into the darkness. "Is my sister pretty?"

Danny laughed. "She's your identical twin, Gillian! Of course she's pretty. She's beautiful, just like you."

Gillian sniffed. "Maybe I should be jealous!"

"Oh, please. Let's not start that." He choked back his laughter. "I love you and only you. Juliana looks like you, but she's not my girl, sweetheart."

"Is she like me in other ways?"

"Hmmm...that's a good question. Remember, I've only met her once in person. I'm not sure speaking on the phone counts. She's a nice girl. Quieter than you, I think."

Gillian giggled. "Are you saying I talk too much?"

"Don't go putting words in my mouth, woman!" Danny planted a kiss on the top of her head and gave her a gentle squeeze. "I just meant from the little I saw of Juliana, she seemed less...what is the word? Lively?"

A moment of silence followed before Gillian spoke again. Her voice sounded mousy and frightened, even to her. Not in the least vivacious or "lively."

"What if they don't like me?"

Danny turned and pulled her into his arms. "They'll love you, Gilly. They won't be able to help themselves."

"You really think so?" Her voice was muffled against his chest.

"I know so, sweetheart."

Once they arrived in Bakersfield, they needed less than an hour to settle into their rooms. The ride hadn't been a long one, only a little over two hours, but the old folks oozed exhaustion. They seemed almost as edgy as their granddaughter, and they were unaccustomed to traveling. The combination of the tiring trip and their nervous excitement had worn them out, and the elderly couple lay down to rest as soon as they were checked in.

In the room next to theirs, Gillian and her mother unpacked their suitcases. The older woman tried to keep up a cheerful face, but it was plain she was wound up tight as a clock spring. The trip was wearing on her, and Gillian reminded herself that her mother was still recuperating from a lengthy illness.

"Why don't you lie down, too, little Mother?" She pulled her into a tight embrace for a moment. "You could use a rest."

The answering smile was shaky. "I think I will, darling. I am a bit tired."

Gillian turned back the covers on the bed. "Come on, hop in."

Her mother crawled between the sheets, and Gillian pulled them up over her then bent to kiss her cheek. Perched on the edge of the bed, she took one cold hand between both of her own.

"You're not losing me, you know." Her voice came out a bit husky, and she felt the sting of tears in her eyes. "You couldn't, even if you wanted to. You'll always be my little Mother."

Though she tried hard to smile, Mary Helen's face suddenly crumpled, and she was crying instead. She turned her head away, and Gillian knew she was ashamed of this moment of weakness. Despite her fear of losing Gillian to her birth mother, she still wanted her to have the opportunity of knowing that mother, as well as the sister who was her twin.

"I'm sorry, Gilly Bean. I guess I'm feeling a bit insecure. Isn't that just the most ridiculous thing?"

Gillian crawled onto the bed and curled up next to her. "I don't think it's ridiculous at all. I feel kind of uncertain myself."

"Really? Why, darling? They're all going to love you!"

As she had hoped, her mother felt stronger just thinking Gillian might need her. And to her own surprise, she found that she did need her...desperately, at the moment.

"I don't want things to change between us. You've always been the best little Mother anyone could ask for. You and Papa made my childhood so perfect. You always put my needs ahead of your own. No matter what, you always made sure I was happy. I know you thought I didn't notice, but I did. Did I ever just say 'thank you' for being wonderful parents?"

Her mother relaxed against her pillow. A smile played around her lips, and she finally met Gillian's eyes.

"You're welcome, Gilly Bean!"

They lay silently for several moments, Gillian's head on her mother's shoulder. A knock at the door startled them both.

"Stay there, Mother; I'll get it." She jumped up and hurried to swing the door open.

Danny stood there, grinning from ear to ear.

"Danny! Are you all settled in?"

"I sure am. I thought you and Mrs.—uh, Mom—might want to see a bit of the town."

"No, you two go ahead." A drowsy reply came from the bed. "I think I'm going to have a little nap."

Gillian hesitated only a moment before kissing her mother's forehead. "Are you sure?"

"Couldn't be moreso. Go on, darling!"

So Danny and Gillian set out on their own to explore Bakersfield.

"Where are we going first?" She turned to face him as they pulled away from the hotel.

"How about we go by Voice of Hope and visit your cousin?"

"Good idea! I'd love that." Then she realized something. "But…Juliana will be there!"

Danny nodded. "I know. I thought it might be easier for you to meet her first. Maybe it won't be so overwhelming if we split up the introductions a little. What do you think?"

Gillian's mouth was suddenly dry as sandpaper, but she nodded. "Okay, Voice of Hope it is."

They walked through the double glass doors at the magazine offices only a few minutes later, with Gillian mentally sorting through a hundred different ways to greet her sister. She was totally unprepared for the exuberant welcome she received from the fresh-faced receptionist.

"Juliana!" The attractive young lady jumped up and dashed across the lobby to meet them, throwing her arms around a startled Gillian. "I have missed you, girl! Are you coming back? Oh, please say you are!"

Not waiting for an answer, the fiery redhead grinned up at Danny. "Hi, Mr. Collins! Nice to see you again."

She rounded her desk but appeared far too excited to sit. A huge grin threatened to split her face in two. "Is Will expecting you?"

Gillian shook her head, unable to find her voice, and Danny made no attempt to explain the receptionist's error. They watched her push an intercom button, bouncing up and down as she waited.

When Will answered, the young woman responded in a voice just short of a yell. "Will, Juliana's back!"

She listened a moment, nodded, and hung up the receiver. "He said his door's open, and you know the way."

Gillian flashed a shy smile then followed Daniel through a door at one end of the lobby, grateful beyond measure that he did, indeed, seem to know where they were going.

Will heard the soft tap on his door and called out a welcome, fully expecting Juliana to enter. Instead, Gillian walked in with Danny, and he wasn't fooled for an instant. Without a second's hesitation, he knew that the young woman with the copper-haired preacher was his cousin Gillian...not Juliana.

He jumped to his feet and hurried to greet them. Despite a twinge of disappointment when he realized Juliana was not back, after all, he was thrilled to see Gillian.

"Look at you, little one!" He hauled her into his arms to bestow the bear hug he had mistakenly given the wrong twin some time ago. "Why, you're pretty as a picture!"

Gillian smiled, standing on her tiptoes to kiss his cheek. "And you're still handsome enough to break hearts, Cousin Will!"

"Hey, stop it, you two," Danny grumbled. "That's my girl you're manhandling, Dawson!"

"Deal with it!" Will shot back, grinning broadly. "Cousins get certain privileges, especially long-lost ones."

"Yeah, yeah!" Danny pretended to be out of sorts.

Laughing, Will motioned his visitors to the two wingback chairs in front of his desk. Instead of returning to his own seat, he dragged another chair from across the room, joining Danny and Gillian in the sitting area.

"What brings you two to Bakersfield? Don't tell me you went and tied the knot without inviting me?"

Gillian blushed, shaking her head in protest as she reached for her fiancé's hand. "I wouldn't do that! When we do get married, you'll know about it."

"Well, of course he will. I'm hoping he'll be my best man!"

Gillian looked as surprised as Will felt at the unexpected announcement. He had only met Danny once. Still, he had to admit the two of them had felt a special connection—once Danny decided not to hurt him—and he approved of his cousin's choice of men. Apparently, whatever problems the two had been having when he last saw the young preacher had been worked out.

His heart contracted painfully at the thought. He was thrilled for Danny and Gillian, but he wished his own matters of the heart had ended as well.

"I'd be honored to be best man at your wedding. When is the big day?"

"We haven't set a date just yet."

"No, but the sooner the better." Danny took Gillian's hand with a warm smile. "I can't wait to make her my wife."

"Well, congratulations, both of you!"

"Thank you, Will. Hey, where's Juliana been?" Danny flashed a grin. "The receptionist out front—what's her name…Claudia? She didn't give us much chance to point out her error, but she seemed mighty excited to think Juliana was 'back' from somewhere."

Will drew a deep, bracing breath and looked away. "Juliana doesn't work here anymore. She decided freelancing was more to her taste, and she's been gone a couple of weeks now."

"Oh!" Gillian sounded deflated, and Will realized she had

hoped to meet her sister.

"I'm sorry, honey. I do have her phone number, if you'd like to call her at home."

Will squirmed but managed to keep smiling under the other man's narrow gaze. He was grateful when Danny made no comment, simply shook his head in response.

"I've made arrangements for Gillian and her family to meet the Camdens tomorrow. I just thought it might be easier for the girls to meet first. I'm afraid it's going to be a bit overwhelming for Gillian."

"I'll be fine. I would have loved to meet her today, but apparently God has other plans." Gillian grinned at the two men. "You boys just stop worrying about me!"

"Yes, ma'am!"

Gillian gave her fiancé a regal nod of her head, and Will couldn't help laughing.

"Are the two of you in any hurry?" A sudden idea came to him. "I know Dad would love to see Gillian. We could make a quick trip over there. I wish your mother were here, too!"

"She is here in Bakersfield," Gillian told him. "So are Poppy and Grams. But they're all resting back at the hotel."

"Hotel?" Will shook his head. "Why didn't you tell us you were coming? You could have stayed at my place, and I know Dad would have welcomed you at his, as well."

"We know that, cousin." Gillian's smile was so like Juliana's that he felt yet another crack open up in his battered heart. "But Poppy and Grams are with us, and it just felt like too many people to crowd in on anybody. We do want to see Uncle Otis and Aunt Ellie while we're here, of course."

"Well, come on then! We can pop in on them now, and the others can come later." He paused. "You may not be able to see Mom—depends on what kind of day she's having. But

I know Dad would love it if we dropped in."

"How is Aunt Ellie?"

"Not well, but Dad tells me he's hired someone to help with her, and Mom seems to be thriving under her care. She's taken a real liking to this woman—seems to genuinely think she's an angel." His short laugh sounded a little hollow, even in his own ears.

"Well, that's great! If she's good with her, the caretaker can relieve Uncle Otis of a lot of pressure."

"I'm sure you're right about that." Will stood to his feet. "Come on, then. Let's do this!"

He gave the front door a couple of light raps but didn't wait for an answer. Instead, he used his own key to open it and stepped inside, motioning for Gillian and Danny to follow.

"Pops?"

"In here, son."

Will and his guests stepped into the living room, where his father sat hidden behind a newspaper. "I've brought someone to see you, Pops."

Otis dropped the paper to his lap and looked up with a smile, which froze on his face as he stared at Gillian. She laughed self-consciously and hurried across the room to place a kiss on her uncle's cheek.

"Hello, Uncle Otis. You haven't aged a day since I saw you last!"

Will's father seemed to be having some trouble finding his voice. Will watched him closely. *What on earth is wrong with Pops? He looks like he's seen a ghost.*

"Gillian!" The older man made an effort to regain his composure, drawing his niece into a gentle hug. "Look at you, child. You're all grown up!"

Will flashed a wicked grin toward his cousin. "She grew up quite nicely, didn't she, Pops?

"Will!" His father scolded, noticing the pink in Gillian's cheek. "You're embarrassing the girl."

"I know! That's what cousins are for."

Danny stood back throughout the pleasantries, until the older man smiled across the comfortable room. "And who is this young man, Gillian? Aren't you going to introduce him?"

"Yes, I certainly am!" Gillian grasped Danny's hand and drew him forward. "Uncle Otis, this is my fiancé, Danny Collins."

"Fiancé!" He took Danny's hand in a firm grip. "Well, well! When's the big day?"

"Soon, sir." Danny's warm gaze rested briefly on Gillian before returning to the older man. "We don't have a date yet, but tomorrow's not soon enough for me."

"Can't say I blame you, lad. Well, it's nice to meet you. Now sit down, all of you. Can I get you something to drink? Water? Iced tea?"

Will took a quick glance at his companions, then answered for them all. "No, but thanks, Dad." He motioned Danny and Gillian onto the sofa and seated himself in an easy chair next to his father, who seemed to be trying not to stare at Gillian.

"Pops, are you okay?" He lowered his voice and briefly touched his father's arm.

"I'm fine, son." Drawing a deep breath, the older man met Will's concerned gaze with an intense one of his own. A worried frown cut two little grooves between his eyes.

Is he trying to tell me something? Why doesn't he just say it?

"Why don't you step in and say hello to your mother? I'll visit with our guests for a moment, then perhaps Ellie would like to see Gillian and her young man."

Will hesitated. Visiting his mother was more pain than pleasure these days. He had hoped she'd be sleeping, and he could avoid seeing her.

"Go on, son. It'll do her good." His father's voice urged him gently. "Julie's with her, so you'll have a chance to meet her, as well."

Please, God, don't let him see how badly I don't want to do this. Will forced a smile and nodded reluctantly. "Okay, Pops."

Chapter Twenty

HE STOOD AND TRUDGED SLOWLY out of the room, knowing he must look like a child on his way to the principal's office. He hated himself for dreading the visit with his mother, but it hurt so badly to witness her steady physical decline.

Will, be honest with yourself. It hurts to see her like this, but it bothers you even more to look at her and know this could be your future.

The short end of the L-shaped hallway between the living room and his mother's bedroom led into the kitchen on one side and a guest bathroom on the other. A staircase leading up to the master bedroom where his father now slept alone was located at the bend. Three smaller bedrooms branched off the long arm of the hall. The last one, at the far end, was his mother's room.

Will stopped as he rounded the bend, cocking his head to listen. Someone was speaking softly…reading? Yes, his mother's new companion was reading to her. Another couple of seconds and Will recognized the words from one of the psalms, though he could not place it in a certain chapter.

Oh, magnify the Lord with me, and let us exalt his name together.

That voice. It had a familiar ring to it. But the woman was soft-spoken and reading quietly. Will decided most voices sounded pretty much the same in a whisper. Perhaps Julie, the new companion, was hoping to lull his mother to sleep.

He took a few steps closer to the room then leaned against the wall to listen. If his mom would sleep, he might not have to deal with a visit today.

The angel of the Lord encampeth round about them that fear him, and delivereth them.

Oh, taste and see that the Lord is good: blessed is the man that trusteth in him.

Will closed his eyes, resting his head against the wall behind him. The voice from his mother's room soothed him, as did the beautiful words. How long had it been since he, the editor of a popular Christian magazine, had actually taken refuge in God's Word?

The young lions do lack, and suffer hunger: but they that seek the Lord shall not want any good thing.

Come, ye children, hearken unto me: I will teach you the fear of the Lord.

What man is he that desireth life, and loveth many days, that he may see good?

Keep thy tongue from evil, and thy lips from speaking guile.

Depart from evil, and do good; seek peace, and pursue it.

The eyes of the Lord are upon the righteous, and his ears are open unto their cry.

Lurking in the hallway, Will swallowed the large lump in his throat but was unable to stop the tears that coursed down his face as he absorbed familiar scriptures from various portions of the Bible.

His problem had been pointed out to him by the very Source he should have turned to all along. When had he stopped seeking God and God's plan for his life? He clearly saw the manner in which he had tried to take matters into his own hands. Rather than trust the Lord with his life and his future, he took it on himself to decide he could never marry, sending away the one woman he would ever love. Panic beat within his heart as he realized that he had rejected the precious gift God sent him.

Without conscious thought, he crept closer to his mother's bedroom where the door stood open. His feet made no sound on the carpeted floor as he eased into the entryway.

His gaze fell reluctantly on the form in the bed, and he stifled a gasp. Someone had prettied her up, and for the first time in far too long, his mother resembled the woman she had been years ago.

A colorful scarf was wound, turban-like, around her head, leaving a fringe of hair peeking out in front. "Someone" had also powdered her face, brushed her pallid cheeks with a touch of pink, and even moistened the dry lips with a softly tinted balm. She lay there, her eyes closed, her breathing even. Will thought she was asleep, though a contented smile curved her crooked lips.

The young woman sitting next to the bed continued to read. She faced away from Will, but there was no mistaking that familiar dark hair and the petite lines of her body.

Confused, he tried to remember the name his father had given when he told him about the new caregiver. Not Juliana Camden! Jill? No…Julie. Julie Kelly. Of course. Why hadn't he seen through it immediately?

The Lord is nigh unto them that are of a broken heart; and saveth such as be of a contrite spirit.

Many are the afflictions of the righteous: but the Lord delivereth him out of them all.

He keepeth all his bones: not one of them is broken.

Evil shall slay the wicked: and they that hate the righteous shall be desolate.

The Lord redeemeth the soul of his servants: and none of them that trust in him shall be desolate.

"That's me, Lord!" Will cried out in silent supplication. "I am broken-hearted and contrite, and I do trust in You. In spite of my self-serving actions, You know that I do. Please don't leave me desolate! Let her love me in spite of my arrogant attempt to work things out without You."

Juliana closed the Bible and bent to place a soft kiss on his mother's forehead. "Sleep well, sweetie!" The soft whisper of her voice was barely audible.

"Amen!" Will kept his voice low too.

She whirled to face him, her eyes more golden than ever in the dim room. Will's heart pounded hard in his chest, and he realized he was terrified she would turn him away.

"Will!" He backed into the hall as she moved toward him, allowing her to close the door between them and his mother.

"What are you doing here?"

"I might ask you the same thing."

She blushed but stood her ground. "I'm taking care of my friend."

"Why?" He was puzzled. Why would she bother with anything that mattered to him after the way he had behaved?

Her eyes were guarded but unflinching. She shrugged. "It's what I felt God wanted me to do." Her enchanting little chin shot upward. "Believe me, I'm not here to get close to you. You needn't worry about that. You've made yourself quite clear."

He sighed, finally allowing his gaze to caress her face.

"What if I said I was wrong? What if I said I can't live without you?" Dropping to one knee, he reached for her hand and brushed it softly with his lips then held it to his cheek as he looked up into her disbelieving eyes. "What if I begged you to forgive me and asked you to be my wife? What then?"

For a moment she just stood there, staring at him as though she thought he'd lost his mind. But then one tear slipped from her eye and trickled down her cheek. Then another. She tugged on the hand he held, and he stood, never taking his eyes from her face.

She's crying. Is that good or bad?

"Why don't you try it and see, Will?" Her voice was soft, as were the eyes she lifted to his. "Try saying all of those things."

The tightness in his chest began to loosen. *Perhaps there is still hope....*

"I was wrong, sweetheart." He lowered his head a little closer to hers.

"Yes, you were."

Nothing like an honest woman. He moved closer yet, close enough to smell the sweet wildflower fragrance of her hair. "I can't live without you, Juliana. You are my heart, my life...I can't breathe without you."

"Yes?" She cuddled into his arms. Her cheeks were still wet with tears, and he used his thumb to catch a little drop of moisture as it fell from one thick eyelash.

"Yes. I've been such a mess, sweetheart. God will forgive me, I know, for not trusting my life into His hands. But can you? Can you ever trust me again?"

"Hmmm..." Juliana's luscious lips curved upward in a teasing smile. "I'll have to think about that."

"Well, while you're thinking, decide whether or not you could stand me for a whole lifetime, because I want you to marry me." It came out sounding like a warning. "And the sooner we can make it happen, the happier I'll be."

Juliana's smile was radiant, and Will could no longer stop himself. He gathered her into his arms and claimed her lips with his own. He wanted to be gentle, but it was no use. Groaning, he kissed her deeply and hungrily.

After a moment, he drew back, searching her face for a clue. "Say something, my love. Tell me I haven't lost you for good. Say you'll marry me!"

She placed a hand on the back of his head, gently coaxing him close again. With her lips touching his, she whispered, "The lost has been found, my darling. Is there a minister in the house?"

"Will!"

His father's incredulous voice brought Will to his senses. He released Juliana and stepped back, grinning, not in the least abashed.

"Pops! You didn't tell me you'd hired the most beautiful girl in the world to take care of Mom."

"I…uh…well, I take it you and Miss Kelly knew each other before now…?" His heavy eyebrows seemed set on climbing right up into his hairline.

Will burst out laughing. "Sweetheart, do you make a habit of kissing perfect strangers?"

"I do not! And whoever said you're perfect, anyway?" Will heroically bit back the impulse to laugh again. Juliana's valiant attempt at humor was a blatant ploy to hide her overwhelming embarrassment. The crimson in her cheeks and the moistness of her beautiful eyes told him she was mortified.

"Pops, this young lady is Juliana Camden. I'm sure I told

you about her. She worked at Voice of Hope until a couple of weeks ago, when my stupidity drove her away. I thought she was lost to me until I found her in here reading to Mom."

"I see. But you didn't tell me she was the mirror image of Gillian, did you, son?"

Slightly embarrassed, Will shook his head. "No, sir. I'm sorry, Pops. It's a long story."

His father's gaze was fixed on Juliana. "I knew you looked familiar that first day. But it's been several years since I saw my niece, and I just didn't make the connection." He shook his head, openly studying her face as if he'd never seen it before. "Juliana Camden." He spoke slowly. "Not Julie Kelly?" Juliana briefly averted her gaze. "No. I'm really sorry, sir. But I didn't lie to you, Mr. Dawson. It's…well, it's a long story, like Will said."

"So I gather." He eyed them both for a moment, finally focusing his attention on his son. "I expect to hear the entire explanation, long or not. For now though, what do we do about the young couple in the living room?"

"Oh!" Will had forgotten about Danny and Gillian. "Well, actually, they came by the office hoping to see Juliana."

"Who did?" She lifted puzzled eyes to his.

He sucked in a breath, realizing he had not yet told her who was with him. Taking both of her hands in his, he came straight to the point.

"Sweetheart, Danny Collins is in the living room. Gillian is with him. Are you ready to meet your sister?"

He expected shy reluctance, maybe even tears, so it was a pleasant surprise when her eyes lit up like two golden lamps.

"Gillian's here?" Without waiting for an answer, she rushed down the hall toward the living room, with Will and his father hurrying to keep up.

Gillian sat close to Danny on the sofa, their heads bent over a large photo album. Most of the pictures depicted Will in various stages of growing up. One was captioned, "8th Grade Formal" and showed him standing with his chest out, head high and a smug expression on his young face. He appeared quite taken with himself, if not the bespectacled girl at his side. Gillian couldn't help a little laugh at the obviously overconfident youth.

"Gillian!"

Her heart responded to the breathless half-whisper as if it had been a jolt of electricity. Gasping, she jumped to her feet, and the album fell to the floor with a thump. Before she even saw the owner of that voice framed in the arched entryway, she knew.

"Juliana!" Her voice trembled, and for some reason she was crying, but it was okay because tears streamed down her sister's face as well.

She had no memory of crossing the room, but somehow they met halfway and fell into each other's arms, laughing one moment and crying the next.

Will motioned Danny out into the hallway. He stood for a moment with his father and his future cousin, all of them wearing sappy grins even as they brushed oh-so-casually at silly tears that blurred the touching scene before them.

But only for a moment. Soon Pops reached out and tugged on the pocket door, and it slid closed without a sound, cutting them off from the most beautiful sight Will thought he'd ever seen in his life.

"I believe your young ladies have some catching up to do, fellas." His father's voice was husky.

He cleared his throat a couple of times then took Will firmly by the arm, tugging him along like a recalcitrant child as he started down the hallway. "I've got plenty of iced tea in the kitchen, and I think we probably have time for quite a lengthy story!"

He was right. It was almost an hour before the girls joined them again. They entered the red-and-white kitchen arm in arm, unable to wipe the bemused smiles off their identical faces.

"Would you look at that? I think I'm having double vision! Pops, what did you put in this tea?"

Will's father shook his head, rolling his eyes hopelessly. He turned his attention to Juliana and Gillian with a kind smile. "I hope the two of you had a pleasant first visit."

"Oh, yes, sir!" They answered in unison then stared at each other in surprise, bringing forth a burst of laughter from the men.

Will and Daniel jumped up to pull out chairs for the girls while the older man filled two more tall glasses with amber liquid. "I assure you there's nothing in the tea except ice, ladies. I hope you'll pardon my son's lack of good manners."

Another good-natured burst of amusement followed his quiet remark and then they were all talking and laughing as though they had known each other forever.

Calls were made to Corman's Corner and then the hotel where Gillian's family waited. Will knew from Juliana's end of her conversation that Annie wanted to come to Bakersfield that very moment to meet her long-lost daughter, but somehow Juliana persuaded her mother to wait until the next morning.

By the time Danny and Gillian said good night and took their leave, a plan was in place for Will to meet Gillian's group at the hotel early the next day. They would follow him to Corman's Corner and the Camden home.

Just as the door closed behind them, Ellie's little bell rang, and a querulous voice informed them she was thirsty. Juliana turned to go to her, but a hand on her arm held her back.

Otis Dawson smiled and shook his head. "Not this time. You don't need anything unpleasant to mar this moment. Besides, I think I want to hold my wife's hand for a little while."

Will stood with his arm around Juliana's waist, watching his father hurry down the hall and around the corner. Then he looked down into the radiant face of the girl at this side.

"Will you walk with me in the moonlight, my love?"

Her answering smile told him all he needed to know. He took her hand, and they slipped out into the night.

Chapter Twenty-one

JULIANA AND HER FATHER PUT forth their best efforts, but Annie could not be kept calm. She paced throughout the house, dusting a picture here, rearranging a piece of furniture there. Juliana worried that she would make herself sick, yet she had to admit her mother had never looked healthier—or more beautiful.

Her hair was swept up into a smooth French twist, with little tendrils left loose in the front, softening the strained lines of her face. She wore a simple, light blue pleated dress with a belted waist that accented her petite frame.

Clarence's big hand closed around Annie's wrist as she reached for a bottle of glass cleaner with an eye toward the huge bay windows at the front of the house. He pulled her into the circle of his arms.

"Stop, Annie. The house is perfect, and so are you. Come on and sit down. You don't want to smell like ammonia when you meet Gillian."

Juliana smiled, imagining herself and Will at her parents' age. *Will will be gentle and kind, too, just like Daddy.*

Her mother rested her head on Daddy's broad chest and drew a ragged breath. "I just can't seem to sit still."

He looked like a big bear beside her tiny mother, but one massive hand rested ever so gently on her waist as he led her to the sofa. "I know, sweetheart. Waiting is hard, but it's almost over."

"Daddy?"

"What is it, Julie girl?"

She hesitated. "Nothing, I guess."

"It's obviously something, so tell me."

"I just wondered…you said you actually ran some kind of ad trying to find Gillian?"

"Yes, I did. Once a month that first year then once every three months…every year since."

"Ever since?" She was shocked at his quiet tenacity. "For twenty-three years."

"That's unbelievable! Were there ever any replies?" Anni aked.

"Oh, yes. There were scattered calls and letters from people. Some folks were sincerely trying to help while others thought there might be something in it for them. But none were from the Parsonses. You have to remember, my distribution doesn't extend past the county line."

Juliana nodded, her eyes on the gentle face of the man who had raised her as his own. "Of course, and Gillian's family settled in another county." She shook her head. "I can't believe you kept printing it for so long."

He wrapped an arm around her mother, and she laid her head on his broad shoulder. Annie was clearly making an effort to remain seated and stop fussing around the house.

"I had to, Julie girl. My Annie lost something she loved with all her heart. By faithfully running that ad, I felt I was doing something to try and get Gillian back for her."

A knot formed in her throat, and a familiar burning at the back of her eyes threatened a downpour of tears. "What did it say?"

A small smile tugged at the corners of her father's mouth. He tilted his head against the high back of the sofa and fixed his eyes upward, as though reading the words off the high ceiling.

"Wanted: Return of baby G. Sale not valid. Money back plus generous reward and clear conscience. No law enforcement."

"People actually responded to that?" Juliana shook her head, amazed.

"Oh, yes! You'd be surprised how many people would sell their own souls for a 'generous reward.' I could have bought babies right out of their mothers' arms a few times."

"That's awful!" Her heart ached for the children who had never known the kind of love she was so abundantly blessed with. "How did you know they weren't the right people?"

"None of them had the right answers.

"Answers to what?"

"Well, first I asked in what specific location the transaction had been made. I believe someone did come up with Corman's Camp once. But the second question weeded them out every time."

He paused, and this time, it was Mama who nudged him, none too gently, with an elbow in his ribs. "Well? What second question?"

He shrugged, as if there could be only one answer to that. "Why, I asked the eye color of the man who delivered the merchandise. Not once did anybody say they were golden."

The buzz of the doorbell interrupted their laughter.

Mama sprang to her feet as if the sound were wired directly to her nerve center. She stood trembling, one hand clamped over her mouth below enormous blue eyes.

Juliana hugged her. "She's here. Are you ready for this?"

The firm little chin went up a notch. Mama pulled in a deep breath and exhaled slowly then gave Juliana a tremulous smile. "I've been ready for twenty-three years. Let my baby in!"

"That's the spirit! I love you, Mama."

She touched her father's cheek before going to the door. "You know you're my hero, don't you?"

He tugged on a strand of her hair and winked. "And you are mine, Julie girl!"

She marched to the door and swung it open.

Waiting outside, Gillian's heart pounded so hard she thought it might burst right out of her chest. Her stomach fluttered as if a million butterflies had taken up residence there. Had Danny not supported her with an arm around her waist, she was certain she would have fainted dead away.

"You okay, sweetheart?" His brows drew together in a worried frown.

Her fingers stroked the soft pink yarn in the little crocheted blanket she held. "I'm fine. Just a little nervous."

She turned to check on Will, who was helping her mother and grandparents out of the car. He had suggested Gillian and Daniel come to the door first, and she knew he was trying to give her a brief moment with her birth family without her mother in the room.

"We'll be right along." He smiled and waved to her. "You two go ahead."

Behind her, the door opened, and she whirled to see Juliana smiling out at her.

Reaching for Gillian's hand, her twin sister pulled her

into the entryway and hugged her. "Please come in. Where is everyone?"

"Will and Mother are helping my grandparents. They'll be here in a moment. Grams doesn't move so quickly anymore, and she's been cooped up in the car too much the past couple of days."

"Well, that's okay. Will knows the way in. Did you want to wait for them or go on into the living room with Mama?"

"Let's go on in." Danny touched her hand, and she realized she was twisting a strand of hair around one finger. She had been trying to break that nervous habit for years. *Apparently you haven't tried hard enough, Gilly Goldeneyes!* She half smiled, remembering her Papa's pet name for her.

Juliana led them down a short hall and through a wide archway.

"Mama, this is—"

"Gillian! Oh, my sweet baby!"

Out of nowhere it seemed, a tiny woman appeared, reaching out to place a cool hand on each of her cheeks. Gillian numbly took in the tears pouring in steady streams down the unexpectedly familiar face and allowed herself to be pulled into a warm embrace.

Over her birth mother's shoulder, she caught a glimpse of Danny's stunned expression, and it somehow brought her to her senses. She eased away, shaking her head in disbelief.

"Oh! I'm so sorry. I didn't mean to smother you. Please forgive me!"

"No, that's not it." Her voice was choked. "It's just that—"

"Gillian?" Even Juliana seemed concerned.

She sucked in a breath of air, determined not to pass out. Turning to the older woman, she reached out to gently stroke her cheek.

"You look like…" She shook her head, unable to believe her eyes. "You look exactly like my mother!"

But those oh-so-familiar blue eyes had moved past her now and were fixed on something over her shoulder. The big man standing behind her mother's doppelganger stepped forward and slipped an arm around her waist, but he also wore a stunned expression as he gazed past Gillian to the doorway.

"Luanne!" Mary Helen spoke from the arched entry, where she stood clutching Will's arm as if it were a lifeline on a raging sea.

Is that really you, my beloved sister?

Vaguely, she registered the presence of a large man and a young girl, the mirror image of Gillian. Juliana, of course. But it was the petite woman leaning weakly against the rather oversized gentleman who commanded her utmost attention.

"Luanne?" She desperately wanted it to be so yet dared not hope.

"Mary Helen!" The other woman whispered her name then gracefully wilted, as if performing some kind of dream dance, into her husband's waiting arms.

Mary Helen rushed across the room to the twin sister she hadn't seen in close to thirty years.

Annie opened her eyes to find Juliana running a blessedly cool washcloth over her flushed face. Behind her daughter, Clarence hovered, a worried frown knitting his brow. She smiled shakily, eager to alleviate his concern.

"There, Mama." Juliana's voice was concerned but

thankfully not panicked. "You're okay. Just got a shock, I think."

Annie closed her eyes again for a moment. "Yes, I...I...thought I saw someone..." *How can I tell them I thought I saw the twin sister they don't even know I have? And Gillian—oh, Gillian must think me such a weakling!*

With the thought, she struggled to sit up. "Gillian!"

"I'm right here." First she heard the voice of her long-lost daughter then her face appeared over Juliana's shoulder. The double-vision effect almost had Annie swooning again.

"Please don't worry. I'm not going anywhere."

Pushing at the hands holding her down, Annie peered around the room. She had not been dreaming!

"Mary Helen!"

Her sister hurried over to sit beside her. "Yes, it's me."

With a strangled cry, Annie opened her arms, and Mary Helen fell into them.

"I can't believe it's really you." Annie shook her head, dazed. "You raised my baby girl?"

Mary Helen nodded and dabbed at her eyes with a lacy white handkerchief. "I know it seems too fantastic to be real, but it is. William and I raised Gillian. We loved her so much, Sissy, right from the start! But I swear to you I didn't know she was yours. I thought her mother didn't want her."

Annie patted her hand. "I know what my husband did, and I'm just so glad she had a mother like you. Oh, Mary Helen, I can't believe you're here. I have missed you so! And to think you were just down the road from me."

"And I've missed you, so much! There were times I thought my heart would surely break."

From the far corner of the room, a spirited voice interrupted their conversation. "Well, mine did break—and more than once through all these years. Luanne Dorton, why didn't you contact me and Papa?"

Annie's lips parted, but she could not force a single peep past them. She whipped her head around toward the new voice, where an elderly woman stood with her arms crossed obstinately over her breasts. Tears streaked down her lined cheeks as she fixed Annie beneath sharp, wounded blue eyes.

"Mama!" Annie hurtled across the room and pulled her mother into her arms. She wasn't sure how this precious woman had come to be here in her home, but right now, she didn't care. Questions could be answered later.

Content to be wrapped in her mother's arms, Annie was none too pleased to find herself pulled out of them and into someone else's, until she looked into the still familiar and beloved face of her father, the Reverend Ben Dorton.

"Oh, Papa, Papa!"

Standing between her parents, she gazed in stunned and delirious joy around the room, taking in all the happy, if more-than-a-little-befuddled, faces. *God still loves me, in spite of my stubborn will!*

"Why didn't you write to me and Papa, Luanne? All these years! I thought I would lose my mind worrying about you."

Without warning, sobs wracked the older woman's body, and she buried her face in both hands. Annie drew her mother gently into her arms.

"Mama, I'm sorry!" Tears rained down her own face as she realized the depth of pain her beloved parents had endured over the years. "I'm so sorry!"

Her father moved close to them and placed a hand on her shoulder. "Did you think we would stop loving you, child?"

Someone slipped a tissue into her hand, and she took it without looking up. "No, Papa, I knew better than that. At first, I was just embarrassed. All the years you and Mama spent teaching me right from wrong…all the plans you had for me…and I just threw it all to the winds and eloped, with a man I knew you wouldn't approve of."

"Luanne…Annie…" He corrected himself, apparently accepting that she had been Annie for more years now than she had ever been Luanne. "We were disappointed, I won't deny that. But surely you knew, no matter what, we loved you. Nothing could change that."

"I did know that, Papa. I told myself that when Jack and I got to California, I would write. But by the time we got here, I already knew I'd made a horrible mistake. Jack was drunk all the time. We had no money. There were days when we didn't eat. I was mortified at the thought of telling you what was going on…and I couldn't bring myself to lie to you."

She sniffled and met her father's steady gaze. "So I decided to wait a little longer, just give us time to get ahead. I thought I could change Jack, talk him into giving up the alcohol, and then things would be different."

"But it never happened, did it?" That was Mama, wiping at her eyes as the outburst of tears began to subside.

"No. If anything, he got worse, and I became bitter and angry. I was mad at myself for being such a fool and even miffed at God for not stopping me from making such a horrible mistake."

Her father's lips twisted in a well-remembered, lopsided smile. "Did you think He might've reached down and physically barred your way, child?"

"No, of course not!" She blushed, in hindsight seeing the foolishness of her reasoning. "But He could have kept me from meeting Jack, couldn't He?"

"Sure He could. But God loves us enough to give us free will, Lu—Annie. He lets us make our own decisions, even when they're not the right ones."

Her mother touched her cheek, urging her on with her story. "Go on, dear. What happened then?"

"We wandered around for a while, moving from place to place as Jack heard of work here and there. I was becoming more and more embittered. Even when we were temporarily settled in different locations, he wouldn't let me go to church. He even hated it when I read my Bible, so eventually I just stopped. It was easier than dealing with his rages. Then I stopped praying, too."

She looked up, forcing herself to look into the dear faces of her parents, hoping they would understand. "But I told myself I would again, someday. When we found a place to live and I could find a church, I would go, no matter what my husband said. I meant to find my way back to God."

She paused, momentarily lost in the past. Her father touched her hand, urging her on. "Tell us, Annie."

"Not long after we landed here, I realized I was expecting a child. Back then this place was just Dale Corman's farm labor camp. It didn't become Corman's Corner until several years later. Jack and I were lucky enough to get one of the few houses available, instead of having to take a tent. I can see now that God was watching over me, even then. He knew I was going to need this house after…after Jack was gone."

"I don't know how you survived!" A frown creased her mother's forehead. "You should have contacted us."

Annie met her husband's eyes, and a smile teased at her lips. "Well, I couldn't see it then, Mama, but that's when God sent my own guardian angel to take care of me. Poor Clarence! I was such a mess that he ended up having to marry me to get the job done."

"It was my favorite assignment ever." Her husband's warm gaze caressed her face.

"Anyway." Annie's eyes sent a warm message his way, but she continued with her story. It had been a long time coming. "Jack was not happy when I told him I was expecting, but he knew how much I wanted a baby." She smiled across the room at her daughters, sitting between Daniel and Will.

"If he had known I was carrying twins, I think he might have disappeared before they were born. But of course we had no way of knowing that, and Jack really seemed to be trying to be happy about having a family, even after I insisted he quit drinking."

With a wry twist of her lips, she added, "I think he was afraid I would up and go back to Texas if he didn't 'play nice.'"

Her mother's blue eyes snapped angrily. "That's exactly what you should have done, too!"

"Perhaps. But Mama, you and Papa taught me that marriage is for keeps. I had made my bed, and I felt duty-bound to sleep in it. Besides, Jack seemed to be trying."

Ignoring Grams' disbelieving expression, she continued. "We were both shocked when I had twins. Dale Corman's wife delivered them—she seemed to make a business of sorts out of midwifery. I had never seen a doctor prior to delivery, so we had no way of knowing I was carrying two babies. Funny, isn't it?" With a thoughtful little shake of her head, she went on. "It truly hadn't occurred to me that there might be two of them, even though I'm a twin myself.

"I was so happy, because I knew Jack didn't plan on allowing me to have another child. Having two at once was the perfect solution." She smiled at Mary Helen. "I named them both after you, Sister."

"Oh! Oh, my goodness!" Mary Helen exclaimed. "I thought it was such a wonderful coincidence that Gillian's middle name was Mary. It seemed she was born to be mine. But my 'adopted' child was actually named for me!"

"My middle name is Helen." Juliana gave her new aunt a shy smile. "I never knew until now why Mama chose that name, but I'm honored to share it with you."

Mary Helen swallowed hard and sent a warm smile to the niece who was a carbon copy of her daughter. Turning back to Annie, she gently encouraged her to finish her story. "Go on, Sissy. We still want to know about your life."

"Well, this is where it became unbearable, because five days after the twins were born, Gillian disappeared."

Chapter Twenty-two

ANNIE WEPT AS SHE TOLD them how she had awakened to find the crib her twins shared half empty. By the time she got through the story, every eye in the room was moist with tears.

"That was the last straw." Her voice broke with little hiccupping sobs. "By the time Clarence showed up here to tell me about Jack's 'death,' I thought God had abandoned me, and I never intended to speak to Him again. I was devastated. If not for Juliana, I think I would have simply lain down and willed myself to stop breathing."

Papa took her hand in his and gave it a gentle squeeze. "And of course you didn't notice that special angel God had sent you?"

"No, I didn't. But Clarence never gave up. He just kept showing up at my door, again and again. I was too far gone to notice that my cupboards never ran out of food, and it was a long time before I realized no one had been around to collect rent on the house, not that I could have paid it if they had. I was worried that Corman would realize his lapse and evict me and the baby, so I finally mentioned it to Clarence.

That's when he told me that he bought my house from Dale Corman the first day he met me."

"And I never could get her to leave it." Clarence's low-toned voice took up the story. "I wanted to buy a bigger house in a better location after we were married, but Annie wouldn't leave. She insisted that whoever took Gillian had taken her from this house, and she wanted to be right here in case they, or Gillian, ever came looking for her. I knew that Jack had taken the baby, but I didn't want to tell her that. So I built on and around the old house, and eventually it became what it is now."

"He was my earthly savior," Annie admitted. "I don't know what made him keep coming back. I was such a mess!" She turned to her mother. "After I married Clarence, I did write to you, Mama. Many times. All of my letters came back."

Grams looked stricken. "Oh, dear me! That must have been after William brought us out here to live near Mary Helen. Ben, didn't we leave a forwarding address?"

Papa shook his head. "Probably not. Most ever'one in Conlen knew us and knew where we were headed. I guess we just figured we'd be easy enough to look up, if anybody came lookin'."

"I kept writing for about a year before I gave up." Annie's eyes misted, and she closed them briefly. "I decided you must not want to hear from me, after all, and I didn't blame you. It never occurred to me that the two of you would have left Texas. In my mind, it was just one more way that God had let me down."

"Oh, Luanne!" The old lady's tears began to fall again, and Annie and her father moved in close to hug her.

After a moment, she reluctantly pulled free of the loving arms. Smiling through her tears, she addressed the roomful of emotional occupants.

"Let's move this party to the kitchen. I'll put on some coffee and bring out the chocolate cake."

Juliana helped her mother get everyone seated around the table, which wasn't easy with all of them chattering like magpies. They all seemed to think they could bridge a gap of nigh onto three decades in a matter of twenty minutes if they talked loud enough and fast enough.

Finally, though, everyone had a chair, and her mother was slicing cake onto dessert plates. She glanced around the little crowd of excited faces.

"I need coffee. Anyone else?"

"Can I help you get it?" Gillian half rose from her chair, but Juliana motioned her back down.

"Not yet, but after it's brewed, I'll let you help me pass out the cups."

She busied herself with the coffee pot, half watching, half listening to the conversation at the long dining table.

"We may never know God's reasons for all we've been through." Her grandfather's vivid blue eyes moved around the large table, resting briefly on each face. "But here we sit, all together again, and for that I am most grateful!"

"Amen!" Grams declared, waving a gnarled hand in the air.

Juliana smiled, thrilling to the sound of the elder voices. *I have grandparents!*

She began pulling coffee mugs from a cabinet and sloshing them around in a basin of soapy water. Some hadn't been used in quite a while. Picking up a dishcloth, she thrust her hand into the first cup, still only half paying attention to the task at hand as she listened to the excited voices behind her. With a loud crack, the cup shattered into pieces, one of which sliced into her right hand.

"Ouch!"

"Ooww!" Behind her, Gillian echoed her cry.

Will was at Juliana's side instantly, thrusting the injured hand under cold running water, while her mother dashed off to find a bandage.

"It just shattered for no reason!"

"It must have been cracked already, sweetheart, and you didn't notice."

The jagged, one-inch cut wasn't as deep as the amount of blood had seemed to indicate. Within moments, the wound was treated with iodine, and Will had applied a neat bandage.

"I think you all need to see this." When the room quieted, Danny spoke up.

"What is it?" Mary Helen demanded.

Juliana was letting the water out of the sink in order to fish out the slivers of dangerous glass. Hearing the alarm in her aunt's voice, she whirled in time to see Danny pick up Gillian's left hand and turn it to face the others, revealing a bright red, jagged line across the top. In size and shape, it mirrored Juliana's wound, although the skin was not actually broken. Rather, it looked as though an attempt had been made to cut through her hand from the inside, resulting in an angry, raised welt.

Momentarily forgetting the glass in the sink, Juliana rushed to her sister's side.

"You felt my pain!" Recalling the discussion with her parents regarding this subject, she was excited to discover they might have been right on target.

"Yes, and I don't think this is the first time."

"I don't either. Did you injure your arm somehow when you were about…." She glanced at her mother. "Six or so?"

"Yes, you were six." Annie nodded, her eyes glittering her excitement.

Mary Helen, too, sat gaping at the implication.

"I did hurt my arm!" Gillian's voice reflected the awe Juliana felt. "Danny and I were playing at the park. I climbed to the top of the monkey bars and fell. Somehow I landed in such a way that I fractured my right wrist and had to wear a cast for several weeks."

"This is unbelievable!" Juliana stared at her sister. "I was sitting right here in the house, playing with my doll, Jelly Bean…" She stopped when Gillian gasped and turned to look at Mary Helen. Her aunt smiled and nodded.

"What is it?"

"I'll tell you later. Go on."

Juliana was puzzled but continued. "For no reason, pain literally ripped up my left arm. It stemmed from the wrist, but at the time it hurt so badly I found it hard to pinpoint the source."

"We rushed her to the hospital." Her mother spoke up, remembering. "She cried all the way, poor child, just writhing in pain. We were terrified, because there seemed to be no explanation for her discomfort. Her wrist was swollen by the time we got there, but the doctors couldn't find a thing wrong with her arm. X-rays revealed no broken bones or anything else that might have explained the pain or the swelling."

"I couldn't use it for a couple of weeks." Juliana lifted her left arm, turning it this way and that as if to test for residual damage. "The swelling went down within a few days, but if I tried to lift it, the pain was unbearable."

"I believe I've heard of things like this." Will stroked his chin thoughtfully. "There's been some new research dealing with an extraordinary chemistry between some twins, in which they feel each other's pain, or lead highly parallel lives—even those separated at birth. Some even claim to have some sort of mental connection."

"Well, don't discount that last one too quickly." Juliana looked at her sister. "Gillian, you mentioned in the letter you wrote me that you refer to Aunt Mary Helen as your "little Mother.'"

"I do, yes."

Juliana told them about the night her father had to awaken her from a nightmare in which she was calling out for her "little Mother."

"She was completely absorbed in the dream." Daddy spoke up, corroborating her story. "I've never seen her so panicked. Even after she awakened, she kept referring to her 'little Mother,' although she's never called Annie by that term."

Mary Helen and Gillian exchanged startled glances, and Gillian shared her own nightmare in which she had also awakened screaming for her little Mother.

"She hasn't had such a troubling nightmare since she was very small," Mary Helen told them. "I had to sleep the rest of the night in her bed."

The ensuing discussion revealed a number of times during the past twenty-three years in which it seemed Juliana and Gillian might have shared one another's pain, excitement, terror, or joy.

"How about you two?" Gillian's gaze moved back and forth from her mother to Juliana's. "Did the two of you ever experience anything like that?"

"Nothing so dramatic." Mary Helen's eyes twinkled as she smiled at Annie. "Though we were always able to finish each other's sentences. And we could never keep secrets from one another—the other one always knew."

"I wish you'd figured out what your sister was up to before she ran off with Jack Kelly!" Grams shook a twisted finger at Mary Helen.

"But Grams, if they hadn't run away together, Juliana and I wouldn't be here," Gillian reminded her grandmother.

"Well, there is that," Grams grudgingly conceded, bringing a burst of laughter from the others. After a moment, Grams' lips twitched a little, then she was laughing, too.

Clarence wandered outside for a breath of fresh air, leaving the reunited family piecing together their broken relationships. His heart was full, and he needed a moment alone with God, just to say "thank you."

In all the years he'd been married to Annie, he had never seen his wife so alive, so vibrant. He'd always thought her lovely, but even he had never realized the full extent of her beauty. The sorrow that cast a constant shadow over her heart had dimmed it.

Lowering himself into a wooden swing hanging from the branch of a large old cottonwood, he spoke aloud to his Best Friend.

"Thank you, Father, for bringing Gillian back to Annie, and for putting that happy light in her eyes. I feel so blessed right now, Lord, I may never ask You for anything again."

A soft chuckle from the darkness startled him, and Clarence spun to see who had intruded on his quiet time. Off to the side, a lank figure leaned against the thick trunk of the cottonwood. Though the man stood completely in shadow, Clarence had no trouble seeing his visitor.

"I hope that weren't a promise, Camden. You ought not make promises ya can't keep, 'specially when you're talkin' to the good Lord."

Clarence relaxed, chuckling. "So. I get a visit, too. Hello, Travelin' Jack."

"Yeah, you're the last one on my list. Funny, ain't it? You trip over a man on the sidewalk one day, and ya end up married to his woman and raisin' his child—oh, and talkin' to angels when no one's a-lookin'."

Clarence shrugged. "Well, if I've learned any one thing about my heavenly Father over the years, it's that I should never second guess His plan of action. He always does it just right, even when it looks all wrong."

"Yessir, that He does."

A brief, comfortable silence fell while Clarence basked in the golden glow of a heavenly presence. He figured Jack would say what he'd come to say when he was ready and not a second sooner.

Finally, the glowing form stood erect, and Clarence heard him sigh. "I'm bein' summoned, Camden. Guess I need to give you my message now."

"I'm listening."

"I wanna thank ya, 'cause you've done real good, man. I saw somethin' real in you that day, and I never forgot it. When the Lord jerked me up outta the pit, I took to makin' decisions based on how I figgered you might make 'em."

Clarence attempted a reply but choked on a rather large lump in his throat. It didn't matter, anyway. Ol' Travelin' Jack wasn't finished.

"You did just what I hoped you'd do when that ring showed up. I didn't want my Annie sittin' here waitin' for a man what might never come back. It was time to let 'er go." He scuffed a toe into the soft soil at his feet. "I wudden ever good 'nuff fer Annie nohow."

"But just look at you now, Jack!" Clarence smiled at his unearthly visitor.

The other man's lined face split into a big grin. "Yeah, I'm walkin' in high cotton now, ain't I?"

"You certainly are. And Jack, I have a message for you, too."

"Yeah? What's that?"

"Thank you. You gave me the greatest gift of my life when you sent me to Annie. I want you to know that I love her with all my heart."

"Well, o' course you do! She's Annie!"

He's right. I never had a choice.

"You've got a point. Nevertheless, I thank you. And thank you, also, for bringing Gillian back to her. Now Annie can live again."

"Well, it took me a mite longer'n I planned, but I reckon the good Lord has His reasons for that, too. Point is, they're all together now, so my work here is done." He looked straight into Clarence's eyes. "The rest is up to you, friend."

Turning, he moved further into the darkness. When he stopped and turned, Clarence caught his breath. All he could see of Jack now were his eyes, glowing softly golden in the night.

"My girls—they're special. You take good care of 'em."

"I intend to."

"I know you do." Jack lifted a hand. "See ya on the other side."

And then he was gone.

Clarence sat alone for a long time, thinking about the changes that pitiful drunk had made in his life. Yes, he owed a lot to Ol' Travelin' Jack.

He rose early the next morning and drove into Lamont as he did every day. But this time he bypassed the Limelight and drove straight to the sheriff's office. Sheriff Headley had retired some months ago, but he could still be found most mornings right there at his old headquarters, having coffee with the boys.

A pleasant, booming voice greeted him before the door swung shut behind him. "Mornin', Mr. Camden! Don't tell me...you need a shoeshine?"

Clarence smiled, meeting the merry eyes of the new sheriff as he shook the younger man's hand. "As a matter of fact, I do, Vergil. Any idea where I can get one?"

"Try the kid on the corner."

"The one who looks a lot like you?"

"That'd be the one." Virgil Campbell's grin was every bit as contagious as it had been when he himself was the local shoeshine boy. "What can I do for you this morning, sir?"

"I'm looking for Sheriff Headley."

"Well, I reckon ya found me." The dry, raspy voice came from the corner of the room.

Vergil chuckled and headed out the door with a friendly wave. Clarence joined the older man who sat in a rocker near the coffee pot, peering up from behind a copy of the newspaper.

"How are you, Sheriff?"

"Ain't the sheriff no more."

"I guess you'll always be the Sheriff to me."

"Hmph!" Headley's head disappeared behind the newspaper. "Well, spit it out. What can I do for ya?"

Amused, Clarence shook his head, eyeing the top of the other man's balding head. Sheriff Headley never had been a man of many words.

"Mind if I sit down?"

"Suit yourself."

He seated himself across from Headley and waited for the

other man to look up from the paper. He didn't.

Clarence sighed. "I'm here to keep a promise I made you a long time ago."

At last he merited some attention. The old man raised his head to frown at him across the short distance. He folded the newspaper without looking at it and let it drop to the floor.

"What's that?"

"I want to tell you now what I didn't tell you then."

Headley leaned back, his old eyes keen with sudden interest. "I don't believe it. You're talkin' about Jack Kelly."

"I am."

"Well, this calls for breakfast. Come on, let's go see Bonnie. I'll pay; you say."

Clarence hurried to hold the door open for his old friend. Headley picked up an old-fashioned derby hat and placed it on his head. Passing by Clarence on the way out, he paused to fix him under a stern gaze.

"And while you're sayin', I expect to hear about that ridiculous ad I've had to read for years in that rag of a paper, too. You know the one. 'No law enforcement,' indeed!"

Clarence laughed outright, feeling younger than he had in at least a couple of decades. "You've got it, my friend. From here on out, it'll be the truth."

"The whole truth!" Sheriff Headley shook a finger in his face.

"And nothing but the truth." Clarence clapped the old sheriff on the shoulder and grinned. "So help me God!"

About the Author

DELIA LATHAM lives in East Texas with her husband, Johnny and their pampered Pomeranian, Kona, who kindly allows them to share her home. She enjoys multiple life roles as wife, mother, grandmother, sister and friend, but above all, she loves being a princess daughter to the King of Kings. She admits to a lifelong, mostly un-battled Dr.  Pepper addiction, and loves hearing from her readers.

Acknowledgments

As always, my most heartfelt gratitude goes to my Lord and Savior, Jesus Christ…for being my Best Friend, my Guide, and my Teacher, and for giving me the desire and the ability to write. I also thank Him for giving me the incredible gift of my husband, Johnny…my tower of strength and daily support, who puts up with the unmade beds and backed-up laundry so I can write. He's more familiar with the kitchen than I am, and thanks to him, I rarely miss a day's supply of vitamins or any other necessary medications I would most certainly forget to take if he didn't place them in my hand. You still make my heart smile, Johnny Latham.

I'm deeply appreciative of my children and grandchildren, whose belief in me is more encouraging than I can say. You are my life.

Sally Laity, Reta Fields-Cortines, and Saundra Randolph…thank you for looking over my manuscript with nit-picky honesty, for finding the errors I could no longer see, for pointing out the inconsistencies and questioning minute details that didn't fit the timeline or the character or the story. I owe each of you more than I can ever repay.

God's blessings on all the friends and family who supported, encouraged, and prayed for me while I wrote. I could not have done it without them.

A Sneak Peek into...

Glorious Gift of Hope

Coming Soon!

Chapter One

NO WAY OUT. NOWHERE TO GO.

Beams of bright light sliced through the darkness, straight toward a yellow Volkswagen bug. An expertly painted, long-stemmed rose trailed along the driver's side, lending the car a jaunty, fun-loving appeal.

The blinding glare grew larger and brighter in the instant between heartbeats.

In the last split-second, Alayna Brennan's gaze flew to her husband, Scott—the man she'd loved since the first day of the second week in third grade. Mrs. Engles seated the new boy next to Alayna and—bright blue eyes twinkling like miniature stars—he shot her a big, broad, beautiful smile.

That was that. Little Alayna Bellamy's eight-year-old heart fell at his feet.

Nineteen years later, with disaster barreling toward them at ninety miles an hour, those same mesmerizing eyes pierced into hers. Scott's lips didn't move in his ashen face, but she heard the words as surely as if he spoke them into her ear. "I adore you, my Laynie-Love!"

She nodded, unable to push a single word past her frozen lips. Yet she never doubted he heard her heart's response, as well.

A loud, vibrating roar thundered through the vehicle. The runaway semi was upon them.

Scott! Oh, my sweet, sweet love!

And then…nothing. Just deepest darkness.

Alayna bolted upright. "Scott!" The scream raked her throat like sharp, piercing talons. Her heart pounded—a massive fist, intent on escaping the prison of her ribcage. "Scott…"

A soft breeze drifted through the window screen and stirred the lightweight curtain panel. The fabric brushed her cheek, and she caught her breath as the room came slowly into focus.

A dream. Another horrid dream that refused to stay away.

Harsh sobs rent the air. She wilted back onto the bed and buried her face in the pillow. Why couldn't she accept her husband's death and learn to live without him? After five years, shouldn't the dreams have stopped? Shouldn't the heartache have alleviated, at least to some small degree?

"God, is it me? Am I doing something wrong, something that keeps me from letting go?" Tears soaked the pillow Scott's head once rested on every night. Alayna still slept in the same bed they'd shared during the six years they were married before—

She jumped up and whirled to stare at the tangle of sheets and the dusky purple comforter—rumpled, as usual, from her flailing about during the night. Breath came in jagged, painful gasps as her gaze roamed the space.

Oh, how she loved the bedroom furniture they'd chosen together. The bright luster of cherrywood brightened the room, even in the dim light of a morning barely post-dawn. A tall, double chest of drawers filled a corner space. Alayna's lips twisted into something that wasn't quite a smile. Scott had insisted on referring to the piece—in his horrible fake-British accent—as a "proper gentleman's highboy."

One hand slid over the footboard of the bed as she drifted across the room and into the hall. Gorgeous Tiffany-style wall lamps dominated the long, narrow space. Scott had spotted them on one of their "Dream-Big Days"—when they'd spend hours wandering through high-end shops that catered to folks with budgets the two of them couldn't even imagine.

"But we can dream," he always said, and laughter would crinkle the skin around his eyes and mouth. Even the memory of that smile set Alayna's heart to a lively canter. "And we will…until we can make our dreams a reality. Then, my Laynie-Love, we'll dance!"

He'd spotted the hall lamps on one such day, his attention drawn by a rather intimidating gentleman who stood straight as a ramrod while affixing bright red tags to the fixtures.

"Look, Alayna! I think those lamps are going on clearance."

"Ohhh!" Alayna tried to bite back the exclamation but wasn't quite successful. If Scott thought she admired something, he'd overspend to make sure it was hers. But those exquisite lamps cost far more than she and Scott could afford, even at clearance prices. She didn't even need to see the prices the salesman was jotting on the tags to know that. "They are beautiful, honey. We'll have to dream a little longer though…can't dance just yet."

Scott nodded, but his gaze remained on the man applying red tags to each, individual fixture. After a moment, he patted her hand. murmured a quiet, "Be right back," and headed across the sales floor.

Oh, no.

They left the store with six matching Tiffany wall sconces. By buying out the remaining inventory, Scott had talked the manager into a deal that even Alayna agreed they couldn't afford to pass up—even though they'd be paying larger payments on their single credit card for quite a while.

But now, with Scott gone, that special day filled her mind every time she walked down the hallway. The gorgeous lamps had become all about the bittersweet memory. She loved them, but they brought Scott so vividly to mind, she half expected him to stick his head out the bedroom door and wink at her.

Headed for the living room, she stopped and shook her head. No more. She'd asked God for help, and He was showing her a way out of the constant sorrow…if she was willing to take the painful, but necessary step onto the right path. The time had come to let go of the "stuff" that trapped her in the past and kept her from following whatever plan God had for her future.

After a quick shower, she settled into the breakfast room window seat with coffee and her cell phone, then punched in a familiar number and sipped the hot French roast while the phone rang in her ear.

"Good morning! Rachel's Love-Again Loft."

Alayna grinned. If her sister's cheery voice couldn't get a person in the right frame of mind for a beautiful day, nothing could.

"Morning, sis. Got a minute?"

"For you, I've got three." Soft, warm laughter filled the line. "What's up, Laynie Blue?"

Alayna rolled her eyes. A girl's night out as part of her bridal shower had included tasty wine drinks called Something Blue— served exclusively that night, in honor of the upcoming wedding. Rachel'd dubbed her Laynie Blue before the night ended. Didn't matter that Rachel, not Alayna, had consumed most of the torrent of drinks the guests showered on the bride-to-be. Despite her initial protests, nothing moved her sister. Alayna would forever and always be Laynie Blue to Rachel. Since she only used the silly nickname now and then, Alayna didn't argue…much.

"Rachel, you're the only Blue in this conversation, and you know it." She sighed. "Anyway. So you asked what's going on. Maybe a lot. Do you have room in the Loft for a few really special items?"

"Depends on the items, and to whom they belong."

"A variety of excellent quality items, and they belong to your sister…that's me, you know."

"Whaaat?" Rachel's soft voice rose by an octave and held the note for a couple of beats. *"You're* gonna part with something? I don't know, Alayna. My insurance may not cover the losses when my roof falls in."

"Ha ha." She forced a smile into her voice. "Well, either you make room, or I'll ask down at the Rose of Sharon. Miss Sharon's always after me to let her take a look at all the 'absolutely *dahlin'* treasures in my '*chahmin'* little *manah.*'"

Rachel snorted laughter—that snort being the one less-than-refined part of her personality. When she burst into genuine, belly-shaking laughter, she…oinked. Unable to prevent what she called her "inner pig," she rarely laughed in public—not true laughter that came from the heart. She reserved that particular charm for sister time with Alayna, who wouldn't have it any other way. She loved those moments when Rachel let herself be Rachel.

"So." One last mini-snort. "I can't believe you're going to get rid of anything. Don't you still have the doll I gave you for your sixth birthday? The one whose hair I later dyed, making it a bright purple mini-'fro?"

"Yes, I do, but you will never find her. Miss Grape-ilocks has a new life, safely hidden away by Witness Protection. Mad Color Monster can't hurt her anymore."

They shared another laugh before Rachel's voice took on that professional tone that told Alayna a customer must've walked into the Love-Again Loft. "How much space do I need to clear out for you?"

Alayna paused, then heaved a sigh. "Well, sis…you might need a bigger shop. Or I suppose you could have one of those estate sale things."

Rachel gasped. "You're getting rid of that much?"

"All of it, sis. What's that term they use at those sales?" She sighed. "Oh, yeah—everything must go."

Having decided, she couldn't afford to give herself time for second thoughts.

Alayna said goodbye to Rachel and called her landlord to submit a six-week notice on the condo. The place had originally been Scott's—she'd simply moved in after they were married. Following his death, she'd signed a month-to-month rental agreement of her own and stayed on, alone with her memories and the possessions they'd shared.

But no more. Within a couple of hours from the moment she awakened that morning, still tangled in the throes of the nightmare that had haunted her sleep since Scott's death, the tapestry of her life took on a new thread.

The sisters met for lunch at their favorite tearoom the next day. They settled in at a small table next to a window that overlooked a small-but-charming rose garden and chatted about nothing important until their food arrived. Instead of releasing her sister's hand after saying grace, Rachel tightened her grip and leaned in to capture Alayna's gaze.

"Sis, are you sure about all of this?" Her eyes, the same vivid emerald as Alayna's, clouded beneath a furrowed brow. "I know I've bugged you to make these changes ever since Scott's death. I do think a new start in new surroundings is a great idea, but you were insistent on staying where the two of you shared the time you had together. Now, from somewhere out of the blue, you're in a huge hurry to leave it all behind. I'd hate to see you regret it later. Are you sure you don't want to give this a little more thought?"

"I'm absolutely certain." Alayna gently pulled her hand free, picked up her knife and cut the crescent sandwich on her plate in half, then met her sister's concerned gaze. "God says it's time, so it's time." She sighed, captured her lip between her teeth for a second or two, and then released it with a somber smile. "Will it be painful to say goodbye to the 'things' Scott and I collected together? Yes. But I've made my peace with it, sat in front of each item and had a good cry, enjoyed a few memories, and then gave it all to God. I keep coming back to Jeremiah 29:11—you know the verse. 'For I know the plans I have for you, declares the Lord...'"

Rachel whispered the rest of the scripture along with her. "'Plans to prosper you and not to harm you, plans to give you hope and a future.'"

Alayna nodded, and offered a smile she hoped was reassuring. "Hope, Rachel. And a future. It's time for me to step into whatever God is urging me toward in the next weeks and month...maybe even years. If I don't do it right now, while the unction is strong, I'll talk myself out of it, and I don't want that to happen. This is right, sis. I feel it in my soul." She touched her sister's hand, still resting atop the table. "Will you help me make it happen?"

Rachel slipped her hand free and used it to flick away a tear. "Do you even need to ask? When we leave here, we'll go straight to your place and you can show me what you want to part with."

"I already told you. All of it."

"*All* of it? Are you serious? I mean, I know you said, 'everything must go,' but I thought you were speaking at least somewhat generally."

"Well, you know. My clothes are mine, and nobody better touch my shoes!" The resulting burst of laughter relieved a moment that had swung too near the danger zone.

Alayna knew without even a faint shadow of doubt that her decision was God-inspired. She also knew Satan would be all too ready and willing to talk her out of that conviction, and she'd determined in her heart not to backtrack. No changes of mind or intentions. "No U-turns," she'd whispered to the rather pale redhead in her mirror this morning. "No turning back. When God says move, you gotta move."

Rachel nodded. "All right then. We'll get 'er done."

They talked of other things after that, and Alayna was grateful for the brief reprieve. The moment she and Rachel entered the condo after lunch, her life as she knew it would be over. God's plan would be in action.

Rachel insisted on picking up the tab. While they waited for the waitress to return her credit card, the sisters wandered the quiet tearoom, admiring the plethora of handmade items for sale, along with country-themed wall art and other home decor. As they discussed the simple beauty in an oil painting that depicted an entire hillside covered with bright orange poppies, a little tug on her skirt drew Alayna's attention. She glanced down and gasped.

A small girl of maybe seven or eight, with a smile like morning sunshine, looked straight into her eyes.

For a second or two, Alayna's heart stood still. The child mirrored her own appearance at that age. Sprinkled across the tiny nose, faint freckles dotted porcelain skin. Bright red curls framed a delicate, heart-shaped face dominated by huge eyes of the same emerald green she and Rachel had both inherited from their mother.

"Hi." The cheery little voice held no hint of shyness, only friendly, open admiration. "You ah so *pwetty*!"

Beside Alayna, Rachel gasped. "Alayna, do you see—?"

She gave a slight nod but addressed the child. Rachel would deal with the shocking resemblance.

"Thank you, sweetheart. So are you." She handed her purse to her sister and knelt, putting herself at the child's eye level. "Did you come over here just to tell me that?"

Bright curls bounced with the up-and-down movement of the little girl's head. "Yep. You ah *beautifoh,* wike an ange-oh." Without hesitation or permission, she reached out to stroke a strand of hair that draped over Alayna's shoulder. "My name is Hope Annaweese Townsend. What's yoah name?"

"Alayna," she breathed. "I'm Alayna. And this is my sister, Rachel." She glanced around the room for an adult that might be with the sweet child, but only the three of them occupied the space. "Honey, where's your mommy?"

A shadow flickered over the bright expression, and then it was gone. "Mommy don't wiv wif us."

"Ohhh. You must miss her terribly."

A nonchalant shrug. "Daddy said she's happy, b—bw— *bwowin'* in the wind."

Blowing in the wind? What a strange thing to say. Did it mean the child's mother was alive, somewhere? Or was the phrase the father's way of telling his daughter that her mother, although physically dead, would always be with her?

"I'm sure he's right, Hope." Alayna tweaked the little nose and offered a weak smile. "Thank you for saying hello."

"It's okay. I—"

"Hope!"

The deep baritone voice, while not loud, held a note of harshness that stole Alayna's breath. She looked up on a sharp gasp.

Steel gray eyes glinted a hint of icy blue. No smile relieved the hard line of the man's jaw—part of an undeniably perfect bone structure. Dark eyebrows drew together over those chilly orbs. Alayna didn't take time for a full assessment of the stranger's frame, but he seemed exceptionally tall...maybe because she was hunkered on the floor next to the child.

She rose to her full height, but even the lift to three inches over five feet didn't diminish the newcomer's towering presence.

"You know better than to walk away by yourself." Two long strides brought him far too close, especially when he turned that unnerving gaze on Alayna. "Please excuse my daughter for bothering you ladies."

"N—not at all." Alayna wanted to kick herself for stammering. "Hope is quite the little charmer."

"Thank you. She can be, but disobedience tends to spoil the usual effect." He gave his daughter another scathing glance. "She knows better than to go off by herself and speak to strangers."

Something almost obstinate shadowed the child's face but disappeared so quickly Alayna couldn't be sure she'd seen it at all. "Miss Awayna's not a stwange-oh, Daddy. She's my fwiend!" The sunny smile wavered but held. "Isn't she *pwetty?*"

Heat rushed upward from Alayna's neck and all the way to her hairline. By now, she no doubt boasted that vivid hue of embarrassment only achieved by true redheads. *Not the best example of pretty...*

"She's—" He broke off, as if only that moment truly seeing the two women with his daughter. His gaze flicked to Rachel and bounced back to Alayna. Seemingly unable to look away, his narrowed gaze traveled her face, head tilted to one side.

Alayna struggled to draw a breath. She wanted to turn away but found herself unable to move a muscle. Even her eyes lacked the strength to break his hold.

"She's very pretty, Hope." He picked up his daughter and looked from her face to Alayna's. "You should be happy about that, munchkin. You look a whole lot like her."

"I know." Hope giggled. "I'm pwetty too. Miss Awayna said so."

Alayna's breath released on a burst of laugher. Beside her, Rachel emitted a quiet snort…which only increased the merriment.

Even Hope's intimidating dad chuckled a little.

"Again, I apologize for my naughty child's intrusion on your lunch."

He nodded, swung on his heel, and walked away without another word. Over his shoulder, Hope waved and grinned.

"Bye, Miss Awayna! Bye, Miss Waycho!"

They smiled and waved, but the moment the tearoom door closed behind father and daughter, both women sank onto the nearest chairs. Alayna fought for breath, while Rachel heaved a deep sigh.

"Cute kid." Alayna aimed for the safer subject.

Rachel shied away from nothing.

"Cute dad! Laynie Blue, in case you didn't notice, we've just been treated to a delicious frozen dessert. On a silver platter, no less, with presentation, as they say, being everything. Five star all the way."

Alayna wanted to argue and opened her mouth to do exactly that. But why fight the obvious? Her chin bobbed up and down and she ever-so-slowly released a pent-up breath. "I'd say at least eight stars out of a possible five."

Her sister giggled. Alayna followed suit, and soon they were laughing so hard tears ran down both sets of cheeks.

TAKE A LOOK AT...

Yesterday Again

CHAPTER 1

Porterville, California
Late September

HANNAH JOHNS' SULTRY VOICE FADED into the last soulful note of one of her favorite melodies. She sang no less passionately for the practice session here in the empty dining room than she would for a full house. But the song was over, and even before the final echo died away, she dropped the cover over the ivories and whisked her handbag off the floor beside the piano stool.

With the self-imposed hour of rehearsal completed, she threaded her way through the maze of linen-covered tables toward the big double oak doors. She was almost there when her employer's voice halted her flight.

"Hannah! Wait up."

With a regretful sigh, she stopped and turned back. She hoped to spend some extra time with her son, Davey, before coming back here for the evening's performance. This interruption threatened those plans.

Despite her irritation, a familiar twinge of sadness clutched at her heart as she watched the wiry white-haired man make his painful way across the polished wood floor. Kip Cavaness birthed the elite Porterville establishment some thirty years ago, nursed it through its delicate infancy and made it a huge success. Kipper's Dinner Lounge was a popular spot for upper echelon visitors, and not only on a local level. Every night brought in visitors from as far away as Los Angeles and Sacramento, all of whom appreciated the tasteful décor and fine menu.

Hannah loved the outspoken old restaurateur like a father, and it was obvious he adored her. But every day his aging body surrendered more fully to the debilitating rheumatoid arthritis that held it hostage, threatening to force him out of the business far too soon.

They had discussed the possibility of Hannah buying the lounge when the time came. She pinched every penny, but at this point, her savings still lacked enough pennies to make it possible. She sighed again, watching the old man hobble toward her. Judging by Kip's appearance today, her dream of turning the place into a Christian bookstore-cum-coffee lounge stood little chance of coming true.

She greeted him with a fond smile. "How's it going, you handsome old devil?"

Ten years dropped off his lined face when he grinned. His answer borrowed words from the song she'd just finished. "Almost like a song, sweet pea!"

It was a lie, and they both knew it. Still, Hannah laughed and gave her friend a hug, a little over-long and a bit too tight.

Blinking back tears, she noted the frailness of his body through the thin summer clothing which, typically for Kip, he continued to wear even though the trees outside showed the first hints of autumn in their changing wardrobe. Losing her old friend would leave a huge empty place in her heart. *Nope, not going there.* I'm far from ready to face that gloomy prospect.

"You're a pretty good liar, sweetie." She gave his thin arm a gentle squeeze. "But you can't fool me. It's bad today, isn't it?"

Kip allowed the forced grin to slip a little. He rubbed a trembling hand over his face and nodded. "I've had better days. But I'll make it, don't you worry about me."

"I'm allowed to worry." Her mocking frown and bantering tone concealed the heaviness of her heart. "I care about you, remember?"

He waved a gnarled hand in dismissal, but the twinkle in his eyes revealed his pleasure at Hannah's concern. "Oh, yeah, that. Well, it'll just put lines on that pretty face of yours." His eyes narrowed as he cocked his head to the side in a patented Kip-look. "Don't you have enough to worry about without adding me to the mix? How's Davey Crockett?"

Her three-year-old son's impish face flooded her mind, eliciting a doting smile. If Lori were here, she'd accuse Hannah of wearing her "dopey mama face"—and she'd probably be right on target. When it came to sizing up people, her best friend Lori Mahoney almost always got it right.

"Davey is wonderful." Just the opening she needed. "I was actually trying to sneak out the door and spend a little time with him before I have to come back for tonight's performance. Did you need something, Kip? 'Cause I really need to get moving."

"Well…." A troubled frown shadowed the old fellow's lined face. "I really do need to talk to you. Can you spare about ten minutes?"

His somber tone arrested her attention. "Of course I can. Let's go into your office so you can sit down."

"No, no!" Kip spun around. Moving as quickly as his painful joints allowed, he made his way to the polished ebony baby grand Hannah had just abandoned. Lowering himself onto the end of the bench he patted the space beside him and motioned her over. "Just sit right here with me for a minute. This won't take long."

She obeyed, her eyes fixed on her old friend's face. Kip never, ever talked business outside his office. Why was he in such an odd mood? Hannah's heart beat out a funny little tattoo as her imagination shifted into overdrive.

Kip picked up her hand and patted it, chuckling. "Don't worry, sweet pea, I'm still good for a few more days. Get that look off your face!"

Hannah couldn't find a smile. Not yet. "You're not worse?"

"Nope. Fit as a fiddle." He twisted his lips sideways and hiked his brows, sending her a familiar, comical look. "An old fiddle, beat up some and a little worse for the wear, but still good for a song or two."

"Then what is it? What's wrong?" Something weighed heavily on his mind.

The cocky grin disappeared. When he raised his gaze to meet hers, she found herself fighting tears yet again. Kip's once-brown eyes, faded now to an odd amber shade, still held so much life. It hurt her to see his body wear out before his heart and mind caught up.

"I've got news you're not gonna like, Hannah." Kip cleared his throat then sat silent for a moment, staring down at the spotless floor with unnerving intensity.

Hannah held her breath.

Finally her boss heaved a dismal sigh and looked up into her eyes. "I've sold the lounge."

Typical of him not to beat around the bush. "The easiest way to say a thing is just to say it!" How often had she heard him toss out that sage bit of wisdom?

She'd learned early on not to hem and haw when she talked to Kip, and he returned the favor.

Always. Even now.

She felt the blood drain from her face. "S–sold the lounge? But…but…when?"

He took her cold hand and gave it a squeeze, his kind eyes never wavering from her face. Another classic Kip Cavaness trait. "Look a man in the eye when you talk to him, no matter what it is you got to say." She'd heard the words more times than she could remember.

"Today. Just minutes ago, in fact."

Unwilling to believe her dream had flown out the window without so much as a feather of warning, Hannah shook her head. "But, Kip, I—" She swallowed hard and drew a deep breath. "You– you were going to wait until—"

"Until I couldn't do it anymore?" He raised a bushy white brow. "That's what I did, sweet pea. I've lain awake nights trying to figure out what to do. Even took your advice and tried to pray about it some!" He chuckled, and Hannah smiled a little even as she wiped at a persistent tear. She'd spent the past four years delivering subtle messages of Christ to her employer.

"I wanted to hold on until you had the means to buy the place. Turning it over to you…well, that's what I would like to do. I wish I could just let you have it." A wave of dull red crept up his neck and to his ears, revealing a familiar discomfort with voicing emotions. Hannah often wondered if that's why, handsome though he definitely was, Kip never married.

His grip on her hand tightened. "You know I would do it if I could. You know that."

Hannah nodded. Despite the undeniable success of the dinner lounge, the old gentleman's crippling illness had eaten up a large portion of what once was a sizeable nest egg.

"There's no one I'd rather see have it." Kip seemed almost to beg her understanding. "But the fact is, sweet pea, you don't have the money yet, and…well, much as I'd like to, I can't afford to let the place go without it. So I've been worryin' a lot, and prayin' a little, and well, today the answer just walked through that front door over there."

"The answer?" Hannah couldn't resist a little reinforcement of her spiritual time and effort. "Answer to what?"

He grinned. "To those practice prayers of mine, I guess. That what you wanted to hear?"

She nodded and kissed his leathery cheek. "Yep."

Kip shook his head, and Hannah bit back a giggle when a strand of flyaway hair, white as a bleached cotton ball, stood straight up and waved at her.

"You're something else, Miss Hannah Johns." Kip shook his head, his lips twisted in a lopsided half-grin. "In all my sixty-eight years, nobody else ever talked me into havin' a conversation with Someone I can't see or touch."

"But it worked."

"Well, something worked." His admission was grudging at best. "Because this afternoon, who should walk through that very door there but my old buddy Luke's son? My godson!"

Hannah had heard his late friend Luke's name a few times. She did not remember hearing about a godson, but it was possible she had. Kip sometimes went off on tangents of such mind-numbing detail that she couldn't absorb it all.

She shook her head. "I don't think I knew about him. But that's OK. Go on."

"Well, the boy's been gallivantin' off here and there for a lot of years, and as it turns out, he's done all right for himself. Not that he needed to, you know." He shook a long, gnarled finger in her direction. "Luke left his family well provided for. But anyhow, now he's back in town, lookin' to start a business and settle down at home."

Hannah closed her eyes, absorbing the shock as her fondest hopes died a sudden, wrenching death.

Kip went on, gently but without faltering. "He offered to buy Kipper's, and at a price I never would have thought I could get. I had to accept it, Hannah."

She swallowed hard, drew a shaky breath, and smiled at her boss. "Of course you did, Kip. I understand. Really."

He dropped her hand in favor of wrapping an arm around her shoulders. "I knew you would." The husky note in his voice wounded her heart. "I always know I can count on you."

She swallowed a gargantuan lump in her throat and dropped her head onto his thin shoulder. "When did it happen?"

"It's a done deal, sweet pea. We made a gentleman's agreement and shook hands on it just a few minutes ago."

Jerking upright, she fixed her eyes on Kip's face. "Well, but...how long before he actually takes over management?"

Kip bit down hard on one side of his bottom lip. Bushy eyebrows rose high on his forehead, and his eyes darted everywhere and nowhere at the same time.

Hannah knew that look. No matter how justifiable his reasons, her boss was not happy about giving up his baby.

"I've already taken over." The voice was deep and resonant. Hauntingly familiar too. Not too mention all too quick to supply the answer Kip could not bring himself to give. Hannah sprang to her feet and whirled. Who had invited himself into this conversation?

He stood, one arm resting on the baby grand's closed lid, lazily taking in the cozy scene between Hannah and Kip. Six-feet-two if he was an inch, the intruder sported a golden tan that surely meant hours or days beneath a tropical sun. He studied Hannah through half-veiled eyes.

Kip struggled to his feet. "Hannah Johns, I'd like you to meet my godson, Brock Ellis. I told you about Hannah, boy."

"Yes, I remember." The newcomer moved around the piano toward them. A cool smile touched his lips but did nothing to soften the steel gray eyes. His clipped tones scraped across her ragged nerves, and she wanted to scream in protest. "You can't possibly be the paragon of virtue Uncle Kip believes you are, Miss Johns."

As each step brought him nearer, Hannah flashed cold, then hot, and back again in rapid succession. A crushing wave of darkness pressed against her eyelids. The hand he stretched out toward her looked far too large for the rest of his body.

He reached her just as she crumpled to the floor.

Her eyelids weighed somewhere around two tons. She forced them open, and then wished she hadn't. Her new boss stood over her, his gray eyes dark with what, in anyone else, she might have called concern. And a flicker of something else, but she had no time to analyze it.

When Brock Ellis realized Hannah was conscious, his chiseled features snapped back into the lazily arrogant expression he'd worn earlier.

"Well? You OK?"

She nodded, but refused to make eye contact.

Mortified, she realized she was stretched out on the worn sofa in Kip's office—no, this man's office. Had he carried her here?

He narrowed his eyes, studying her, and finally spoke again. "Well. I certainly hope you don't make a habit of this sort of thing."

Angry heat rose in her cheeks and she sat up, one hand flying up of its own volition to smooth her hair.

"I've never fainted before in my life!"

"Good. Glad to hear it." He handed her a glass of water. "What brought it on today? Are you sick?"

"No, of course not. Where's Kip?" She ignored his first question.

"Right here, sweet pea." Her erstwhile employer made his slow, shambling way through the doorway.

"I called Lissy." Kip kept the phone number for Davey's babysitter on file in case of emergency. "She's fine to keep Davey as long as you need her. I tried to reach Lori—thought maybe she could pick you up—but she didn't answer."

"I don't need anyone to pick me up, Kip. My car is here."

"You're not driving anywhere." Brock's dark eyebrows shot high, and the line of his jaw grew rigid. "Not after that little swooning stunt you just pulled."

Spotting her purse on the floor beside her, Hannah scooped it up and rose to her feet in one motion. She swayed a little but remained standing, and the wave of dizziness passed.

"That's my decision to make." Lifting her head in a show of defiance, she marched to the door.

Behind her, Brock chuckled, and she gritted her teeth. Had he always been so annoying? Even more maddening, a familiar little jangle accompanied his derisive laughter.

Slowly she turned. Her keys swung between his thumb and forefinger. "I had a feeling you'd be hard-headed, so I took the liberty of borrowing these while you were, uh…sleeping."

"You…you…!" Furious, she turned to Kip. He sat in a nearby armchair, looking miserable as he watched the sparks fly between her and Brock.

At Hannah's beseeching look, however, he shook his head. "You really shouldn't drive. Hannah, you just fainted."

She sighed, frustrated. "Kip, trust me—I'm fine. Would you please just tell your godson to give me my keys?"

"Don't waste your breath, Uncle Kip." Brock never took his cold gaze off Hannah's flushed face. "I'll take her home."

She opened her mouth to protest, but he held up a deprecating hand. "Don't bother!" His curt voice sent stinging barbs of anger throughout her rigid body. "Come on, let's go."

Silence reigned, thick as cold butter, inside his shiny silver BMW. Hannah refused to speak, and Brock had his hands full for a moment navigating traffic.

How could this be happening? Why would God allow this man, of all men, to buy her workplace?

Finally he spoke. "My guess is you're a little concerned about how all this might affect your job."

As if she would admit that to him. She said nothing but, as she expected, her silence did not buy the same from him.

"You should know that your position is secure—at least for the next three months."

Now he had her complete attention. "Three months?"

"Uncle Kip insisted on making that a condition of our agreement." His laughter mocked her, but when he spoke again, genuine affection took the edge off his brusque voice. "The old goat wouldn't sell the place at any price unless I promised not to send you packing without giving you a fair chance. So you've got three months to show me what you can *do*." "

"What I can do?" Stop parroting the man.

"I suppose it's only fair to tell you, Hannah—I really don't care for female lounge singers."

"Do tell." Had there ever existed a man more arrogant and annoying?

Brock shrugged both broad shoulders. "Call me old-fashioned, but I don't think a lady belongs in a cocktail lounge."

"Kipper's is not a cocktail lounge. It's a dinner lounge, a very elite dinner lounge."

He grunted, twisted his lips, and raised those cocky eyebrows. "Hmph. Well, not anymore."

Her jaw dropped and she snapped it back into place.

"It will be a cocktail lounge as of the end of the year." Brock's relentless voice persisted in saying things she didn't want to hear. "It will also cater to an elite clientele." He chuckled, and the sound ripped at Hannah's ragged nerves.

"But the only food served will be basic appetizer fare." He shook his head, quirking an eyebrow in her direction. "It will not be a dinner lounge."

Tears burned the backs of her eyes. *Oh, Kip! What is this ...man...doing to your baby?*

But it wasn't Kip's baby anymore. Brock Ellis owned it now, and what he chose to do with his business was just that—his business.

"I'll look for other employment."

"That's probably wise."

Hannah waited. Would he bring up the past? She refused to be the first to broach the subject. But Brock said nothing, and perhaps it was best. Still, it bothered her that he could so easily ignore the fact that they once had an intimate, if brief, relationship. How could she have been such a poor judge of character?

Had it really meant so little to him?

Don't be an idiot! Brock showed exactly how little it meant to him when he walked away without so much as a good-bye.

Well, thank goodness she no longer cared. It only irked her that this man's sudden reappearance so swiftly sent her into emotional regression. Here she sat chastising herself for something she had come to terms with long ago. Not that some good hadn't come of it. If not for that one life-altering mistake, she'd have no Davey, and Davey was her world.

"Hmmm. So you do know how to smile—a little."

Brock's deep voice interrupted her reverie. "Why am I so sure it isn't meant for me?" He paused, shooting her a brief glance. "I get the distinct impression you don't like me at all, Hannah Johns."

She bit back a blazing reminder that he had done nothing today to change the opinion he'd left her with at their previous encounter.

"I barely know you." A true statement, in spite of everything. "But, to be honest, I don't have a burning desire to change that."

Brock nodded with a wry twist of his lips. "That's your right. However, I'm afraid you're going to be forced into my company, like it or not, until you find other employment—or until the three months expire. I'll try to make it as painless as possible.

"In the meantime…" He grinned. Hannah's heart skipped a beat as she caught a glimpse of another Brock Ellis, one she had known a long time ago. "A penny for the thought that made you smile."

"I was thinking about my…" She faltered, not sure she should mention Davey.

"Your boyfriend?" Brock provided. "That dreamy smile had lo-o-ove written all over it."

"My personal life is none of your business, Mr. Ellis."

Brock laughed outright. "That's true, and I apologize. But surely you don't intend to call me Mr. Ellis for three months? That'll get a little old, don't you think?"

Of course it would. But she had forbidden his name to so much as cross her mind for so long that she could not imagine allowing it to pass through her lips—and to his handsome, arrogant face, no less.

"I'll work on it." She made no effort to hide the annoyance in her voice.

"You do that." His obvious amusement irritated her. "Turn here." Her voice was curt. She couldn't help it and didn't want to. "I have to pick up my son."

There, it was out. Maybe Brock would let it slide.

"Uncle Kip told me you have a son." He turned where she had indicated. "How old is he?"

She panicked, then decided to be truthful. She was a horrible liar, and Brock was certain to see Davey at some point during the next three months anyway. Not that he would make the connection, although Davey's face and behavior all but mirrored the man. And if he did…well, let him think what he wanted.

"He turned three a few months ago."

"I see. And how long have you been divorced?" His wolfish grin aroused an almost uncontrollable itch to slap his lying lips. "Sorry, couldn't resist. Uncle Kip also told me you're not married."

She gasped. How could he ask such a ridiculous question? When sh could breathe again, Hannah spoke quietly. "I'm not. Kip was right. On the other hand, I'm not divorced either."

"I see." Those clipped tones must be his own special trademark for disapproval.

Fury washed over her in a sudden, unexpected wave. She emitted an icy little bark of laughter and shook her head. "Do you, though? I can't believe you, of all people, can get that look on your face because I have a son without the benefit of a husband at home. At least I'm there for my son, and I will be as long as God allows me to walk this earth. I would never, under any circumstances, abandon someone I love. *Never.*"

She pointed a trembling finger at Lissy's house and fumbled for the handle as Brock swung the car to the curb. By the time he brought the vehicle to a full stop, she had the door open and one foot outside the car. Tears burned her eyes, but she refused to let them fall.

"Hannah, I—" Brock's bewildered expression almost passed for convincing. "I'm sorry, really. I didn't mean—"

"Lissy will take us home." She ignored his apology, then slammed the car door and marched up the sidewalk, head high, back ramrod stiff.

Davey flew out the door to meet her, dark curls bouncing. "Mommy! Mommy, I missed-ed you!"

Hannah picked him up, hugging him to her. "Hey, big guy! I missed-ed you, too." She rarely encouraged his mispronunciation of words, but at the moment she wanted Davey to stay little for a very long time.

"Who's that man, Mommy?" One arm around Hannah's neck, her son pointed to the car. Brock remained in place, watching them. "Huh? Who is he?"

"Nobody, Davey."

She set the small boy on his feet. Taking his hand, she led him to Lissy's door. Behind her, the BMW's engine purred as Brock pulled away, but she refused to look back.

"Mommy! Who was that man? How come you got in his car? You're not 'pose to get in a car with a strange-oh."

Oh, he's not a stranger, sweet boy. He's your father. But he'll never know about you, son. I'll never let him hurt you like he hurt me.

Don't miss your opportunity to add this dynamic *re-release* to your library. I promise you will not be sorry!
Watch for *Yesterday Again.*
Coming soon…again.

Printed in the USA
CPSIA information can be obtained
at www.ICGtesting.com
LVHW092106250823
756273LV00004B/672

9 798223 954057